THE
FOUNDATION GAME

Beginning

A Novel by
Brenda Kempster

Cover design by Heinz Pohlmann

ISBN-13: 9781735194707 (pbk)
ISBN-13: 9781735194714 (e-book)

Appreciation to the characters in my life
who gave me inspiration and support.

What if this is just the beginning?

*"Life is what happens while you are busy
making other plans."*

John Lennon

THE
FOUNDATION GAME

Beginning

CHARACTERS

Jonathan Ross	President of the Foundation
Andrew Benton	Chief Financial Officer
Margaret Maxwell	Executive Director
Rolf Schwartz	Scientist, Deutsche Pharmaceutical
Helen Nelson	Board Member
Maureen Sloan	Board Member
Johann	German Baker
Lawrence Hollingsworth	United States Senator
Eleanor Hollingsworth	Wife of Senator
Henry Ramsey	Department of Justice Asst. Attorney General
Bob Harris	Investigator for Assistant Attorney General
Scott Jenkins	Political Consultant
Megan Jenkins	Scott's wife
Rosario Ortega	President of La Clínica, Costa Rica
Jack O'Riley	Journalist

Ken Miller	*Journalist*
Jose Luis Maldonado	*Colombian Businessman*
Mario Garcia	*Colombian*
Edward & Gina Collins	*San Francisco socialites*
Geoff Collins	*Son*
Mike Bergmann	*Boyfriend of Margaret*
Helga	*Rolf's twin sister*
Pat Wilson	*Liverpool Lass*
Jodie & Frankie	*Daughter and son of Margaret*
Jeff Peterson	*FBI*
Laura	*Margaret's secretary*

Prologue

In 1969, President Richard Nixon signed the Tax Reform Act incorporating into tax law the nonprofit corporate designation of a 501(c)3.

In 1976, Congress passed a law that nonprofits could spend up to $1 million per year on lobbying efforts, allowing a greater voice in the government.

By 1980, the nonprofit sector, following the public sector and corporate sector earned recognition as the "third sector".

Some executives of nonprofits soon discovered that this opened the door to legally accept the price of unethical behavior as a means to achieve more wealth and power.

During the Clinton Administration, the lines between the three sectors became even more blurred. Public and private sector partnerships were encouraged as a legitimate way to collaborate.

Nonprofit organizations saw the benefit of teaming with the private sector for joint ownership in product development, trade marking, and patents that formerly were sole domain of the private sector.

Since the Millennium, the third sector has become a much more powerful vehicle for corporations, business interests, and the socio-economic elite to team together. This partnering allows them to secure billions from government funding, private donations, and online funding sources.

Nonprofits may own property, develop products, own trademarks, file copyrights, and operate corporations such as hospital networks, public health organizations, sports teams, educational institutions, among many others.

This is all legal; all tax free as long as profits roll back into the 501(c)3 to further corporate social responsibility.

The third sector primarily operates under the oversight of a self selected Board of Directors. Donors and funders, for the most part, may serve on the Board and may receive honorariums, expense allowances, and personal tax deductions.

Groups of like minded individuals frequently pool resources to form complex nonprofit global partnerships that may conceal real intentions, and perhaps further personal goals.

Corporate and personal interests, rather than charitable or social priorities, can influence an agenda when unethical players are in the mix.

According to the National Center for Charitable Statistics (NCCS) by 2015, more than 1.5 million nonprofits were registered in the United States, with more than 3.5 trillion dollars in assets.

Zenkon Foundation is a fictitious "third sector" player with substantial assets.

The

Foundation Game

Beginning

Germany

Earlier in the afternoon, Rolf celebrated his last hours on earth by enjoying a few beers chased along with a matching count of *Jägermeister* shots in the local tavern, with no idea that he was in fact bidding a final farewell to his friends and neighbors.

His killer, Andrew Benton, now kept a focused gaze on the autobahn as a light drizzle coated the windscreen of the rented Mercedes. He exhaled a deep lungful of cigarette smoke, and literally felt hours of pent up stress slowly easing, allowing him to breathe freely again. In fact, he was experiencing a rare moment of unexpected calm after the storm.

The initial adrenalin rush and accompanying panic of murdering someone had completely worn off, and he found himself feeling a genuine sense of undeniable relief. The plan he had long envisioned was falling nicely into place, better than he had hoped, and as kilometers were left behind, his delusional mind convinced him that killing Rolf had been the best solution.

In life, Dr. Rolf Schwartz had always carried the physique of a heavy set man who obviously enjoyed his food and drink. So it had been quite a fete for the slight Benton to muster the strength necessary to drag his victim's lifeless body to a final resting place in the dank cellar of the cottage.

He pulled him with great effort down the narrow stone steps, figuring that at least the moldy smell of the old cellar might mask the creeping stench of death from any near term unexpected caller.

Benton, now speeding along the highway, calculated that the doctor would stay put undiscovered at least long enough for him to make a clean escape out of Germany, and that the timing of his encounter with the scientist had in retrospect been a blessing in disguise. He grinned at the notion that his victim had even cooperated by neatly packing his own travel items earlier in the day, and conveniently placing them, ready for departure inside the front door of his cottage.

Of course, Rolf was always well organized and meticulous about details, some would say to the point of being obsessive about everything. He had taken particular care that all was ready for instant loading in the car after his afternoon send-off festivity at the tavern.

Benton wickedly smiled to himself as he sped along, figuring that Rolf was actually in character by playing a part in the arrangements of his own end. His carefully planned Central American trip had just been routed to a more permanent eternal destination.

Rolf's tattered for wear red luggage, along with his worn black leather computer case containing his German passport and cell phone were now stowed in the trunk of the rental car, and like the killer on their way to Frankfurt Main Airport.

The disposal of the body was less planned. It had succumbed to being unceremoniously stuffed into large double strength heavy duty trash bags, and then

2

rolled for extra padding, and perhaps some semblance of dignity, in one of the posh oriental rugs gracing the old wood floors of the chalet's hallway.

The scientist's remains were now at rest in the dark cellar. His well used old medical style ice chest, serving as a makeshift unmarked tombstone.

Benton was confident that it would be weeks, perhaps months, before anyone would even become suspicious of the scientist's disappearance.

Associates and close friends were quite accustomed to his habit of extended trips and self imposed seclusion, often burying his head in his Petri dishes and glass tubes, and then consuming long periods with complicated research, endless experiments, and data analysis. They would think nothing out of order or suspect regarding his latest absence. Thoroughly expecting him to be ensconced in the rain forests of Costa Rica without any expectation of a word for months, they would wait to cheerfully welcome him home as he reappeared with a jovial greeting at the pub.

Years prior, his beloved partner Tristan shared in the excitement of his successes. He would talk for hours with Rolf in his engaging British upper class accent. He had a ritual of lovingly bringing him an afternoon tea and slice of cake and smiling at him, instinctively knowing that not a single word was needed. Sometimes, Rolf completely buried in his data not noticing he had passed through with the sweet token of affection. This made his partner love him even more for his dedication to cause.

They had fantasized about the discovery of the great cure that would bring fame and fortune, and how they would have sufficient money to travel the world in early retirement from the patents. But it was not in their fate. Tristan had died of Lou Gehrig's disease, a loss that haunted Rolf in knowing that even with all his knowledge of cures and remedies he could not save him from an inevitable fate.

So in an effort to compensate for enduring pain and unbearable loss he had pushed himself into an even more recluse and research devoted lifestyle as an escape from his loneliness. Perhaps there was a speck of comfort in Andrew's deed that they were together once again.

Rolf had widely announced to family and friends his intent to take leave from his beloved homeland for a six month work assignment at a remotely located Costa Rican research facility. The center was owned by the Zenkon Foundation, an organization where Benton until recently served as the Chief Financial Officer before tendering his resignation to the Board of Directors.

Benton calculated that technology could assist him in maintaining a false sense of normalcy that the scientist was working on the project in the rain forests of Costa Rica by creating a virtual reality. He would use Rolf's social media presence, cell phone and his e-mail accounts to keep him alive. The world could be misled regarding the actual circumstances. He thought that if he were to regularly send text message responses to any calls the scientist might receive and post occasional updates on the progress of the research via the scientist's blog and social media sites that his death would be electronically concealed.

Benton's first step in accomplishing this was to forward the deceased's home telephone to the cell phone now hidden in computer briefcase in the trunk. He expected to be safely away from the crime scene and in another country by the time any questions were raised regarding the whereabouts of the researcher.

As far as he was concerned, killing Rolf had been an unfortunate necessity. There was no purpose in second guessing, and no sense in lamenting what was done.

He had seen no other option to directly dealing with the researcher once he had learned that Rolf had grown suspicious of Foundation investments. Rolf had begun asking probing questions about the Miami distribution operations of the Foundation's health and homeopathic rain forest products.

In fact, Benton was quite shocked to learn that his nemesis, Jonathan Ross, the President of the Foundation, had recently been in contact with Rolf asking other awkward questions with reference to sales of the pharmaceutical lines.

Ross asked Rolf to return immediately to Costa Rica to check things out, enticing him with the promise of new funding for experimental vaccines if he were to also watch over what might be going on with the production and distribution. Ross had said that he needed someone he could trust to keep a closer eye what was going on, particularly since they were close to a new break through.

In reality, it was Ross needing to monitor Rolf so as to not upset any plans with new and lucrative investors he planned to line up from China.

Jonathan Ross' timing could not have been worse for Benton. As far as he was concerned, he was the reason he had already been unceremoniously dumped from his position at the Foundation. Here he was meddling again, just he was close to cashing in on a retirement nest egg in a well hidden Swiss savings account.

Benton calculated that he had worked way too hard, and it was too risky to have any internal auditing, or even worse, the whiff of an internal investigation leaking to the media. In no time it would be like sharks on bloody fish bait, likely leading to a political scandal and putting him at risk of losing everything. His savings and nest egg had disappeared once in the Great Recession, and he was not about to let it happen twice.

He figured that he had learned the hard way how to take care of himself, no one else would, and that was for sure.

Besides, he self justified, what he had skimmed from government grants was peanuts compared to the constant flow of billions in padding and bailouts to politicians and bankers, to say nothing of the regular insider stock trading to feather nests.

Benton had intended to visit Rolf unannounced in his cottage near Nuremberg. He only planned to apply strong pressure and to put a stop to any questions or suspicions that might call attention to activities. As a backup he figured he might be able to buy loyalty with additional funds from well placed investments about to pay off. Either way, he intended to make sure the scientist was on his team.

However, it became clear from the start of the unanticipated confrontation that the scientist's personal ethnics and rigid German view of rules and situations would be a problem for Benton.

For Rolf the world was either black or white – no middle ground. His personal integrity and decency were traits undoubtedly seen as uncompromisingly stubborn and naive to an unethical and desperate Benton, who realized quickly that the scientist's unyielding stand ended any hope for a compromise or payoff.

The scientist was caught off guard by the unexpected appearance of the former Foundation executive. He had his antenna up from the get go and easily figured that Benton was up to no good.

Under pressure to leave on the trip, the few drinks he had partaken at the bar permitted him a little more verbal bravado than his usual reverence and regard for superiors normally allowed. A sudden argument took place, making it quite clear that the scientist wanted no part of any scheme.

He became more and more convinced that Jonathan Ross had indeed been correct in believing that there were unlawful activities going on with the distribution process.

The escalating argument propelled the increasingly unhinged and nervous Benton into an uncontrollable rage, and resulted in a dreadful shouting match. It became obvious to Benton that hush money was not in the cards at all.

He had more trouble on his hands than he had anticipated.

It was not a premeditated act but rather impulsive one. As if it were animal instinct, Benton plunged down towards the hearth in the midst of his anger and grabbed the heavy brass poker resting inconspicuously against the stone chimney of the fireplace.

With one swift and well aimed swing he delivered a single fatal blow to the right side of the scientist's skull. He became like an enraged animal protecting his territory. The hard blow emitted a devastating crunching thud. Rolf never even had time to see it coming. His bulging eyes were the only witness to the shock and disbelief he must have felt as his lifeless body collapsed to the floor.

Mercifully, death was almost immediate.

A few moments of sheer panic ensued before Benton could compose himself. Breathing hard, he involuntarily let the poker slide from his grasp, his body sinking into the worn leather recliner chair at the side of the fireplace, unable to remove his gaze from the buckled body of the scientist.

His heart was racing and his pulse was pounding loudly in his ears. His palms began sweating, and he felt a wet stream run down his back under his jacket, uncomfortably drenching his shirt.

Then out of the blue, like a slowly rippling wave on a serene pond, he began to feel a sense of calm and ease come over him. He felt a despicable self congratulatory pride that he was able to carry off a killing with minimal effort and rather skilled composure.

Months of anger and resentment toward unfair treatment and unwarranted dismissal from the Foundation seemed to be in tandem released from his trembling body leaving him with a bizarre sense of calm. True, the scientist had not been the main cause of his bitterness, but he symbolized the problem.

The very act of killing him had been somewhat therapeutic and well deserved.

Benton was certain no one had actually seen him arrive at the chalet. His immediate thought was to escape by quickly driving away, leaving the body to be found by friends or relatives. He could arrange the scene to look like an accident. It would be easy to assume the scientist had slipped and cracked his skull on the hearth having imbibed a few too many drinks earlier in the afternoon.

Thinking through it, though, and noticing Rolf's briefcase and packed suitcases at the door, he realized that friends at the tavern would confirm that the researcher had been relatively sober by German standards when he left the establishment. He would have been mindful of the fact that he had to drive to the airport to catch his flight to Costa Rica.

The intended departure, however, provided an even more brilliant option to Benton.

He decided the most logical choice was to arrange the death scene as if the scientist had simply left as planned. If he hid the body, and took the suitcases with him, no one would be suspicious of the missing man, at least not for a while, and certainly long enough for him to depart the country.

He surveyed the small cottage and quickly found the old black oak door leading to the scientist's lab. It was conveniently located down a narrow stone staircase only a short distance from the lifeless body. He opened the heavy portal and flicked on the light switch to illuminate the well lit laboratory below.

In one corner there stood a stainless steel work table. Above were shelves filled with manuals, specimen jars, and files. A lonely reading lamp stood on the worktable, no doubt well used by the scientist on his late night projects; opposite was an old bar sized refrigerator in which the researcher kept his samples and pharmaceutical supplies. All was immaculately kept.

Benton contemplated perhaps disposing of the body by stuffing it into the cooler. Then he noticed that the floor was designed of interlocking wooden slats fabricating a suspended decking about half a meter above the dirt below.

He smiled and nodded to himself, realizing that he would be able to actually wedge the body between the dirt floor and the tiles without the extra undertaking of having to take time to dig a hole to bury it.

Once he had figured out his plan, the entire effort of wrapping the body in the trash bags and carpet and hiding it beneath the old wooden slats had been mechanical and unemotional for Benton. In his own opinion all had been accomplished perfectly.

The now brilliant scientist and former President of *Deutsche Pharmaceutical Research Foundation* was no more. He had been regarded by peers and philanthropists around the world as a likeable person with a passion for humanitarian science.

The self-possessed perpetrator was already well away from the chalet, coasting along the autobahn; occasionally moving to the right as upcoming drivers impatiently flashed their headlights to speed past him. Their unremitting pace did not bother him at all.

He continued unrushed on his own purposeful journey, calmly lighting another cigarette and taking a deep satisfying drag.

Defying rules, he glanced at the *No Smoking* sign above the console, and murmured *fuck you.*

He had the scientist's luggage, computer, and mobile phone in his possession, and would simply keep the victim alive electronically for as long as might be necessary.

He decided that his mission to Germany had been marvelously accomplished, giving himself a mental pat on the back.

Pushing Rolf's death out of his thoughts, he allowed his mind to drift back nearly ten years to the day the Foundation had first been formed in San Francisco.

He remembered the day as if it were yesterday.

San Francisco, ten years earlier

The original team had congregated in the lavish Executive Board Room of the Pacific Rim Telecom Company. The impressive expanse of the Oakland Bay Bridge provided a magnificent backdrop through the huge picture window framing the length of the Board room.

Ten new corporate board members were in attendance – some having commuted north by car to San Francisco from nearby Cupertino, heart of the Silicon Valley.

Participants were now seated around an impressive antique mahogany conference table.

A giant flat screen monopolizing the wall at the head of the room displayed the digital image of a newly designed logo. In boxes to the side of the logo, were the faces of four Board members who would be participating from Washington, D.C. and Los Angeles locations. The screen portrayed an impression that they were larger than life, and each too busy to take time out of hectic schedules to attend the meeting in person.

Benton recalled the countless logistics needed for setting up the foundation. Selecting the board members and maneuvering through the legal ramifications and government tax regulations had been a tedious task. It had required opinions from attorneys and advice from consultants to make sure it was done within legal and tax guidelines.

Yet, he recalled, once the required formalities and technicalities were all worked out, the actual procedure of activating the organization by voting the new Board of Directors into existence was over in what seemed like the unremarkable span of a heart beat.

The entire meeting to make it all official had lasted less than two hours. Benton recollected that the well rehearsed business agenda moved quickly and flawlessly.

Each of the founding board members was a highly accomplished professional who had made the commitment to serve as a director only provided it took up no more than a minimal amount of valuable time. Their priority was on more important business obligations. Clearly details and nonprofit organizational minutia were better left to be trusted to and managed by the foundation staff.

Taking another puff at his cigarette and remembering well the details of the brief session, prominent in his mind was the image of a young liberal San Francisco activist named Jonathan Ross. He was elected unanimously to the position of President of the Board of Directors.

He smiled to himself when he remembered how easily the immature upstart had been to read and to manipulate.

Benton had picked up early on Ross' hunger for power and prestige while the Foundation was still in its formative stage. He knew that the fast talking and charismatic Ross was seeking upward mobility in the Bay area's nonprofit world, and would be satisfied with no less than the high profile role of President of the Board.

As far as Benton was concerned, controlling the finances offered far more influence in the long run. So, he willingly conceded the top title to Ross early in the game in order to set things in motion. Ross had then been more than happy to reciprocate the good deed by agreeing to shore up Benton for the position of Chief Financial Officer.

At a trim and fit fifty-five, Andrew Benton was already eligible for early retirement after twenty-five years of continuous corporate service in the communications industry.

Long term executives had been offered lucrative buy-outs to make room for whiz kids and developers streaming in from Silicon Valley start ups, and promising to transform telephone and cable companies into global multimedia giants.

Benton had experienced the impact of the *dot.com* bust from 1999-2000 on the workforce and the mindset of his company. Many mid-level and union workers lost their jobs due to greedy company executives self dealing in risky spin off startups that turned into worthless paper stock.

Faster digital computers were replacing hundreds of workers in switching offices and systems management. A small centralized team could now literally manage an entire state or even global network service.

He knew that technology was passing him by, and calculated that it was the right time to take his chips off the corporate table and move on.

Quite frankly, he was already beginning to feel a little out of step with the rhythm of the company that had provided him a long secure career. Now, as it transformed itself into an information age multi-national digital media conglomerate, he had no interest in keeping up with the ever-changing technologies.

The Foundation provided an opportune and logical segue into a new lucrative career in the nonprofit sector. For a decade or so, he would have the chance to further supplement his retirement benefits and golden parachute. The CFO position could offer him the opportunity to maintain the lavish lifestyle to which he was accustomed.

The younger Ross, on the other hand saw the role of President as a gateway to building political influence in the San Francisco Bay Area. He had worked his way up through a number of smaller and moderate paying non-profit organizations. He wanted a career in politics, was challenged by fresh ideas, and looked to an exciting future that would give him the esteem and remuneration that he felt he deserved.

He planned to one day run for political office in the freethinking Bay City. To win the hearts and support of many liberal minded voters meant needing to punch his ticket in the non-profit do-good arena by funding many special interest projects.

As president of a foundation, Ross would have a vote on the Board as well as the responsibility of lead manager in day to day operations. He projected this would give him policy credibility and the necessary visibility in the media to build his image with future constituencies; and of course, access to funding to build his political constituency.

Politics makes strange bedfellows, as the saying goes.

Andrew Benton with his conservative corporate history was now teamed with the more impulsive and idealistic Jonathan Ross. Together they were prepared to pull off the business of building the charitable Zenkon Foundation for their own respective self interests.

The business savvy Benton, eager for a home turf advantage right out of the starting gate, had offered to host the first meeting of the Board at the corporate headquarters of Pacific Rim Telecom, or PRT. He was confident that the impressive location gave him the added ease and prestige to guide the gathering to the important conclusion he had planned for months with his cohort.

The venue was an imposing gothic structure located south of Market in an area considered primarily low rent before the nineties *dot.com* boom. As with all of real estate in the Bay Area, the south of market properties became high rent status as the Silicon Valley outgrew its geography and continued expansion north to the downtown areas of San Francisco and Oakland.

The original building occupying the site was constructed by AT&T in 1925, and at the time was the tallest structure in San Francisco, climbing twenty-six floors.

It is believed that in 1929 Sir Winston Churchill while visiting the building made his first transatlantic telephone call, phoning his London home. Since then, the edifice has been home to many tenants, the latest being PRT.

PRT is surrounded by high rise neighbors.

Gigantic contemporary glass structures protrude thirty and forty stories into the skyline, defying fears of earthquake country. The 1906 quake is long forgotten. Skyscrapers are now built on postage size lots, cleared of the homeless and local pawn shops.

The glass and concrete neighbors could not compare in quality to the white Venetian marble of the PRT building. Fluted columns capped with elaborate Corinthian capitals, high ceilings, and expertly fitted and gleaming hardwood floors are unmatched.

However, there was an absence of one glaring amenity. There was no central air conditioning ever installed in the historic building.

Only the areas that housed the sophisticated computer equipment of PRT had the benefit of a cooling system. Some of the upper floor executive offices also had wall or window units rigged into them.

After all, this was San Francisco, and the thermometer rarely ventured much past eighty degrees. If it did, a natural breeze from the Bay was sure to quickly cool things off. Everyone joked that summer in San Francisco could come for a day or so in April or October. It was anyone's guess.

Usually, the old window air conditioning units remained off. The office staff tolerated the occasional day of warmth by merely removing their jackets and ordering ice-lattes from the abundance of trendy cafes located all around the building. Guessing which days management would actually turn on the portable units was a regular game among the workforce.

This particular day the weather was sunny and clear and could certainly be classified as one of the few summer days of the year.

Consequently, by time the meeting convened in the early afternoon the temperature was already uncharacteristically warm, and the old window units hummed away in the background.

Each new Board member, eager to move the session along, focused on their individually labeled briefing packets displayed carefully on the table in front of them.

Margaret Maxwell, an independent consultant, walked around the long table making sure all the attendees had their packages. She had carefully prepared the materials and compiled each binder the previous evening.

Her knowledge of the organizational process and her personal associations with most of the newly appointed board members overruled the personal dislike Ross and Benton had for her.

Actually, Margo had been the one who had conceived the original concept for the Foundation. She took the idea to Ross at the People's Rights League and to Benton at PRT a year earlier.

Ross and Benton had both seen the potential for leveraging her Silicon Valley corporate contacts into more interesting and lucrative possibilities for themselves. They eagerly signed on to her idea of creating an international philanthropic organization with the technology power brokers. Deep pockets would be targeted as donors in exchange for good public relations.

Benton retained her as a long term consultant. Chemistry and personalities clashed between the two. He tolerated her consulting work in order to recruit just the right mix of influential board members to guarantee success in building their long-term plan.

Figuring that he and Ross would have the upper hand and control of finances as key officers, he had conceded to support her interest in a permanent position as Executive Director of the Foundation.

The brief meeting focused on logistics such as the approval of the articles of incorporation, voting officially for the members of the board of directors, the election of the officers, and compensation packets for the managing executives.

These procedural steps were necessary according to the state requirements. The Foundation would then receive an official stamp of approval with the California Secretary of State and the State Attorney General allowing operation of the newly formed California tax exempt corporate business.

Typically, once the procedural documents are prepared and filed with the California Attorney General, and state approval is obtained for a foundation, the board is rarely involved in the day-to-day operations – perhaps meeting only once or twice a year either in person or via electronic communications for approving tax filings or annual reports, and the subsequent year expenses.

Benton and Ross intended to have as much independence as possible from what they saw as unnecessary bureaucratic oversight or micro management by Margo. The fewer the meetings they had the better as far as they were concerned.

Most of the new board members were wealthy entrepreneurs who had arranged to contribute generous seed funding from their own corporations. Some had willingly provided sizeable personal donations just to enjoy the benefits of a tax-deductible contribution in exchange for positive media exposure. All members would most likely rely on corporate and personal tax accountants to keep required paperwork straight.

The initial fund of the Zenkon Foundation easily topped more than sixty million dollars – an impressive amount for a new foundation. It was more than enough to provide a solid base to create a diversified portfolio of interesting charitable projects as well as investments in for profit business ventures.

The Zenkon Foundation was allowed to pay salaries to board members and executive staff, along with fringe benefits. The law permitted it to hold property, invest in stock portfolios, and in general engage in any lawful activity consistent with the corporate mission statement.

Jonathan Ross and Andrew Benton considered the delegation of management for the Foundation the most important agenda item of the short meeting.

The duo had agreed that Margaret, or Margo, as her friends called her would begin the meeting with an opening welcome and a few brief words of appreciation to the benefactors for their financial support and volunteerism as members of the new Board of Directors.

Margo took her seat at the table and then pushed the activation button on a control panel in front of her.

"Good afternoon," she began.

"Welcome to your first meeting as the new Board of Directors of the Zenkon Foundation."

She glanced around the room and smiled warmly at each of the six new founders with a genuine gesture of appreciation. For effect, she then looked directly into the camera to draw the remote participants more fully into the occasion. She was proud of the solid line up of influence she had managed to corral.

She then continued with her prepared remarks.

"Your overwhelming generosity and personal involvement in seeding this new organization will benefit many needy causes around the globe. It is heartwarming to know that the financial success of each of your companies has now enabled us to begin our journey of social responsibility that will improve the lives of many individuals in many countries.

With your guidance and support, we will pledge to make this a unique enterprise. Again, many thanks for pioneering this effort with us."

Several of the attendees nodded in consensus, and Ross encouraged their mutual support by initiating a polite applause.

"I would now like to turn over the meeting to our colleague, Jonathan Ross who will get to the business at hand. Jonathan."

She smiled as she indicated to Ross to continue with their well rehearsed program.

"Thank you Margaret," said Ross, clearly keeping the tone on a business level with her, and obviously enjoying the opportunity to seize control of the meeting for the first time.

He began by dutifully acknowledging her role in the origin of the Foundation, and segueing into remarks about her new role.

"We have been fortunate over the past year to bring your vision to reality, and look forward to working with you as the new Executive Director for the Zenkon Foundation per approval of item number four on our agenda this morning."

"It will be my pleasure to serve the Foundation in that important role, assuming the Board will approve the agenda item." Margo responded with poise and deference.

Ross smiled agreeably, paused for effect, and then continued to work down the list of action items that had been detailed by Margo on the prepared agenda. It was really only a procedural exercise to legally record the votes. Margo had individually briefed each of the board members in advance. Each trusted her judgment and recommendations, and none had any personal interest in the mundane operational aspects of the Foundation, nor objections to Margo managing the Foundation.

Most of the Directors occupied seats on several boards. More importantly, they had global corporations to run requiring more than their full attention. All were happy to defer management to capable staff.

The Board would rely on Margo to maintain the records and keep them informed. They trusted she would act in compliance with the legal regulations- under the delegated direction to Jonathan Ross and Andrew Benton, as elected officers of the Board.

"We are anxious to hear your recommendations for worthy projects," said Ross in closing the meeting.

"Our mission and objectives for the Zenkon Foundation focus on global research for improving health and education. We understand that this is an ambitious undertaking. Nevertheless, rest assured that with your support and the work of our executive management team, we will identify and invest in those projects that will benefit the neediest recipients.

"Our first order of business will be to secure office space and hire support staff within the next month. Then we will embark on identifying projects worthy of our mission.

"Margo will keep you informed via e-mail and quarterly updates. We look forward to working with each of you."

Ross glanced around the room, catching Benton's eyes, to signal that their strategy had been executed without a flaw.

In less than two hours, the two smooth operating co-conspirators had won the confidence of the other appointed directors. They had taken control of more than sixty million dollars of newly designated nonprofit corporate assets.

Both of the new managing directors considered this sizeable amount merely initial seed funding for their ambitious future undertakings.

"As your new President of the Board, it is my honor to now adjourn the first meeting of the Zenkon Foundation." Jonathan said, smiling triumphantly and closing the blue binder containing the meeting materials.

Germany

Flashing lights in the rear view mirror abruptly brought Benton's thoughts and attention back to the present.

As he had drifted in memories of the past, he had unintentionally slowed down in the fast lane of the autobahn. Now an irritated driver in a large late model car was eager to pass by and with unabated annoyance signaled him to move over by again flashing his headlights.

Benton immediately veered into the right lane, deciding that perhaps he should alter his route from the autobahn to the lesser traveled road, after all he still had plenty of time before he needed to arrive at the airport. He allowed the impatient car to effortlessly speed by him.

Disobeying the strict German obsession in keeping the highways clean, he defiantly flicked the butt of his cigarette out the window onto the pristinely maintained hedge of the autobahn.

Thoughts of what he had done to Rolf were becoming increasingly easier to handle with each kilometer gained.

He sped self-assuredly onward to the next exit.

His mind drifted once again to the Foundation and his oust by the Board at the last annual meeting.

He recalled the deteriorating relationship between Ross as President and himself as Chief Financial Officer. The differences had come to a head, leading to a predictable showdown at the last Board meeting.

The hostility between them left option for the Board than to accept his resignation.

It had taken five years of filings and annual reporting, before Zenkon was approved for permanent non-profit status by the federal government. This elevation in rank gave it the legitimacy for opening the doors to even more lucrative international donors.

Permanent non-profit tax exempt status had become very difficult to achieve because of vigorous IRS oversight of charitable organizations under the post 9/11 National Patriot Act.

The National Security Agency, CIA, FBI and others, collectively known as the *intelligence community,* convinced that Al-Qaida and other terrorist organizations were using non-profit organizations to launder money for nefarious causes, placed all charitable operations under the microscope. This had effectively slowed down approval processes to nearly a stand still.

. Benton had to admit that even with all the tension between the three managers that it had still been a good ride. Ross and he both read each other pretty well and so for the most part aligned when needed. Each had looked the other way when individual interest was obvious.

It was more of a dance with Maxwell. She was a play by the book type, and even though she had seen a few things in Washington, both men knew she would be Pollyanna about anything off color close to home base.

Benton was now out, but not before he made sure he would be more than comfortable in retirement. He had no regrets about a few side deals negotiated on his own behalf along the way.

He was not about to have red flags raised that risked federal investigations, or worse. Opening up a Pandora's Box could certainly put a damper on plans.

That idiot Ross had no idea how dangerous it could be. He should have just left well enough alone, and been content with his own damn side deals.

Senator Lawrence Hollingsworth wiped the sweat from his brow. He was a seasoned politician experienced in the Capitol Hill power plays, and normally completely in control. However, the phone call had unnerved him.

His hand was shaking as he replaced the black receiver into the cradle. He was a respected elder statesman. No one had the right to threaten him.

Hollingsworth was a liberal Democrat, or progressive as the media liked to refer to him, who had decided that this was to be his last term in office. His decades in Washington were definitely enough.

He had experienced the anguish of the Beltway politics and K Street lobby during the conservative stampede of the Reagan-Bush years, which had almost left him disillusioned, but not defeated.

The Clinton Administration opened the door for more optimism in his progressive caucus, but even then the partisan politics had degraded policy comprise into never ending political gridlock.

Following the Bush Two administration, and the deceptive manipulations that led to an Iraq war, he knew national politics and global stability had changed forever.

He had more fight, but no more appetite for the never ending fundraising and partisan deal making required just to maintain a seat in the Senate. Both parties placed first priority on getting re-elected. The work of the people took a back seat to self centered egos and interests of polarized politics.

Statesman or not, he knew he had to get out, believing that the great American experiment with democracy was sadly headed for paralysis.

He had, in effect, already resigned his Senate leadership position by electing not to seek another term in office, but he did not forsake his convictions. He still cared. In fact, he thought he could be a more effective advocate for his causes behind the scenes as a private citizen, without having to worry about the responsibilities and media concerns of the elected post.

The press had reported that he would soon retire, returning to his California ranch, but the Washington insiders knew better. He could still be a major back scene player. The Party knew it could count on him when he might be needed.

He was feeling tired, and admittedly not getting any younger. He more and more preferred the climate of his bucolic central California foothills home to the relentless crush of the grid locked Capitol Hill.

Yet the idea of keeping active in retirement by helping a philanthropic organization seemed to help rejuvenate his spirits. It was one of the reasons he agreed to work with the Foundation after Andrew Benton had approached him years prior.

He had been on the Board from the first day the video conference connected him to the San Francisco meeting. But he had never been one of the active board members, more a figurehead, allowing the Foundation to use his name to help with causes and fundraising.

But now as he planned to move on, he gave more thought to the mission and the more stress-free philanthropic activities. As a more active board member he might benefit from the social interaction to keep him going, after all it was an enjoyable group.

There was no argument among his peers that Lawrence Hollingsworth had devoted his life to improving the quality of life for middle class and poor Americans. Of course, there were immense political differences, but his integrity and conduct was unquestioned.

He was elected to a congressional seat in the post Vietnam and civil rights era as part of the new infusion of liberal Democrats who ran on the heels of Watergate and a myriad of social issues that rocked the late sixties and mid seventies.

It was during those early idealist days that he had become a tireless public advocate. He learned how to do business in the nation's Capitol. In the process, instead of becoming cynical or on the take, he had become an even more tenacious fighter.

Hollingsworth had weathered his political storms.

Moreover, the struggle had not diminished him. He had earned the term statesman. He was well respected on both coasts – and in both Houses of Congress – because he was a man of his word who went to bat for what he believed in, not for the highest bidder.

He played hard partisan politics but was more broadly focused and social issue oriented than many. This meant he would occasionally publicly disagree with his fellow Democrats if he believed it was for the greater good. For this, media outfits, such as CNN, regularly sought him out for comment on issues, knowing that they were more likely to get a less partisan response. This was, indeed, a rare happening in the brutal political milieu.

It was actually surprising how he could regularly fall out of step with the majority and still be effective. No doubt due to his safe seat as a senator from California.

Extreme partisanship was impacting effective public service. Money and special interests, and party tribalism trumped his causes. He did frequently worry about the great democratic experiment envisioned by Alexander Hamilton and the Founders.

Constant questions haunted him.

Has it already failed? Was it sabotaged by big money? Is it capable of adapting to new technologies? Is it being torn apart by partisan cable news personalities? Can it weather brutal online conspiracies and disinformation campaigns generated within the country and from bad actors globally?

He knew it was time for him to get out.

Holly, as his colleagues knew him, was now the ranking minority member of the Senate Health and Human Services Committee. He had served as Chair of the committee during the days before the Bush Administration had dominated both the White House and the Hill. Nonetheless, even as the senior minority member of the powerful committee, he still carried substantial influence.

The Senate and House Health and Human Services Committees provide oversight and budget allocations to the enormous bureaucracy known as the United States Department of Health and Human Services or HHS.

Congress had recognized the need for a nationwide consumer protection law as early as 1906. Then, in 1937, a public health disaster tragically drove home the need for an even stronger federal law.

Sulfanilamide, the first *"wonder drug"* and a popular and effective treatment for diseases like strep throat and gonorrhea, was formulated into an Elixir of Sulfanilamide and marketed for use in children.

Tragically, the liquid formulation contained a poison, the same chemical used in antifreeze. Before the flaw was discovered, the lethal dosages had killed more than one hundred people, most of them children. The earlier law did not require the drug's manufacturer to test the formulation for safety before it was sold.

Congress corrected this weakness in the law the next year when it passed the Federal Food, Drug, and Cosmetic Act. This law, for the first time, required companies to prove the safety of new drugs before putting them on the market.

The new act also added the regulation of cosmetics and therapeutic devices, and generally updated the law to improve consumer protection.

Congress has continued to give FDA new responsibilities over the years, including the requirement that drugs and medical devices be proven effective as well as safe before they can be sold. Public health and safety has allowed the agency to build up into a staff of thousands, and receive a healthy federal budget appropriation for biomedical research.

By the late nineties, this research allocation had already reached almost eight hundred million a year. Senator Lawrence Hollingsworth had a lot to say in how that appropriation was allocated.

The late evening telephone call had been the last thing he had expected. He had been burning the midnight oil, preoccupied with funding for prescription drugs and social security benefits, and thought the shrill sound of the phone was his devoted, yet forever complaining wife, Eleanor. She would no doubt be calling to complain again about his late working hours.

The Senate office staff had long vacated the building so he answered the ringing telephone himself.

"Hello, Holly here." He answered in his informal tone, fully expecting Eleanor's well intentioned whine.

"Senator Hollingsworth?" responded a deep raspy male voice with a distinct Texas drawl.

"Yes," he responded quizzically.

"This here is Henry Ramsey."

"Oh, yes, Mr. Ramsey. How may I assist you?"

He straightened up in his six-foot frame in the black leather chair, and immediately putting himself on his guard.

Ramsey was a political hack of the highest order handpicked by the Attorney General to stir up dirt for the upcoming election battle by finding any dirt to justify a public lynching of declared or potential candidates before highly publicized Senate Committee hearings.

Of course, the mission of the Department of Justice to serve as the *people's representative* had been high jacked by an Administration that now shamelessly used it in the capacity of a partisan hack force for the White House. Career bureaucrats were being fired or leaving under political pressure.

If DOJ wanted to conceive an investigation it would not matter the veracity. Talking points would have virtually nothing to do with the legitimate work of the committee, or public interest, but rather a way to focus media attention on partisan kangaroo courts in order to scar political opponents via innuendo and scandal.

Ramsey was a former state attorney general from Texas. He was a fast talking, loud mouthed star at playing to cameras.

A call from him personally this late at night was not a good omen.

"Senator, as you know, we are looking into a number of the activities of certain corporate executives. The public is not too happy with the obvious diminishing returns of their stock portfolios."

"I am aware of your investigations, Mr. Ramsey. What is the urgency at this time of night?"

"Well, Senator. The HHSC Committee has a lot of discretion, shall we say, to direct research funds to corporations and foundations. It would be unfortunate if some of those grants appeared on lists associated with questionable activity and investments of certain Boards. Let's say that could cast a bad light on certain members of the Committee."

"I am sure it would, Mr. Ramsey. But what are you implying?"

"Let's just say that we are fully aware of your long term involvement on the Board of the Zenkon Foundation, Senator Hollingsworth, and expect you to be fully upfront in our request for information."

"What do you mean? What request for information? Surely there is no reason to believe any wrong doing with the projects or members of a small charitable organization."

"That may certainly be the case, Senator. Although, *small* would not be my choice of adjective for the projects of the Zenkon Foundation. We expect you to be fully cooperative in our inquiry, or let's say, there might be regrettable consequences for your impeccable reputation."

"I take issue with both your audacity and your implications. I have no idea to what you might possibly be referring, Mr. Ramsey."

"Again, Senator, we will be in touch shortly regarding information you may need to provide for the investigation. It will be worth your consideration to be most cooperative with our inquiry. Good evening."

Holly paled, and was obviously taken off guard as he sank back into his chair. He had no idea what was going on, but knew instinctively that it was not good, and that worried him.

Clearly, Justice had some information or more likely innuendo regarding Zenkon activities. True or not, in the current political climate the media could spin any snippet of information and gossip into a full-blown scandal. If he were implicated in any way, it would be front-page news. If he were cleared, a retraction would perhaps be mentioned on the back page.

He checked his watch, picked up the phone once again this time to reach Scott Jenkins, a west coast based political consultant and confidant.

It was still only nine-thirty in the evening in California, early for the late working former lobbyist.

California

Margaret Maxwell rarely took a day off, let alone unplanned leave time, so she surprised herself by actually calling in to the office and leaving a voice mail message for her secretary, Laura. She informed her that she would be out of the office couple of days.

She needed an escape, and a quick trip down to Santa Barbara to meet with Scott Jenkins was just the thing to kill two birds with one stone.

While he had not gone into any specifics the night before, his tenor was clearly one of concern for the Senator, and he had projected a clear sense of urgency. A trip to get to the cause was all the incentive she needed to act so uncharacteristically impulsive.

Scott had seemed polite but insistent about getting together immediately.

She was actually looking forward to a drive south. Although the coastal town was nearly a full day's journey from her northern California home, somehow it felt like a long road trip and the smell of the ocean breeze might just clear her head.

She rationalized that a quick overnight trip would provide a respite from the past couple of week's stress and pressure in the nation's capitol. She would be back before she knew it. Hopefully more relaxed and with Holly's problem worked out.

At six thirty that morning, she quickly packed an overnight bag, checked her e-mail, threw a few essentials into her briefcase, and tossed everything but her phone into the back seat of the car.

Her flight had barely touched down the night before from the Washington fundraising trip when Senator Hollingsworth called her. He was a bit short, and insisted she contact Scott Jenkins right away. She obliged by immediately calling Scott on her drive home from the airport.

Although she had never met Scott Jenkins, she felt she already knew him from the praise the Senator had bestowed upon him over the years.

It all seemed a bit mysterious, but he had echoed the Senator's wishes that she meet with him as soon as possible.

Since she needed to get away for some private thinking time anyway, this was all the excuse she needed to drive south the following morning. She always did some of her best thinking while she was travelling, normally flying from one coast to the other.

Alone, with the sunroof letting in the big blue California sky, she gave a deep sigh that seemed to help in letting go of some of the past week's built up nervous tension. She had not driven alone down the Central Coast for years, not since she had first put the Zenkon Foundation together.

She agreed to an arrival time that would allow an early dinner meeting with Scott. He had insisted she stay in their guest room. She had hesitated, not having met him before, but he persisted, and said Holly would definitely approve. So she took him up on the offer.

Getting an early start, she set out on a trip that would take her nearly three hundred miles straight down California's Highway 5 until she reached the Los Robles cut off. It was a fast route that would give her all the time she needed for the promised arrival time.

Driving the center of the state through the Central Valley is not as pretty as the Pacific coastline; but it does have less traffic and stops. The route would lead her far enough north for to take pleasure in the picturesque foothills lining the central coastline and the town of Santa Barbara on the final stretch.

She figured it would take about seven hours or so - plenty of time to think and help sort things out.

It was a perfect California morning. The lingering mists of late winter were already being warmed away by the pleasant morning sun of an early spring in the agricultural rich San Joaquin Valley.

As she turned right onto the on-ramp heading in the south direction of the interstate highway, Margo pushed the button on the dash that slid open the sunroof, letting in the cool refreshing morning air.

Starting up the relaxation music the kids had given her for Christmas a couple of years before; she smiled remembering how tickled they had both been watching her opening the thoughtful gift. They were really excited about their precious find.

The kids had remembered that she was forever saying how stressed she was from all the travel. The two had actually walked about half a mile to a local store to ask the clerk to help them find music that would help their mom unwind. Funny, it actually worked just about every time she listened to it.

Jodie is the younger of her two children, and has the world fully by the tail. She bosses her older brother, Frankie, who adores her, never complaining about her strong will to be the head decider and decision maker.

Sharing custody of the two with her ex-husband has always been a challenge. Communications are strained at best, and his new wife's animosity never lets up even after five years. The only saving grace since the divorce and custody battle is that the three adults in the equation at least make a good effort to keep the differences private from the children.

The kids seem to be well adjusted and happy most of the time, handling two homes and multiple parental rules and regulations with reasonable accommodation. At least, Margo likes to think that is the case.

It is usually curly haired Jodie who serves as head negotiator and peace maker if anything looks like it is getting off track, with Frankie as her faithful backup quarterback.

They would both be staying with their dad until the weekend. Margo had to admit the kids were both cared for and safe with their father and step mother.

She left without eating breakfast, opting to get a quick start. Her stomach began grumbling. Stockton, a sprawling valley town about thirty miles to the south of the Sacramento, would be her first quick stop. There was a trendy café just off the interstate where she knew could get a latte and a muffin.

The traffic was fairly light, as usual, on this stretch of the road.

In recent years, the sprawling farms of the San Joaquin valley had given way to track houses of bedroom communities for commuters into Sacramento and the Bay Area. A few untouched expanses of farmland remained so she was able to enjoy the country scenery and vineyards of rural Lodi.

Most folks actually thought this stretch of the road flat and boring. You had to be a Northern Californian, or more accurately, a Central Valley Californian, to fully appreciate it.

It is all a matter of timing. One could just miss the little window of quiet splendor that opens on the Central Valley before the ceaseless heat of the summer. Summer heat is relentless, rendering this same land a brown washed-out desert for months.

It can also be treacherous at times when enveloped in the deathly *"tulle fog"*. It is a low hanging thick mist that blinds motorists and causes multi-car pile-ups in the dead of winter, or completely shuts down all air traffic into Sacramento.

Now, in the springtime, the rains had given the land a brief green-gold wash of color. The satiny cups of bright orange poppies and the brilliant yellow pack of tarweed crowed the roadside and filled the center divider with a vibrant hue.

Margo fully appreciated the landscape, and often drove this stretch of highway on her commute to the to the corporate headquarters of the Foundation.

She was focused on the previous night's strange conversation with Scott. Something bothered her. It was not the tone of the conversation itself, for they had hit it off immediately. Something he had mentioned had caused her to make a mental note to herself, but she could not quite put all the pieces together. It was something he must have mentioned just in passing that really bothered her.

Senator Hollingsworth had been insistent, even uncharacteristically persistent, about meeting with Scott. These thoughts continued to nag at her, but she shrugged them off.

Still listening to the kids' music, she failed to notice a black sedan following her as she neared the muffin and latte turn off.

"Maybe I'll make it a double latte, that will clear my mind," she thought as she pulled into the café parking space.

She ordered the coffee to go, but then changed her mind. Instead, she took a seat at a small table near the door opting to eat her bran muffin inside the café. It would be her first meeting with Scott, and so she wasn't going to chance a spill down the front of her blouse by drinking coffee as she drove.

There is nothing like making a first impression with a stained blouse, remembering an episode of a humiliated female colleague at a tech company presentation a couple of years back.

"Silicon Valley," the reminder of the location jogged her mind, *"that's it!"*

The passing reference from the previous night's conversation with Scott had something to do with some tech meeting she had attended. However, exactly what was still nagging at her thoughts.

Perhaps Andrew Benton had been causing problems again. This would be cause for some concern. Margo was not certain why that would be a reason for Senator Hollingsworth to pressure her on driving to this meeting.

Andrew Benton had been looming in the background for months since he was abruptly dumped from the Zenkon Foundation a few months earlier, but why would that be so urgent?

She would have to probe Scott. Clearly, something was going on. It was just like navigating the politics of the early days of the Foundation, but surely, that was all water under the bridge.

She sped back onto the highway, and remembered an early Foundation meeting when she had become angry with Benton and Ross for some of their suggestions regarding creative financing of new ventures, or as they called it *"thinking out of the box"*.

They were always up to something, and seemed to thrive on finding ways to circumvent the rules.

Margo always felt in a watchdog mode.

Andrew, Jonathan and Margo regularly gave advice to the annual meeting on investments in projects and global initiatives, and were rarely challenged on their recommendations.

Board members, with their insider knowledge on new initiatives at the tech companies, would also advance projects through partnerships,

The Zenkon Foundation owned a diversified stock allocation, real estate, patents and trademarks from the work of the health and pharmaceutical products, and substantial cash on hand. The nonprofit corporation was in solid financial standing, and all ten of the original founders continued to serve on the Board. The track record of investment, profitable returns and host of philanthropic endeavors was impressive – allowing the initial seed money from the benefactors to grow substantially.

The work of Dr. Schwartz had brought prestige to the Foundation in the public health community. He was convinced that inserting genetic information into other organisms, particularly fungi and plants common in the tropical rain forests, would be relevant for human gene therapy.

He was currently working on removing virulent genes from viruses to create vaccines.

It was painstaking work, but Rolf was a major player on an elite global team. Herbal cosmetic products were popular, and the production and exportation enriched the Foundation and funded further scientific research to find the key to efficient vaccine production.

The relationship between Margo, as Executive Director, and the two managing officers, Andrew and Ross, had never been easy. Over the years, disagreements regarding the direction of investments and selection of projects to receive contributions at times grew to explosive confrontations that continued to fester.

She remembered one particularly hostile annual board meeting where she had confronted Ross.

"You keep playing around, and you are going to sink this organization in a scandal. If you want to be a team player then keeping the mission moving forward on the up and up is your best bet," she had said to him. "But if you let your border line ideas and extravagant taste for fun and games hamstring the initiative, you'll pull us all under."

Of course, he had laughed at her, and said she was too paranoid.

Nevertheless, her words had resonated with Jonathan. He knew he had to watch himself, knowing that she would never tolerate his sleazy schemes.

Margo had walked off angrily. She thought all along that he was trouble. She never forgot about the incident, and where it happened.

Laura had booked them into an incredibly lush private setting at the direction of Andrew Benton.

Money was never an object in the early days. Seed money of sixty-million got attention and lots of perks, and money attracts money. In the Silicon Valley there was always another venture capitalist wanting to rub noses with the big guys, so a tax deductable contribution to the tune of a million or two was a rounding error for their accountants, and more fuel for the Zenkon Foundation.

The meeting was held on eight acres of a prime gold country canyon estate fifteen hundred feet up in the Sierra. It was five thousand plus square feet of custom home. The owner had built it through the courtesy of funds contributed by shareholders in his *dot.com* start up. He leased it out regularly to other Silicon Valley insiders – banking a nice extra hidden cash flow on the side.

It had not taken much persuasion to allow use of the estate for the annual board meeting once Benton tempted him with padded invoice he could use as documentation for a lucrative tax write off with the IRS.

Thinking about the Foundation meeting recalled all its colorful members instantly to Margo's mind.

The member who loomed largest was Maureen Sloan. She was the most opinionated voice of the group from day one. They had become close friends, and were kindred souls with a mutual respect for each other's challenges.

Margo admired Maureen's strength, tenacity, intelligence and her impressive political contacts.

They had first met at the University of California in Los Angeles. Maureen was only a year ahead, and had taken Margo under her wing, giving her lots of motherly advice, not all of it solicited. Margo knew that there were times when she may have made serious blunders if not for Maureen. She was a good friend, and why Margo affectionately called her Mo.

Margo hadn't thought to call Mo before leaving for Santa Barbara, but now it seemed like a good idea. She thought to check in to see if she had any idea why Senator Hollingsworth was intent on her meeting with Scott.

She signaled her car phone to connect with Mo's cell number, but got the familiar recording that she was unavailable, and to leave a message.

Rather than leave the message she hung up, thinking she would just call her again further down the road.

Costa Rica

Dozens of small fishing boats dotted the Guanacaste coastline, gliding silently over the deep blue water of the Pacific.

Sun baked fishermen in white shirts and Panama hats pulled in full nets, harvesting the daily catch for the local beachside restaurants and hotels. The multicolored and modestly built wooden lanchas contrasted with the elegant power boats hired by tourists who had paid hundreds to brag back home that they had reeled in the big one on their tropical holiday. All in all, the setting cast a picturesque panorama just a couple of kilometers off the pristine white sand beaches dotted with early morning walkers.

In the evening, the western setting sun would change the impression to a golden backdrop that silhouetted the nearby islands on the western sky, as the birds and monkeys on the shore settled for the night. But at this time in the morning all was just coming to life and readying for another day.

Helen Nelson let out a sigh of contentment, reflecting on her peaceful life in the small Central American country known as the *"Switzerland of Latin America"*.

Now proud that she had her permanent *cedula*, or national identification, she finally felt like a real local.

For years, she had traveled back and forth between Florida and her modest house in the beach resort of Flamingo, but now being an official permanent resident gave her a true sense of pleasure and belonging. The locals, Ticos as the Costa Ricans proudly referred to themselves, addressed her *Dona Helena*. She liked both the unassuming formality and the respect the title afforded her.

Guanacaste is the most northwestern state in the small country, and was formerly Nicaraguan territory. This is a fact that still instills nationalist tension between the two countries.

The white sand beaches merge into the Nicaraguan border. The tropical beauty, climate and easy going lifestyle make the area a popular attraction for American and European retirees and tourists.

Expat gringo real estate agents along with questionable store front lawyers and title companies lie in wait for a never ending stream of first time visitors enchanted by the breath taking views and uncomplicated lifestyle. Fortunes are made from nonrefundable deposits made by dreamy-eyed foreigners. They think they have discovered a retirement paradise among the high-priced ocean front condos and hillside residences.

The sound of the waves and majestic view would never grow old for Helen. She loved to see the variety of houses across the picturesque bay on the hill above nearby Potrero Beach. Expensive beach view lots owned mostly by millionaires, retired airline pilots and corporate beneficiaries of the international technology boom intermingle with the tiny thatched roof abodes of locals.

Impulsive cash buying on properties listed for much more than true value, along with untrustworthy agents making exorbitant commissions in an unregulated real estate market, resulted in prices skyrocketing. Helen had been furious with this. For years she dreamed of investing her moderate savings in a permanent home once she fully retired.

That hope was long gone.

Instead, she rented a more modestly constructed house from a local, but had a priceless view that she now considered her paradise.

Helen treasured it all.

The early morning sound of the phone ringing had startled her from a deep sleep. Answering it, she noticed that it was still dark outside her window.

"*Buenos dias*", said Helen expecting to hear the voice of a neighbor or local friend.

"Hi Helen, this is Jonathan Ross, sorry if I woke you. I know it's a bit early there, but I needed to reach you as soon as possible."

He sounded a bit tense. Hearing Jonathan's voice had further caught her off guard.

For a moment, she wasn't sure if she was actually awake, or this was the end of some dream or nightmare waking her up.

"My goodness, Jonathan, this is a surprise, nothing serious, I hope".

Ross had never called her before, let alone waking her before even the monkeys had begun daily bellowing to greet the morning sunrise.

She hadn't really given much thought to not hearing from anyone at Zenkon over the past few months, and if truth be known she was losing interest in anything to do with it. Retirement pleasures were taking up all her time, and that was just fine with her.

"Well, everyone is healthy and kicking, so nothing to worry about there," bantered the Zenkon executive.

"But I do need to meet with you in person to go over some things, and want to arrange my flight details this morning for a quick turnaround trip."

"Oh, well I suppose so."

"So it would be okay with you, then?"

"Okay with me, what? My goodness, what is this all about?"

She was now fully alert, and a bit hesitant.

"Jonathan, I am just waking up, please slow down. Can we just go over things on the phone a bit later? And why do you need to come so soon?"

"I can explain more in person, Helen. And I want to be there in the next couple of days, if you don't mind making time for me."

"Of course I can take time for you, Jonathan. I am retired and have all the time in the world. I am just wondering what is so urgent with the Foundation that we cannot discuss on a telephone call a bit later today."

"Helen, I would rather not go into it on the phone, but would really appreciate your advice, if that is alright with you. Besides, a quick trip to *pura vida* land is always an added treat. Any chance you could meet me in San Jose the day after tomorrow?"

"Tomorrow, my goodness that is a spur of the moment trip, isn't it? It must be very urgent for you to have to fly so far. So, I guess the least I could do is to drive to the city and meet up with you. Thankfully, it's not as long a drive as it used to be now with the new road open again."

"Good, Helen, I appreciate it."

"Jonathan, we have had such a time with the tail ends of the rains this year. Mudslides have closed the roads, and landslides you know…," but before she could finish Ross cut her off claiming a waiting call.

She had no time to find out any further details, and so reluctantly agreed to make the drive and rendezvous with him.

His abruptness and sense of urgency to fly all the way down in order to meet threw her off guard, and his rudeness made her uneasy. She scolded herself for being so accommodating and letting him manipulate her into a trip she would definitely rather not take.

Nonetheless, she had agreed to meet him in Belen, a small town a stone's throw from the San Jose airport. But she knew that even with the improved road conditions helping mitigate the stress of the last leg of the drive that it was still a long tiring journey from Guanacaste.

No, she was not looking forward to the trip at all. But her sense of commitment, and a bit of guilt regarding her recent absentee involvement, contributed to her accommodating his strange request.

Helen eagerly accepted the invitation to serve on the Foundation Board when Margaret Maxwell approached her years earlier. She saw it as a way to help further her interest in health and quality of life causes for seniors.

She had a vast national network of senior organizations, and was able to leverage her political contacts to get matching government funds for projects funded by the Foundation.

One project in particular came to mind, where the Foundation funded laptop computers for more than one hundred seniors, and provided training so that they could go online to talk with family and grandchildren far away. The funds for the laptops came from the foundation, and the state funded all the needed wiring and telecommunications access needed in the senior care facilities.

Over time, she was able to see the project scaled as a model to dozens of assisted living facilities throughout the country. She still thought about all the nice letters she received from the residents of the homes. They were so happy that they were able to communicate with their families, especially the grandchildren, due to her efforts.

She considered herself so fortunate to still be healthy enough to live independently, but many of her generation were lonely and isolated. Her work to help alleviate that had been rewarding, and felt she owed that to the investments of the Zenkon Foundation.

But age was creeping up on her.

Her energy level had been considerably reduced due to a serious heart condition. The inevitable slowdown that comes with advanced age also affected her. She subscribed to a new philosophy of enjoying one day at a time, even signing up for a twice a week yoga and meditation class on nearby Flamingo beach.

She found herself looking forward to the sessions with the small group of senior ladies and the young handsome instructor, and enjoying how the morning stretch helped keep her limber.

Her body was definitely slowing, but there was no doubt that her mental acuity was as sharp as ever.

A Board meeting months before came to mind.

Ross, learning of her declining health, had been the one to convince her that the pace of the Foundation was more demanding than she needed.

He had suggested her taking a break from committee work. He told her to concentrate on her retirement move, and when settled they would work something out for her to get active again.

She gladly took him up on his offer to serve as her proxy whenever a vote was needed. Besides, on any really urgent matter Flamingo was only a phone call away, so he had said.

Of course, Ross knew that cost of international telephone bills was an issue that really got Helen going. She was proud of the seniors that she had connected to technologies with video talks and modern communications. But, she personally still preferred the old fashioned way of affixing a stamp to a neatly written letter rather calling on a long distance charge.

Costa Rica, with its unreliable mail delivery and spotty telephone access was just the place for Helen, as far as Ross was concerned to get her out of the way for a while. In fact, sending documents or mail could literally take weeks to arrive, even in the twenty-first century.

The country had a cultural adversity to establishing a national address system, formal street names or house numbers. A residential mailing address could virtually consist of *the yellow house fifty meters from the mango tree near the school.* Hopefully, the mango tree was still there as a sign post for the delivery person, or even worse hope that the yellow house had not been recently painted blue.

Ross intended to keep her isolated from the day to day operations and communications of the Foundation, while he put in motion other plans he had for profiting from business dealings in the small county.

Helen still had the call from Ross on her mind when her cheery employee brought her a cup of strong Costa Rican coffee. This was her morning constitution, and the one habit she refused to give up even at the advice of her doctor. Heart condition, or not, she was not going to sacrifice all the pleasures of life.

"Gracias, Daniel." She said as the friendly Nicaraguan employee placed the hot drink in front of her.

She loved this daily pleasure, and was enjoying the aroma even before the rich taste reached her mouth.

"De nada, senora," he politely responded, as usual.

He did not bother to ask her if she wanted anything to eat, knowing Helen's morning ritual by heart. Their routine consisted of him grinding the Arabica bean coffee, pouring it through a rustic handmade filter suspended on wooden frame, one cup only, and then bringing it to her on the patio.

He would then provide her with a Spanish language daily morning paper that he had walked earlier to buy, or once a week bringing her the English language giveaway.

"Le gustaría el periódico?

He asked pointing to the latest edition of *The Tico Times.*

Helen indicated that she would indeed like to see a copy of the weekly, which claimed to be the leading publication for expats residing in the seven-country Central American region.

Unfortunately, due to rising costs, the paper had already announced that it would soon be making a transition to an online only version of the publication. This was upsetting Helen and a lot of other older expats in the area with either no reliable internet access or interest in reading the news online.

The front-page normally displayed pictures of serene beaches and reported the usual articles about the latest union protests, national political feuds, and the growing crime waves from Mexico and Nicaragua, to the north.

This issue featured pictures of migrants and refugees, escaping from the violence and death threats of drug lords to the south, being detained along the border with Panama.

She sighed, frustrated at the changing times of the once peaceful small country now sandwiched in the middle of the growing unrest.

She flipped quickly to the inside back pages to check out the latest prices on local real estate, another habit she failed to break. She knew the properties were all out of the range of her social security payments and depleted post recession stock portfolio.

Not getting as far as the classifieds, her eyes picked up a short article almost hidden on page ten. The subject of the article, Rosario Ortega, was familiar to her.

Former Minister's Account Closed

Banco Alajuela unexpectedly closed a bank account and seized assets belonging to former Minister of the Environment, and current President for the Environmental Trust Fund of the Zenkon Foundation, Rosario Ortega. The personal account was opened four years ago. Details of the closing are unclear, as banking regulations protect client confidentiality and prohibit bank officials from discussing any information related to private accounts. Outraged, Mr. Ortega indicated to this reporter that he would be filing a formal complaint with the Financial Entities Superintendence (SUGEF) regarding the matter.

Helen raised her eyebrows at the short article.

She had only met Mr. Ortega once during an annual meeting of the Foundation Board. He had traveled to California to report on the progress on a number of environmental projects Zenkon had supported.

Well, well, well. She said to herself, thinking the call from Ross was just too much of a coincidence. Her radar was now fully activated regarding her upcoming trip.

Helen hadn't noticed that Daniel had silently returned to the table and was clearing her empty coffee cup.

Her mind had wandered to what was shaping up to be an interesting encounter with Jonathan Ross.

Santa Barbara, California

The Los Robles cut off knifed through the coastal mountain range just north of Santa Barbara. As Margo continued driving down the highway, she wondered what unsavory deal Ross might be up to now.

He had called her earlier in the week while she was meeting with potential funders in the nation's capitol. He had been as garrulous and charming as ever. Nevertheless, she had instantly sensed the pressure and his insincere manner as he wheedled her for information on the upcoming rounds of federal grant announcements.

They both knew that her contacts on the Hill were worlds better than his were. It was no secret between them that, as usual, he would try to milk her for information. And, if she gave him the leeway, he would most likely take the credit for securing funding.

Yesterday's call, however, had found him unusually interested in her personal life, without a doubt a distraction, she thought.

As she drove the sedan closer to the looming hills, the thought of having to keep a closer watch on Jonathan Ross made her stomach sour with the acids of displeasure. All she needed now was to have Ross be up to something, particularly if it were to drag her or any of the others into something unethical or worse.

Holly's nervousness was enough to worry about without any further trouble from Jonathan Ross.

She sighed and glanced in her rearview mirror, catching a glimpse of the dark colored Lincoln that had ridden in her wake since she had pulled out of the gas station in Santa Nella a while back.

The car closed the distance between them and then moved around her to pass on the two-lane highway. The passenger slowly turned his oddly impassive face toward her as they cruised past. For a split second she considered shifting into a devil may care mood and sticking her tongue out at him. She would not have seen much of a reaction from him as his eyes were hidden behind the icy silence of mirrored pilot style glasses.

The car quickly disappeared into the bright gap of mid-afternoon glare.

A large brown hawk majestically glided down from the hills ahead, coasting low and parallel to the earth, effortlessly it moved back and forth across the rich green rows of T's. The empty wooden crosses served to anchor the newly blooming and twisting vines of Santa Barbara's future wines.

Miraculously, the land had resurrected itself from the dead following the fires that nearly devastated the entire area just a couple of years before. Thousands had evacuated family homes, migrant worker camps, and multi-million dollar mansions, as the unrelenting flames burned an indiscriminate path. No one pulled up and moved on though. Insurance companies paid out billions, and the rebuilding and replanting was as if folks were taunting fate.

The Mexican laborers returned to toil the land again. It was a cycle of life the area and the State had lived with for generations.

As the hawk soared closer, Margo marveled at its huge span of wing, nearly seven feet across. It never flapped its wings, riding the silent drafts down from the foothills stretching across the fields. Its great shadow passed over her as they crossed paths, as if an omen of things to come.

A little while later, Margo pulled into the picturesque coastal town, feeling inside her purse on the passenger seat for the scrap of paper on which she had written the directions to Scott's house. Old school in writing directions, she never programmed them into her phone's GPS, preferring to use freeway signs to guide her to Santa Barbara, and then discovering the last mile the old way with written directions and perhaps an occasional wrong turn.

She dug out the paper with the scribbled directions, and easily followed them up the winding hill to the destination.

Old pink adobe buildings cast their early evening shadows. Sunset would arrive soon. The scene was gifting an impression even more beautiful than any of the local artists could even dream of rendering on canvas.

Scott's house occupied a bougainvillea filled hillside with a clear view of the Pacific Ocean. Although the shoreline was not quite visible, the Channel Islands could be seen before the horizon.

Margo parked the car on a pebble stoned driveway landscaped with palm trees and sago. Collectively, it gave a positive impression of inhabitants with pride of ownership.

"Margaret." Scott greeted, extending his hand as he walked out to greet her.

"Hi Scott, nice to meet you in person, and call me Margo, okay? Much less formal," she said, shaking his hand.

"Great. I've probably read every report you have published, so I feel like I know you already," he commented, leading the way down a short hall past the kitchen.

The house was airy with bone white walls, unstained hardwood floors and luscious plants complimenting the natural views of the hillside which could be seen through the large windows.

"Oh, all that tedious advisory committee work. You must think I'm a tight old policy wonk or something. But I must admit that I can't take total credit. We have some good writers on staff with the talent to convert thinking to polished product".

Scott shook his head and laughed, "Don't be too modest, now, every train needs a good engine".

He looked to be in his mid-forties and was tall and trim. She registered that he was probably serious about exercise and health.

"Seriously though, you're one of the few people who actually know how to clearly address the key issues. Not everyone can use reliable data, touch on all the salient points and boil it all down in a very easy to understand way."

"Well thank you."

Margo took a seat on the white leather couch.

"But you're no slouch either. You come very highly recommended from one of the best statesmen in the world. Holly insisted that I make the call to you. I nearly had to promise him in writing that I would come right away."

"That, to me," Scott laughed, sitting down in a contemporary style Italian charcoal gray recliner, "sounds like the Holly I know and love."

Margo laughed with him.

"Indeed," she said, rolling her wide brown eyes in exaggerated exasperation.

"Say," Scott said, sitting up on the edge of the chair. "Would you like something to drink? A glass of wine – we've got a nice Santa Barbara Merlot and a Chardonnay, some bottled water, like High Mountain Sparkle or something. I think Megan has some diet soda in there, too. I'm going to have a beer."

"A glass of Chardonnay sounds marvelous."

"I have it coming right up!"

Scott hopped up and disappeared around the corner into the kitchen.

Margo pushed herself up from the couch and walked across the living room and out the French doors that opened onto the balcony.

The house was set about midway up the terraced hillside and looked out over the western edge of Santa Barbara and the sea beyond.

Scott came onto the deck with their drinks.

"This is a breath taking view, you are very lucky."

"Yes, fortunately we moved here years ago. I guess these days we probably wouldn't be able to even consider buying in this neighborhood – even with the fires!"

She agreed on what a disaster the fires had been over the past five years.

"Do you want to sit out here and unwind from the ride before we get you settled in?"

"Sure. And thanks again for the invite, clearly it is lovely."

They sat and sipped in silence for a while. Scott leaned forward and placed his glass on the wooden coaster resting on the smoked glass tabletop.

"So your trip down was okay, I take it."

"Fine, actually much more than fine, the drive is relaxing. It's easy to take for granted how beautiful our state can be, although climate change is definitely taking its toll."

"I nearly forgot, you just got back from DC, and here you are on the move again," Scott lamented.

"You must have been running on fumes this morning."

"Oh, I'm used to it. I commute into the Bay Area almost weekly. I have a little café about halfway between my house and the Silicon Valley that has a great latte and muffin."

They sat a bit awkwardly, as the sea slowly engulfed the sun. Scott stood, offering her a quick snack, which she politely refused.

"Then let's go settle you into the guest room. We have a couple of hours or so before dinner, so if you like you can refresh or just relax till it's time to go. The restaurant is just down the hill, and casual."

Margo obediently followed Scott back through the house. He proudly toured her through the home, talking about how they had renovated it after the purchase.

It was now decorated in contemporary design, simple lines, clean, plenty of space and definitely uncluttered. It offered the luxury of space for husband and wife to avoid bumping into each other while not being forlorn or lonely.

The guest room and bath were on the lower level, providing privacy from the main house and master bedroom.

Scott took leave of Margo, explaining that he needed to go back upstairs to his study to do a little work before dinner, and before Megan, his wife arrived home.

Margo lifted her travel case up onto the comfortable looking queen size bed, adorned with pillows in all the shades of the ocean and sand. She removed a change of clothes for the evening and hung them on the closet doorknob.

She took her toiletry case and small bag of makeup into the bathroom. The polished stainless fixtures gleamed highlighting the pristine white porcelain countertops.

Back in the bedroom, she moved her bag to the floor, relocated some of the pillows to a spare corner, and stretched out on the bed, remembering that she still needed to make the call to Mo.

She dug in her bag for her phone, just as it set off a warning beep that she was out of range to make a call.

Tired from the drive, the fresh sea air and glass of wine were proving soothing sleep enhancers. She easily dozed off, only waking to the sound of a closing door, hurried steps and faint voices in the kitchen above. Checking her watch, she was surprised that she had napped for nearly an hour and a half.

She quickly showered, dressed in a pair of skinny jeans and white blouse, and went upstairs in the direction of the sounds.

"I am really sorry, Sweetheart," the woman was saying as she picked up the briefcase by the entry to the study.

"But we have a major crisis down at the Center. I have to run damage control."

Striding down the hall towards the front door was a stunning blond, briefcase in hand, speaking over her shoulder to Scott who followed in her wake. The woman straightened, and turning, saw Margo.

"Hi!" You must be Margaret," she said coming forward, hand outstretched.

"I'm Megan, and so sorry that I am just running in and out at the moment".

"Margo, please. It's a pleasure to meet you"

"Megan can't join us for dinner, some disastrous tangle down at the Center, so it looks like it is just the two of us".

"Oh, I'm so sorry to hear that. I was so looking forward to visiting with you as well. I hope it's nothing too serious."

"Not if I can get back there and get in front of the media before anybody else does. Our clients may be undocumented, but they are still entitled to their rights and legal counsel. As long as I can fend off the press until we can sort through the wreckage of an ICE raid this afternoon on the vineyards it will be okay. Hopefully, it shouldn't get more serious than a few noses bent out of shape and a big embarrassment for someone."

"Yeah and it means I'm saving a couple of bucks on dinner," said Scott trying to make light and nudging his wife.

"Listen to him, will you?" frowned Megan. "Anyway, sorry I can't join you, but I have to go."

She pushed past Scott into the study where she began searching through a tall file cabinet. She found what she was looking for in a green folder, put it in the briefcase, kissed her husband and headed for the front door.

"I hopefully won't be too late. We will catch up later, Margo for a night cap".

*****

The restaurant was a fashionable affair on State Street that specialized in California Nouvelle Cuisine. Margaritas were part of the regular fare, and Scott with Margo's concurrence ordered a couple of *House Top Shelf* on the rocks with salt and a side of guacamole and chips.

Margo was wondering what the connection really was between Scott and Holly. But Scott insisted they first enjoy a tasty meal and the relaxing ambiance, saving the serious talk until dessert and coffee.

Setting down his coffee cup, Scott, almost reading her mind, volunteered, "I'm actually under contract to Holly to help him navigate his transition from public to private citizen."

"Oh, I didn't know that, Scott."

"You would be surprised at the complexity of issues and maze of rules and regulations governing what elected officials can and cannot do even after they leave office."

"I am sure with Holly's reputation that he has more than enough options."

" He has offers coming from left and right, and, of course, wants to be squeaky clean on any semblance of conflict with corporate interests should he decide to stay involved."

Margo nodded, curious.

"I had heard that the Department of Justice was given marching orders to dig up some new dirt on corporate scandals. But Holly can't be concerned about anything to do with that?"

"No, but there's going to be an avalanche of serious reform proposals on the Hill to help push through the Administration's clean house initiatives. Talk about hypocrisy, right? But regardless, Holly doesn't want to have any bleeps on his radar screen. His expertise and connections will be very valuable to any client he represents, should he decide to move in that direction."

"So then why the sudden concern now with the Foundation?

"That is exactly what we want to get to the bottom of, Margo. He had a call from DOJ with some insinuating remarks that caught him off guard."

"Holly has always played by the book. He is always the one on the Board that insists on everything thoroughly researched and documented, from personnel to financials before we sign off on a project or grant. Sometimes he even questions the cost of a meal at a meeting, making sure it won't come back to haunt him that he took some sort of a favor."

"You and I know that, but these days reality is what you make it, and a few well placed conspiracies, and you are guilty of taking kick backs with a long road to proving yourself innocent."

"That is for sure, Scott. It is disgusting how much innuendo gets reported as fact."

"Plus, inquiries on the Hill have been making some folks uneasy. So far, it has only been informal inquiries with seemingly innocent questions – but your President Jonathan Ross is tooting his horn all over town. That is a problem, and he is casting unwanted attention at Holly.

"Ross enjoys his image as poster boy for the fat cats." She was starting to get a bit worried.

"Look, Margo, Holly is very uneasy about his name being raised along with Ross' in conversations regarding the Foundation investments and some of the federal programs he has supported."

"But the Foundation is clean. We have always played by the books."

"Are you sure about that?"

"Of course we are. What are you trying to insinuate?" She responded more defensively than she had intended.

"Just be careful, and watch your back, things may not be as straightforward as you think. Holly tells me that he thought Ross was always a question mark. His true colors may be starting to show."

"What do you mean?"

"Margo, you have been around the Washington scene for long enough to know that nothing is the way it seems, and everyone is out to get as much power and fortune as possible. Jonathan looks out for his own interests, you know that, and maybe, shall we say, he has gone too far."

"Go on."

"Look, I am not implying anything remiss on your part."

"Well I certainly hope not, I have never, and I mean never done anything unethical regarding Zenkon.

"But Ross has had free reign and built up quite an international network on some of these projects over the years. Are we really sure on everything he may have had going?

"I see what you are saying."

"And, remember, this is election year politics. If the opposition can throw a bone at the media or even create any reason to hold congressional hearing on questionable use of federal funding they will do it.

"Especially involving a senior senator such as Holly."

"Yes, and it certainly would take the heat off them on some of their own shortcomings this past four years. Diversions are what they need, and we want to make sure we are not the ones to give them cause, right?"

"Now you really have me nervous."

"We don't want you nervous, Margo. We want you on guard, and to help us think through this."

"Holly apparently did not send me down here just to talk possibilities. What do you both know is going on?"

"We know nothing for sure at the moment. But let's say that Andrew Benton may be bent on singing a tune that the Administration wants to hear now that he is a free agent. That would place him in line for a nice post if the election goes right."

"Well I can confirm that he made no secret about the idea of living in style as an ambassador somewhere in Europe."

"We suspect Ross has been feathering his nest on either deals with Benton or even solo."

"You can't be serious! How could they fool the entire Foundation?"

"Let's just say that you may have been manipulated big time without knowing. You may have worked on some grant or project that they used as a front for their own self interests. And if that is about to backfire big time, we need to move to figure out what and how – and quickly head this off at the pass. Holly's reputation and perhaps the future of the Foundation depend on us getting to the bottom of it."

"This is really hard to believe, Scott.

"How could they have fooled me and all the other Board members?"

"Look, Margo, it may be hard for you to accept and swallow your pride, but you know as well as I do that nonprofits have served as havens to cover up national and international misdeeds for decades. I am not saying that is what is going on here, or what those two were plotting. Nevertheless, Holly is convinced that we do have a problem here, and we need you on our side to help figure this out.

"For right now, continue business as usual until we get more data. You have to deal with Ross as if all is normal, and keep the Foundation activities operating as if all is normal."

She stared at him dumbfounded, and he continued.

"At the same time we need to do a lot more digging to find out why Ross was so adamant about getting rid of Benton. It was obviously more than the managerial style differences he touted at the last Foundation meeting. Once we know that then perhaps we will be on the road to figuring the rest. Then we decide how best to handle it."

"I still don't believe it."

"Believe me, we all need to work together make sure that we come out clean for everyone's sake. Hopefully it can be handled internally."

"Oh God, if they have set us up, it will bounce right back to me. I will never be able to show my face again."

"Listen, according to Holly you are the one with the best grip on the thinking of the Foundation. You understand the motives that drive each of the players. Right now we need you to stay solid. Put your thinking to good use to figure out what the hell these jerks have going."

Margo stared, unable to speak.

"Look Margo, sorry that I was the bearer of this bad news, but can I count on you to hold strong and help sort this out?"

She nodded, trying to look calm, but under the table both her hands began shaking on her knees.

As the delicious meal had been, it now felt more like an unwanted hard brick in her stomach. She wasn't sure if her legs would actually hold her up as she rose from the table.

*****

She lay on the bed in Scott's guest room, restless and unable sleep. Her thoughts took her back to the day she and Ross had worked together to refine the idea for the non-profit Foundation. It had been after she had approached the Silicon Valley giants with the original concept.

Margo had a strong feeling that some sort of public interest philanthropy, financed from major contributions by the *dot.com* success stories, could actually help them demonstrate good intensions and a semblance of social responsibility to regulators and the cynical press.

Even at the height of the stock boom, the young rich entrepreneurs were taking hits on their self-centered attitudes, and for good cause.

To succeed, the Foundation, as a whole, would have to represent diverse social agendas and contribute to a wide range of global causes. The members themselves needed to be a balance of big donors and advocates with unquestionable reputations as champions for the underdog.

The corporate guys would build their social standing as philanthropists. Special interest advocates would get their projects for the poor, underrepresented, and general social good funded.

Ross was a mid level staff director of the People's Rights League, and while his character was personally offensive, the involvement of his organization could not be ignored if the credibility of the Foundation's mission was to be publicly accepted.

PRL was a liberal national lobby group, and had a good reputation for protecting the interests of the underrepresented. PRL's reputation was impeccable, and would be just the balance to the *dot.com* guys.

Jonathan Ross was not the PRL representative she initially wanted for the Foundation. She wanted his boss. Public buy-in to the project rested heavily upon involvement of a good guy group, and the head of PRL was the one with the squeaky clean reputation.

However, she could not convince him to sign up. He could not bring himself to personally work on a project with the high tech sharks, no matter how altruistic – so he offered Ross as the sacrificial lamb, if for no other reason than to get the inside scoop on the operations and keep tabs on what was going on.

Ross was a newcomer at PRL, but there was no doubt that he was not going to let the grass grow under his feet.

Like Margo, he had studied the Japanese business models in college and sensed the opportunity. He was a Beverly Hills rich boy playing at social justice – a true limousine liberal. As a gifted undergraduate, he was elected student body president in his sophomore year. In his senior year, he represented the Ivy League schools at the Young Democrats national convention.

It was at that gathering that he caught the attention of the national office of the PRL. He made an impressive presentation at one of the plenary sessions, and was later recruited to the League's west coast operation. He was seen as an up and comer.

It was also clear that he saw PRL as simply a stepping-stone to loftier goals. His ambition alone was enough to cast his lot with Margo and get access to play ball with the big boys.

He immediately caught on to her stream of thought about where she was headed with her project, and could hardly contain his enthusiasm of wanting to play a big role.

"So Margo, what you are saying is that it may be possible to design some way to have folks put aside their own self interests and work together on projects that support the greater good?"

"That is the idea Jonathan. Can we make that happen in the world of philanthropy? It would be a wonderful experiment if we could pull it off."

"Sounds like a worthy cause, but where would you even start?'

"I was hoping you would have enough interest to ask that question."

"Consider it asked."

"I think the answer may be in coalition building similar to the model that a Professor Ouchi once proposed. In fact, he wrote the book on the theory."

"So Margo, you are saying that we would be taking the ideas, and experimenting with the real deal."

"Yes, he calls it *Theory Z*."

The Japanese model had been used by academia as a perfect case study of how different political perspectives, particularly government and industry, could set aside differences for the greater social good, focusing on what they could agree upon rather than be divided by their individual diversity.

It was a perfect fit for Margo's idea of consensus global philanthropic efforts to balance incredible amassing of wealth by the few in Silicon Valley.

Ross and Margaret had a common grounding in the approach from the start. The idea of putting theory into practice and making it work for a nonprofit corporation appealed to both of them.

Jonathan jumped in with how he thought it could work.

"First you pull together a truly representative group of public interest advocates, covering all your bases: labor, education, health, government, and so on," he said.

"That will form your working group – The Foundation." She agreed, continuing enthusiastically.

"But remember, Jonathan, we keep them from killing off the project, or each other, by showing them their common interest."

"Well, that should be relatively easy, since all of them can focus on the needs of the underdog against the wealth and greed of the Silicon Valley fat cats!"

"Not so harsh against the donors. We have to let them see mutual interests and then harness enthusiasm for the greater good of both sides. After all, the Silicon Valley type guys will be footing the bill for this. They expect some return on investment."

"The trick will be to keep the investments balanced with social causes, Margo, or else it will look self-serving and defeat the purpose."

"Board members will know that, our job will be getting them to stick to it."

"Well, right now all you need is to get the right folks to buy in on both sides. Then get them all on the same page."

"I agree, Jonathan, but I won't mislead anyone or misrepresent the objectives. I assume once the project gets started it will take on a life of its own."

"You sound pretty confident, Margo."

"I know we can make it work."

"*We?*" he said, trying to act modest.

"Of course, I mean us, unless you don't want to be involved in the project. You are the guy PRL gave me. I guess if you are not up to the challenge, I can give you back!

She knew PRL wanted part of the project, and was sure they would find someone else if Jonathan wanted to back out.

"Hey, don't jump to conclusions. I would not miss this one for all the sake in Japan! I'm in."

Their enthusiasm even had them dusting off old college textbooks to make sure they were on the right page. The buy in pitch to the recruits was to have them see the value in investing for the good of society, and using Silicon Valley dollars to do it.

Margo was also relying on her thinking that the public interest advocates would actually jump at getting an opportunity to deal directly with the new technology economy sector. Although they would never admit it, honorariums and all expenses paid meetings and travel to lavish surroundings appealed to nonprofit staff.

She was convinced that there was enough common ground and self-interest on both sides for a win-win scenario – and a strange political alliance was more than possible.

From the beginning, the phone company had been a perfect target for Margo to hit for financing the Foundation. Whining public interest groups were always on its regulatory back, and it needed all the positive press it could get.

Technology was rapidly transforming the old telephone network to be far more than a wire used to transmit voice calls. The industry was exploding with new high speed data services bringing entertainment via streaming video and interactive multimedia right to every home. Data was driving the new economy, and Silicon Valley had the vision, technologies, and talent to make it happen. This evolution had sparked such a growth that vaporware business plans turned into gold by selling fantasy profit margins to venture capitalists.

Many of the investors had no understanding of what was going on, just that they needed to be players in the game.

Consumers had to be convinced that it was in their best interest to pay higher phone bills to replace old copper telephone wires from the fifties and sixties with new high speed fiber optic or coaxial cable to be able to use all these fancy services.

Margo and Ross wrote up a detailed proposal and were given time on the calendar of the Vice President at the telephone company.

He wasn't much of a visionary. He liked to do things the way he had been trained through years of molding by the Ma-Bell training regime. He proved a more difficult a sell on their proposal that they had expected. He was courteous enough during the presentation, but his vacant nods indicated that he really did not have much of a clue what the hell they were talking about.

The descriptions of a Japanese model they raved on about seemed to go in one ear and out the other – and quite frankly the fact that PRL was involved made him even more determined that this was a crazy deal.

He had promised he would give them an ear so he listened.

Margo and Ross were beginning to doubt they would get his buy in at all. However, he suddenly perked up when they predicted that the Foundation would save him from dealing with lots of groups who constantly approached them for funding various charitable projects.

Now they had his full attention!

If he agreed to buy in, not only would he be rid of them for the rest of the afternoon, but also he could use them to keep dozens of other grant seekers away. They would have to be the ones to deal with all the minority group requests, and consumer groups, and tree huggers, and whoever else might emerge as a thorn in his side.

Now that appealed to him.

He officially signed on with the caveat that one of his Vice Presidents would represent the company perspective on the Foundation – after all, he had to answer to his Board on the sizeable donation.

Andrew Benton would be the designated team player from PRT.

Margo and Jonathan now had clear sailing and enough seed money to pull the rest of the Foundation together.

It took the better part of a year to recruit the other benefactors.

California is the Mecca of public interest advocacy – a cause on every street corner. The list of potentials included political activists, academics, right wing causes, left wingers, environmentalists, ethnic minorities, seniors and children's rights groups.

Margo and Jonathan scrutinized the candidates as if they were the CIA trolling for special deep-cover agents. They left nothing to political chance – the Foundation might be a strange family, but there was no doubt it would be managing a substantial budget.

They needed exactly the right mix. The personalities had to gel.

"How many more candidates do we need to review," he asked as they sat in her office one evening.

"Well, with the last round of eliminations we have about twenty five files that look really solid."

"God, we still have twenty five of them!

"That is right, my friend, we are in California after all." She laughed.

"How are we ever going to cut that list down to the right ten or so members that can work together, yet each brings something unique to the party?"

"We have gotten this far. I can smell success." Margo responded, taking a bite from the pickle that had come with the pastrami sandwiches they had ordered from the corner deli.

"I hope so. My social life cannot take much more of this suffering. Burning the midnight oil here had taken its toll."

"Just hang in there, Jonathan. We should be able to wrap it up shortly."

"Then the fun will really begin." He said.

The process was methodical and an intense intellectual challenge. They both loved it. They were each political junkies of the highest order. This was the best fix of high stakes strategy either of them had ever been close to.

After months of analyzing and scrutinizing, checking and rechecking sources, they finally hewed out the list of the top fifteen names, and were ready to meet with Benton on the final cut.

A couple turned them down outright. Either it was bad timing or they just would not join alliances with either the Telco or the Silicon Valley investors. They preferred the clarity of black and white and declared on which side they remained to fight their battles.

The final selections were made for eight to occupy seats on the new Board of Directors. Ross and Benton would constitute the other two, and agreed that Margo be nominated to serve as the Foundation's Executive Director.

Three of the names were public interest representatives, one a Senator, and four were wealthy technology geeks, whose stock shares plans had turned to gold, allowing them more than enough play money to contribute generously to the cause.

Collectively the members of the newly formed Zenkon Foundation had probably kept at least legal departments busy over the last decade with litigation against each other for one cause or another.

There was not a wilting violet in the group.

Frankfurt, Germany

A monotone electronic voice from the GPS system commanded Benton to keep left and take the A-81 Ausfahrt five hundred meters ahead.

The driver obligingly obeyed the virtual navigator's directive.

The fast pace of the autobahn, along with the lingering strain of the fatal encounter, had been enough for him, and so he decided to take a detour through the back roads. He figured that even if he stopped for a hearty local meal that he would still arrive at the airport in plenty of time to check in for the night at the Airport Sheraton Hotel.

His flight to London was scheduled at seven-thirty the next morning.

Naked grape vines terraced in the Inca style farming, and seemingly out of place in the centuries old German vineyards, indicated the route was nearing the Heilbronn area. This placed the killer only about an hour or so from Frankfurt Am Main Airport. He was confident of his timing and route programmed into the navigation system. German engineering was most reliable.

The female electronic voice came to life again. She instructed him to take the B-27 exit. He obeyed. As he departed the main highway onto the two-lane road, he noticed the collection of small houses topped with brown slate roofs, and marveled at the spotlessly clean streets and front pathways in this working class town of Neckarsulm.

Every Saturday the *Hausfrau* for generations faithfully and meticulously swept and cleaned the front porches, readying them for the weekend strollers' inspecting eyes. The custom and pride in cleanliness had not changed in centuries throughout the German hamlets.

The large grey building of the Audi automotive plant dominated the landscape. Benton reduced his speed to the indicated seventy kilometers per hour. Drivers on the Autobahn broke the speed barriers, but no one drove faster than was posted on the surface streets. That was the rule.

The evening had cast a heavy black shadow over the fields, replacing the haze and brown landscape that the winter sky afforded. A few signs telling daytime signs were beginning to announce that spring might not be too far away, but for the most part the lingering winter remained casting a grey gloom and winter chill.

He continued for about five kilometers and then turned a sharp left at an old cemetery. Gravestones stretched for miles, giving the impression that more residents resided under the ground than above it in the many villages dotting the country landscape.

A momentary chill rippled through his body as the vision of Rolf came to him. The neatly positioned headstones denoted an eternal home to several generations of the town's inhabitants, and seemed much more respectful than the old plastic ice chest over the remains of the scientist.

He intentionally changed his thinking back four months earlier to Zenkon's annual Board meeting. The scene he recollected still made him fume.

He vividly recalled the ungrateful backstabbing from Ross. The relationship had always been one of mutual distrust and suspicion, each hiding a dark agenda. But the little weasel had no idea who he was playing with. He certainly had no concept of the dangerous relationships Benton was navigating in some of his deals.

He tried to give just enough information to keep Jonathan satisfied, but it was never enough to keep him from poking his nose where it wasn't wanted. If he had just minded his own business, they both could have continued using Zenkon's squeaky clean cover without anyone's interference or knowledge.

The idiot had ruined everything with his meddling.

The GPS assistant interrupted his thoughts again. She was now instructing him to follow a winding road. A weathered signpost confirmed that he was near Bergen, another small industry town that specialized in metal works.

A large wooden sign indicating the Alabama Saloon dominated the corner lot, as he turned left, seeming to be misplaced in this land of the *Biergärten* and *Gasthäuser*.

He noticed a small town hall clock ensconced in a pale pink tower indicating that it was eight o'clock, and wondered if he might be able to make it to Heidelberg before dark. The magnificent historic city on the banks of the Neckar River would be ideal for a late evening meal.

He proceeded to drive along at a brisk, but legal, pace, passing through the quaint village of Eberbach just in time to hear the chiming of the church bells signaling the eight thirty evening service.

It was only twenty more kilometers to Heidelberg, and he was now feeling hungry. He was enjoying this brief break away from earlier events, deciding that fatal encounter with Rolf was not going to cast a cloud over his life or his appetite.

Heidelberg is rich in history and architectural elegance, its history spanning at least seven centuries. The Old Bridge, as it is known, is a relatively new feature, having been constructed in 1786. It replaced an earlier wooden bridge that had traversed the Neckar River for centuries.

The immense Castle and surrounding walls date primarily back to the baroque reconstruction of the city about 1700, although the first authentic recording of the town's history is documented from 1196.

Heidelberg University was founded in 1386, and still prides itself on attracting highly qualified scientists from all over the world.

The setting sun in the western sky cast a beautiful orange glow over the towering castle and the Gothic buildings constructed on the steep cobblestone city streets.

The views reminded Benton in a way of the hilly streets of his own San Francisco home.

Viewing the breathtaking German city again, Benton recalled memories of the purpose for his first visit to the town, trying to brush uninvited thoughts of Rolf aside.

It was a scholastic awards conference years earlier that had caused him to travel to the city. During the meeting he was introduced to Dr. Rolf Schwartz, who was then a visiting scholar in biochemistry at the University. Pacific Rim Telecom was a corporate sponsor of the conference. At that time the company was courting favors to make inroads in Europe for an expanding wireless market.

Rolf gave an impressive presentation on the need for corporate social responsibility in addressing the growing risk of global pandemics. He unabashedly requested help with financing his expensive research into developing preventative measures.

Benton had been impressed with the scientist's determination and boldness, and subsequently invited him to the corporate headquarters to pitch his proposal.

The event in California had been a public relations success for the telephone company and raised four hundred thousand dollars for Rolf's effort. More importantly, it had initiated a relationship with Rolf and Andrew that spanned more than a decade.

Zenkon Foundation began contributing to Rolf's efforts. His research was well on the way to protocols for development of experimental vaccines. Benton made sure the scientist was a priority for a sizeable investment by the non-profit organization to assist in both development and eventual manufacturing processes.

The Board of the nonprofit unanimously approved a proposal for the establishment of the *Deutsche Pharmaceutical Research Foundation* during its first year of operation.

Maxwell and Ross were both in complete agreement with Benton that the focus and need for alliances with other countries was well within the organization's mission and focus, and a German location would be excellent. Benton had no trouble in rallying support for a multiyear grant in the amount of five million dollars, providing he could get matching funds for the idea.

International health organizations and other government programs were already warning about preparation for a global pandemic. Benton correctly assumed that he would have no problem convincing Senator Hollingsworth that a federal partnership would be a good idea.

A special research project slipped into the HHS appropriations budget, identified as an international health alliance for developing countries, was secured.

It was listed in the Federal Register as a non-competitive ten million dollars grant for a university and nonprofit partnership program between California and Germany. Research and resulting product production benefits were to be targeted for developing countries.

The Zenkon Foundation was awarded its first federal grant contract for management of a global public health initiative.

The idea of developing generic drugs to provide to developing countries was not a new concept. For years, there has been a bitter divide between drug manufacturers and activists on this issue. Poor countries, generally in the most need of drugs to combat highly transmittable diseases, are least able to afford the cost of the medications.

Billions of dollars from western countries and China are pledged to the World Health Organization and other international relief efforts. Nonprofit organizations apply for international licensing rights to distribute, and in some cases partner in the manufacturing of the drugs. Pharmaceutical companies continue to play a public game of feigning to fight third party generic production or international distribution rights, while in fact a complex web of interlaced relationships, along with blurry lines on what is legal, illegal, or a combination of both, is a challenge to sort out.

Legal drug distribution within the United States is a regulatory nightmare. As many as ten or more stops may be made on the route between a manufacturer and the consumer. The manufacturer of the drug is not required to inform the drug store or the consumer of the distribution process.

The Federal Drug Administration has responsibility for the safety of the manufacturing process, but is not responsible for the distribution chain. This is managed, or more likely mismanaged, by a mixture of bureaucracies in each of the fifty states, all with separate purchasing processes.

States regularly compete with other states for product, pushing up the cost of the drugs for consumers. Cost of the same drug in different states can be quite different.

This shortfall has opened the door to an array of fraudulent handlers and distributors. A paper trail is rarely required by any of the states. The illegal diluting of expensive drugs for cancer and diabetes has become a serious problem, as well as a lucrative business for some.

Andrew Benton brought his thoughts back to the present as he drove the last few meters across the Old Bridge and parked his car on a cobblestone road near the Marktplatz and main gate of the Castle.

He walked a few short steps to the Hackteufel restaurant, and pushed open the heavy old fashioned wooden door. Greeted with the aroma of the cooking pork and veal he suddenly realized how hungry he actually was.

Typically for this time of day, the popular establishment was already crowded with locals enjoying a meal. He approached a small table set for two presently occupied by an older man just finishing his a beer.

"*Guten Abend*," Benton offered in his broken German.

"Guten Abend," the local returned the greeting, and politely smiled as he signaled him to be seated.

A pleasant young waitress brought a well worn menu card from which he made his choice. He then settled down anticipating a tasty meal before continuing on his short hop to the airport hotel where he planned on spending the night.

In the morning, he would walk easily from the hotel lobby to the connected concourse.

He knew that he would be well rested and ready to leave Germany and the remnants of the deadly trail behind him.

San José, Costa

Had Helen Nelson invested a little effort in learning how to use technology as simple as caller location identification perhaps she would have known that Jonathan Ross was already in the country when he called her earlier that morning.

He had already arrived the evening before when he told her he was in process of making his travel plans.

The modern airport facility where he landed is located only a few minutes from the hotel. Like all government projects it is a topic of corruption and political controversy.

Government officials, in a zeal for privatization, turned the renovation project over to a competitive process. It was awarded to an American corporation to oversee the construction and manage the facility for the next twenty years. The company was constantly behind construction completion schedules.

A current investigation alleges the firm has overcharged airport user fees to the tune of more than fifty million dollars. Legal messes and legislative hearings will continue, a few heads may ultimately roll, but no doubt the twenty-year contract will be renewed with promises and winks.

The growing popularity of the small country has expanded the number of international airlines with regular routes from Europe, the United States, Canada, and South America. Tourists are enticed with visits to rain forests, beautiful beaches, and the *pura vida* lifestyle.

Thousands of tourists a day stream into a small customs and baggage area, sometimes having to wait hours for passports to be stamped with the visitor visa. On arrival Ross was trapped among the throngs of passengers.

He was now, however, comfortably settled at the elegant Marriott Resort San Jose. The hotel is nestled on the grounds of former lush coffee fields, and originally built just a stone's throw from the sprawling Intel technology facility.

Intel constructed the factory with great fanfare. The company boasted that it was a replica of the worldwide plant located in Folsom, California. Microchip production, and cottage industries spawned by the plant, for a brief time surpassed coffee production exports for the small country.

Then with the expiration of government waivers, including ten years of tax free operation, Intel deserted the small country. It moved most of the operation to China on promises of a better profit margin. Thousands of locals were left unemployed, and the welfare of the local economy suffered.

Marriott also lost business clients when Intel pulled out. The resort now caters more to the tourist and wedding crowds.

The large Intel building stands as witness to faded hopes for government private sector partnerships.

Ross had become a regular at the luxury hotel during his frequent trips to the Central American capitol city. He liked the convenience, the friendly staff that recognized him on arrival. The great coffee served at the hotel's small corner café was an added treat. It was at the hotel that Ross had first met his main contact in Costa Rica years before.

Corruption of elected officials fosters a culture in Mexico, Central America and the Caribbean to look sideways to money laundering activities. Of course, the locals justify their own actions by being the first to admit that Costa Rica is only moderately corrupt compared to other countries such as Mexico or Colombia.

Even though there has been an attempt at cleansing of the Tico political campaign process, relatively speaking, reforming political processes anywhere is difficult at best.

During the post-millennium election process, all the candidates in Costa Rica made the usual pledges of honesty and anti-corruption. But as with most politicians, the old ways of nepotism and corruption ensconced in elected office are hard to erase.

Moreover, since terms of elected office are short in the small Central American country, and compensation modest, there are always bad apples that for a price are willing to be enticed to feather their nests for the longer term.

Ross found an eager cohort for the deceptive plans he had in mind under the legitimate cover of Foundation business. Rosario Ortega was just the right person.

Ortega was born and raised in the municipality of Cartagena de Santa Cruz, a small farming community in northern Guanacaste near the Nicaraguan border.

As a boy he dreamed of becoming a famous soccer star. He had big ambitions, and was bright. Bright enough to know that he did not have the right stuff to make it as a football player.

Instead, even at age fifteen he witnessed firsthand the growth of foreign visitors to the Guanacaste coast, and quickly learned that gringos would pay good money for a handsome local tour guide. Familiar with the stretches of coastal beaches, he provided adventures for the tourists to capture photos of cappuccino monkeys and sea turtles. He guided trips to snorkel in the turquoise waters off the shores of nearby Catalina Islands.

Rosario had the personality and the business acumen to start his first business before he reached nineteen. By age twenty five he was running four different operations along the western coast. He had a team of employees stretching from Tamarindo in the north to Jaco in the south. He trained them in how to entertain on adventures through the rain forests, on deep-sea diving expeditions, and night time turtle viewings.

It was a natural for him to expand operations to include real estate. Older tourists who could be easily lured into investing in retirement dreams and properties with magnificent views of the Pacific Ocean were always available.

Impulsive decisions and non-refundable deposits on lots with the promise of a newly built home made him a small fortune. More than half of the property buyers backed out of a contract once they returned home, cleared their heads, and realized the challenges of packing up and moving to a developing country with a foreign language was more difficult than they had imagined.

Forfeiting a few thousand on the deposit was a big loss for retirees. But losing a deposit was better than hundreds of thousands more building a home that most likely would not work out for them. Ortega was sometimes able to sell the same lot twice or even three times in one season.

Now he was a confident, if not cocky, self-made entrepreneur.

Yet his humble beginnings, in a class-conscious society, dogged him. It was more a psychological factor than lack of means, but he was insecure socializing with the country's well educated and upper class society.

He had not attended private schools. He had no connections to foreign universities, and certainly not the historical lineage to be connected to the ruling elite. He remained a social outcast, and as far as he was concerned, this gave him personal license to take care of himself.

A self financed run for political office was his proclamation at recognition. Personal assets enabled him to finance a campaign run.

He constructed a first class soccer field in his home town. Then on election day he virtually led a parade of locals from the plaza to the polling stations in their colorful green and blue team shirts.

Loud blasts of *Ortega para el futuro* could be heard through deafening speakers perched on the back of Toyota pickups. He had an election victory in the town of three thousand residents —easily half that number were at the Sunday afternoon soccer game.

Of course, he rarely visited Santa Rosa. He preferred the luxury of his spacious Escazu home. He lacked empathy for his own people; with disdain for what he believed was a lack of drive and ambition.

Two terms as a legislator, and donations to other politicians, secured him an appointment to national office as Minister of the Environment. At the time, he considered it one of his best investments. He soon realized that he had been outsmarted by the political establishment.

89

The appointment was to a position that was gradually being relegated to insignificance as advocates for development and infrastructure were gaining control over environmentalists.

Ross had jumped on the opening. He approached Ortega during the early days of the Foundation with the pitch of setting up a private Environmental Trust Fund with the help of the Zenkon Foundation.

"Look, you could have more control over what type of project to finance, independent of government oversight," lobbied Ross at a reception hosted by the Costa Rican Chamber of Commerce years earlier.

"You know they will be a pain in the ass always trying to put the brakes on environmental oversight. Funding for conservation is already a lower priority with this Congress; a well funded private trust will give you the advantage you need to stay relevant."

"Your suggestion is interesting, but that would take a large contribution. Where would we find interest in that type of investment?" Ortega was cautiously sipping on his drink.

"Well," said Ross, "let's just say that there may be a Board of interested philanthropists that we could approach, shall we say that at this point they prefer anonymity, you understand."

"This certainly sounds like an interesting approach. I would need to know more about your idea."

"If this approach seems feasible to you, I have no problem making a few contacts to check it out, wouldn't take long."

"Certainly, the rain forests and the environmental preserves of Central America are worthwhile causes. A private trust has merit," agreed Ortega.

"My sentiment exactly," responded Ross.

"Let's take advantage of my time here, Mr. Ortega. I will make a few calls to test the waters, and then perhaps you would like to discuss this in more detail over dinner tomorrow."

"I am sure that my calendar can be cleared."

"Perfect. We can meet at *La Monastere* at seven."

"A wonderful choice." confirmed Ortega, impressed with American's obviously extravagant taste and knowledge of the elegant five star French restaurant.

*****

La Monastere, a French cuisine restaurant situated on a hilltop high above the well to do town of Escazu, was renovated from an original monastery from the late nineteen century.

The original chapel presents a delightful ambience and old world charm to the establishment. The location does not disappoint on the magnificent view of the valley below. The venue is graced with an enormous lighted cross as a reminder of its religious origins, and cleverly masks the irreverent conversations taking place at many of the tables.

A seventeenth century monk silently approached the table, presenting Ross and Ortega each an ornately decorated *bill of fare* and wine list. A younger monk unobtrusively filled their water glasses and lit the small red candle in the center of the table.

"Buenas noches señores, que podemos ofrecerles para tomar?"

Ross and Ortega both ordered a cocktail, before turning their attention to the expansive carte du jour.

"The chef is skilled at combining the art of French cuisine with a blend of local ingredients into perfect culinary selection that ranges from frog legs in cream to wild boar with truffles," exclaimed Ortega.

"I hear all accompanied by the most extensive wine list in Costa Rica."

"Yes, you heard right. My wife and I have enjoyed many evenings of dining and music here. She says that it is like a spiritual experience." He laughed.

The waiter returned with the drinks, after which the meal was ordered.

Ross further impressed Ortega further by ordering a bottle of Chateau Petrus to accompany the main course. This was a night that could determine the inauguration of his future, and he would spare no cost.

"Thank you for joining me this evening. I am optimistic that you will think our meeting worth your while."

"The pleasure is mine," responded Ortega, raising his glass, "already your exquisite taste in our local cuisine has made the evening quite worthwhile".

The monk returned in silence, placing a basket filled with a selection of freshly baked breads, and a *pate hors d'oeuvre*, between them.

"Let me first begin by saying efforts to preserve the beautiful rain forests and environmental beauty of Costa Rica has not gone unnoticed by the members of the Zenkon Foundation Board, Sr. Ortega. Our board members care greatly about preserving the planet's most precious riches. This small country is certainly blessed with many."

"I am honored by your knowledge. As we discussed last night, this has been a difficult balance for tight resources when our country has so many other priorities. *Me entiende?*"

"Yes, I understand fully. That is the reason after speaking with the Board of my own Foundation that I am confident you will find they are interested in working with you.

"That is good news."

"They gave me the go head to move forward on a proposal. In fact, they are very interested in working with knowledgeable persons who can develop initiatives consistent with our global mission."

"Please tell me more of your organization," asked Ortega.

"In brief, the Zenkon Foundation is well funded by a group of entrepreneurs who have an interest in giving back to society. They have been successful in earning through their own successful business ventures, mostly in the area of technology. As President of the Board, my recommendations carry a lot of weight in funding priorities."

Ross' remark was clearly intended to position himself. He had Ortega's attention and continued.

"Clearly, environmental preservation is high on the agenda. Your country has the experience and dedicated resources to be a key influence in this area of endowment."

"I could not agree more, Senor Ross. I have a personal as well as a public passion for this issue."

"Exactly, and that is the reason that I thought our meeting necessary."

Ortega visibly relaxed indicated for Ross to continue.

"My thought is to establish an independent corporation to drive our nonprofit investments in this region. You understand that it is important to have a trustworthy partner since our benefactors plan on substantial investments over the long term."

Ortega's interest was now considerably peaked. Ross clearly had his full and undivided attention.

"We propose to identify worthy causes in environmental preservation and education. This will be under the initial investment direction of our Board. Once confidence is established, of course, more independence is inevitable.

"My proposal to you, Sr. Ortega, is to head a corporation. Shall we say as President of the Environmental Trust Fund?"

Ortega looked in silence, and Ross continued.

"We understand that this would necessitate a resignation from your present position. This sacrifice would be appropriately compensated in a salary and benefits package commensurate with your experience."

A brief moment transpired between the two men. The waiter returned and placed the meal on the table.

"This would be a big change for you, Senor Ortega. Do not feel pressured to give me a response this evening. Let's say that the offer is on the table for you to consider."

"I appreciate your understanding, Mr. Ross. There would be sacrifices for me to assist your Foundation. I will give serious consideration to this proposal,"

Ortega was clearly intending to get the best deal possible.

"My Board will take your expertise and connections as a distinguished Minister in the government into full consideration in a comprehensive salary, pension and benefits package.

"Thank you."

"And, of course, there would be a lucrative signing bonus to cover expenses of your situation," responded Ross with a quick grin, seeing that he already had Ortega hooked on the idea.

"Why don't we enjoy our meal and this magnificent view? We can follow up with finalizing the business matters before I leave San Jose tomorrow evening."

"Agreed, and please call me Rosario."

"To our Costa Rican alliance, Rosario." whispered Ross as he refilled both wine glasses.

He then gently clicked them in what he already knew was a triumphant toast of success.

*****

Ross now needed to meet again with Ortega, and this meeting was not going to be as cordial as the initial dinner.

Ross had never entertained illusions regarding Ortega's self interests in the Trust. He knew that despite a lucrative salary he would be a willing player in other prospects for them both.

To be fair to Ortega, Ross had to admit both had handsomely profited from the various deposits to their mutual *sociedad anonima.*

The alliance had made both men very comfortable financially.

In Latin America it is common for private citizens to hold property and business rights under titles of *anonymous societies or SA's*. Such corporations are easily established with the help of an attorney.

Once the appropriate documents are filed with the national registry, no public entity has access to the names of the shareholders of the properties or securities. It is a way to avoid lawsuits potentially confiscating the assets of the wealthy, and an added side benefit is the difficulty that courts face foreclosing on assets of private citizens.

Rosario Ortega was extremely familiar with the workings of the system. His own tourist operation and land development companies operated in this mode long before meeting Ross.

As President of the *Environmental Trust Fund*, he continued to use his network to make sure he was still privy to prime real estate available for purchase. He had inside knowledge regarding protected properties or lots in foreclosure that could be acquired at fire sale prices.

In Costa Rica, more than thirty percent of all land is designated as protected.

A healthy cut of the grants, indicated on the legal books as indirect costs, was regularly deposited in a separate S.A. account.

Ortega would purchase land at a low bid price. Its value, of course, would immediately sky rocket once the he announced investment in the expansion or renovation of a nearby private reserve facility.

The SA owned by Ortega and Ross would then lease surrounding ground space to dozens of small service companies eager to serve visiting tourists.

If a tour bus wanted to park near a reserve then parking spaces had to be leased. Small restaurants needed space and water access, and of course the usual array of other facilities – all owned by the anonymous company of Ortega and Ross.

It was a perfect set up, and Ross and Ortega owned ninety percent of the stock. The brother in-law of Ortega, Gilberto Fernandez Munoz, was attorney of record, and owned the other ten percent.

Ortega had convinced Ross that his attorney would better protect their interests if he were part of the deal. Initially, Ross saw no problem with this since he and Ortega were fifty-fifty on the balance of the stock.

Ross later learned that Munoz was in fact the brother in law of Rosario Ortega, and quickly realized his grave mistake. By not doing his research, he had inadvertently given sixty percent of the company to the Ortega family, delegating himself the minority shareholder.

Ortega had begun to flex the muscle, and Ross was understandably nervous of the precarious situation. He had learned enough that he wanted to pull out his share, and set up a separate operation himself.

Helen Nelson was the target to become a silent minority share partner.

To complicate matters even more, Ross and Ortega had entered into a medical research joint venture that had also turned into the financial crown jewel for Benton.

The project had operated under the radar from the onset. But recently, an eager reporter from the *Los Angeles Times* published an article on natural rain forest cures and skin rejuvenating products. It referenced a donation from Zenkon Foundation to a rain forest research clinic. A flurry of inquiries from baby boomers seeking the fountain of youth had

97

gone viral in social media, briefly crashing the Foundation web site.

Ross was in damage control, and trying to put a lid on it. Benton had not been cooperative. This had ultimately led to the fall out and reason for Benton's recent resignation from the Board.

But another serendipitous encounter several months prior ultimately gave Ross the push to make his move on breaking with Ortega. He decided to attend his twentieth university reunion. It was at the reunion that he had run into his old college dorm mate, Tom Yang.

Yang, now a doctor was living back in his Chinese homeland, had approached him at the reception.

Their chat was mostly bragging back and forth. By the end of the night Ross saw an opening to spread his wings, and at the same time cut the ties with both Ortega and Schwartz.

Yang casually informed him he was now working on infectious diseases and saw a lucrative market for future vaccines made in China. It was just a matter of time, he said, that the next pandemic would hit, and SARS should have convinced the world already that the next wave was on its way.

The seemingly innocent remark was not lost on the naive Ross, thrilled to think about an Asian business connection.

Yang, already well informed on the Foundation work by Chinese government operatives, said they should keep better in touch and share what each was doing. Yang then suggested perhaps even forming a business alliance, off the record for now, of course.

Ross was ready to grab onto an opportunity. He had no shame in providing documents containing some of the confidential research copied from Rolf's journals at the *Clínica*.

He justified that the Foundation funded the work, and so as President he had the right to share it with whomever he wanted.

This he did without the knowledge of the scientist.

*****

The mountainous Arenal area is influenced by the Caribbean slope weather patterns and receives anywhere from three to five meters of rain a year. Even when it is not raining, the climate is cool and foggy. The temperature warms somewhat during the day, but can get quite chilly at night.

Dominating the backdrop, the Arenal Volcano serves as an impressive setting for the modern facility of the *Clínica Salud Del Nuevo Milenio, S. A.* established by Rosario Ortega and Jonathan Ross.

Ross and Ortega had presented a convincing analysis of how the area could be better served by preservation of the rain forest and use of plants for homeopathic research and a state of the art research facility for a potentially lucrative bio-tourist industry.

The policy environment in the small Central American country is friendly toward medical research facilities, and with a socialized medical system encourages exploration of natural medicinal solutions to combat illness.

In keeping the diseases that plague most tropical countries in check, through a system of education and preventive medicine, the citizens consequently enjoy a life expectancy equal to that of North Americans.

Costs of medical treatment are much more reasonable than those of the North American neighbors.

This is one of the reasons a robust medical tourist industry continues to expand. Bio-tourism offers treatments for specific medical ailments and surgeries to dentistry and all forms of elective plastic surgery.

The latest homeopathic and spa treatments and follow up recuperations in scenic settings add to the allure of Americans and Europeans. The pampered treatment includes airport pickup services, luxury accommodations, and personalized medical access.

Rolf and Andrew flew to Costa Rica years prior to meet up with Ortega and Ross for the final board review of the investment into a Costa Rican nonprofit.

Each member of the foursome had his own agenda.

Rolf Schwartz was intrigued with the possibility of researching and experimenting with natural products as the basis for vaccines. He calculated that the location was a perfect natural ecosystem for his work.

The rest of the group was more focused on self interest than any altruistic goals.

Andrew envisioned the results of Rolf's efforts as being the golden goose he would transform into a line of profitable pharmaceutical products.

Ross and Ortega already had ideas on how to enrich themselves from spin off companies.

Within weeks, the international business partnership was formalized and registered under the title of *Clínica Salud del Nuevo Milenio, S. A.* The *acionistas,* or shareholders, were filed with the Registro Nacional.

The corporation had the financial means through the Zenkon grant to conduct environmental research and education, develop products from research, and eventually distribution activities.

Los Angeles, California

Margo got an early start the next morning. She still had not recovered from the unsettling conversation with Scott the previous evening.

It was hard for her to grasp that Benton and Ross would actually have manipulated to such a degree without her knowing anything about it at all. Perhaps that was just wishful thinking.

She should have known that her personal dislike for each of them, and the ever-growing rift, had some concrete basis. She kept asking herself how they could have also fooled an entire board of directors.

Then the impact of the circumstances hit her like a powerful punch to the stomach.

"Oh, my God," she said aloud to herself.

"They were able to do it because of me!

I have been the one from the beginning giving the glowing progress and financial reports to the Board. Of course, they were able to get away with it. I have been their dupe."

The freeway on ramp was just ahead, but she pulled over to the side of the road to settle her nerves.

"No wonder Holly wanted me to get a handle on this right away. If Ross and Benton have been up to nefarious schemes, Scott is right this could be trouble for everyone."

The freeway sign ahead indicated north to San Jose or south for Los Angeles. She decided to head south and talk in person with Maureen Sloan about her conversation with Scott and her growing fears.

*****

The driver of the black sedan picked up his cell phone and speed dialed the number to the Washington, D.C. office.

"Sir, it looks like she is heading south."

"Then keep on her tail. My guess is that she plans to meet with Maureen Sloan. I want to know her every move."

"Yes, will do, sir." Bob Harris disconnected his boss at the DOJ.

He followed Margo onto the 101 freeway and headed towards the San Fernando Valley where the road would eventually merge with spaghetti-like junctions into the sprawling Greater Los Angeles area.

*****

Maureen Sloan had been a natural choice for the Foundation Board from day one.

Margo and Maureen had become close friends during the time on the Foundation. Her Irish face with its long curly hair and her sparkling blue eyes flashed in Margo's thoughts. Both women were strong personalities and successful professionals who had conquered the old boys' networks. They were kindred souls with a mutual respect and admiration for each other's challenges.

Margo needed to see her now, and knew that the best place to find her would be at her office on the expansive university campus in Los Angeles. She pressed on the gas and continued to head due south.

This conversation needed to be in person.

"Margo, what a surprise, what are you doing here!"

Maureen remarked as her friend appeared unexpectedly at the door of her office.

"It's good to see you, too, Mo, it has been too long. But I'm not so sure after you hear what I need to tell you that you still will think it's such a good surprise."

"Don't be silly. It's always great to see you. But I must say you do look a little pale."

"I probably do."

"Here sit down. I'll get us each a cup of coffee."

Margo sank into the large well-worn brown vinyl sofa under the window of the small cluttered campus office. Small in space, Mo's office resembled a large, colorful scrapbook. All the souvenirs were so rich with story that they invited you to ask questions. *"What's this?"* or, *"When did you meet him?"*

Walls were plastered with pictures of political celebrities and candidates, plaques and certificates of recognition for various causes, and dozens of colorful buttons and bumper stickers of campaigns lost and won. There was even an autographed Russian poster dated from a trip she had made to the former Soviet Union with a western media delegation in the early 80's. Next to the poster were smaller, signed photographs of the same trip. Most were now fading from decades of light streaming through the dusty blinds of the narrow office window.

It was clear that Maureen did not shy away from her life of political activism. She exuded in the self confidence to put her history on show for all to see.

Baby and graduation pictures of all her godchildren were crowded on the credenza. Mo doted over her numerous godchildren like a mother hen over her chicks. Never married, she found a motherly joy in serving as a mentor and guide in their lives. She loved the fact that she could spoil them, talk to them frankly, and share secrets that they would never tell their parents, and this gave her joy.

The kids trusted her with their confidences, and her friend Margo did, too.

"Here you go, Margo. A hot cup of coffee will put you right."

"Thanks. I hope I am not interrupting your day too much, but I just had to meet with you right away."

"It must be pretty serious for you to come all the way from Sacramento to see me without even a heads-up."

"Well actually, I did try to reach you a couple of times yesterday, but the cell service in Santa Barbara is not the greatest. One would think with all the money folk having vacation homes there that broadband would have arrived, but I guess not."

"Santa Barbara? I thought you were returning home this week from our nation's lovely capitol."

"Yes, well I did.   But I wasn't there five minutes before Holly was on the phone pretty much mandating me to get my butt to Santa Barbara."

"Whatever for?"

"To meet with Scott Jenkins."

"The lobbyist?"

"Yes, and so unlike Holly to do that, right?"

"That's for sure," replied Maureen staring at her friend with full attention.

"In a nutshell, it seems the world may have turned upside down, and we are all getting thrown off."

"Margo, that sounds a bit dramatic"

"Maybe, but maybe not."

"I am all ears.   I know for sure, that if it is important enough for Holly to send you on such an urgent road trip something important must be going on that he is really concerned about.

"After years in the Senate, there is not too much that gets his feathers ruffled, or that he thinks cannot be handled with a few calls.   You had better give me the details."

The directness of Maureen's Irish gaze indicated that she had shifted from a casual tone to one of concern.

Margo proceeded to fill her friend in on the details of the conversation with Scott.   She was feeling an intense and empowering release at being able to share her concerns with a trusted friend.

She needed a shoulder to lean on. Her friend was the one to be able to help her connect the dots.

Mo was more than bright, and had proven it, too. She graduated from university when she was barely twenty, and then cruised through a doctorate program by age twenty-three. Since then she had been an outspoken voice on social issues.

It didn't take her too long to figure out that Ross and Benton had most likely done something underhandedly.

"This is more than troubling, for sure, Margo. We may find out that at a minimum these jerks have been siphoning off donor funds."

"Well for sure, that is not going to make the IRS very happy."

"It may be worse than that. They may have been using the foundation for other illegal activity that at this point we have no idea of ramifications.

"In either case, this could mean big trouble for all of us — to say nothing of potential criminal charges if the feds get involved."

"I know it Mo. I have been ill with worry since Scott raised the red flag last night."

"The best offense is going to be a good defense working from data."

"I agree."

" For that, we need to gather as much information as we can. We also need to clearly understand who our friends are on the Board, and who might be conspiring with Ross and Benton."

"Oh, Mo, you think others might be involved as well?"

"You will have to go through all the records with a fine toothed comb and see what you can dig up."

"I already planned on doing that starting as soon as I get back."

"In the meantime, I will do some research myself. I can feel out each of the board members. Looks like I may have to call in a few favors myself on this one."

"I really appreciate this Mo."

"There's no other choice. We have to find the underlying cause of this, and the sooner the better. Keep up the spirits, and we will figure it out."

"Okay. I knew you would be a level head for me to rely on."

"Two heads are better than one," she joked, finally getting a bit of a smile from Margo.

"Listen, I am going to run. I can just about make it back to Sacramento just before dark if I get on the road now."

Maureen gave her friend an understanding hug before she headed to her car.

*****

Bob Harris figured it was going to be a very long day when Margo connected from the 405 Freeway to Highway 5 towards Sacramento.

It was easily a five to six hour drive to the capitol city, along a straight and boring route.

It was a straight run though, so he felt no urgency to tail her car. Instead, he pulled into a gas station near Santa Clarita just before the Grapevine. He filled the tank and loaded up on candy bars and a large black coffee to circle back to where he had started early the previous day.

"Great," he thought, *"nearly nine hundred miles in two days and not even a break for a beer — I need a better job!"*

He reported to his boss that he was on his way back to Sacramento. He filled him in that Margaret Maxwell had in fact been in contact with both Scott Jenkins and Maureen Sloan.

He was instructed to stay with her until further notice.

*****

The sun was just setting by the time Margo arrived. The Sierra foothills were already casting their evening shadows over the valley.

Nearing the freeway exit for her turn off, she connected to Herb's home number.

The phone barely got through its first ring when her daughter Jodie breathlessly answered the line.

Just like when they were at home, the kids seemed to be within jumping distance of the phone to see who could answer first. Sometimes Margo never even heard it ring.

"Have you been racing your brother to the phone again?"

"Hi Mom," Jodie laughed. "Are you home now? We've been waiting ages."

The kids were always anxious to return from their father's house.

He was demanding with his children. According to Jodie, he always had a long to do list when they arrived. It included making them clean his house in exchange for outings or other treats during his visitation time. He argued they needed discipline and chores growing up had never done him any harm.

Sometimes Margo felt that she was too soft on them. She rationalized that her permissiveness was more the balance they needed from the militaristic environment and the trauma of an acrimonious divorce.

She could sense the familiar hint of desperation in her daughter's voice.

"Almost there, Jodie," she said. "Are you both ready?"

"Yes mom, we are both ready."

"Make sure you have all your schoolbooks and other things together. I don't want to be driving back and forth."

Jodie assured her that they had everything.

"Good. I will be there in about fifteen minutes. Tell Frankie not to go off anywhere before I get there."

"Mom, we've been cooped up here all week. Frankie has been on restriction since we got here for mouthing off at Dad. He made both of us clean the whole garage as well as the house."

"Oh dear."

"It wasn't even my fault. Come and unlock us from this spotless dungeon!"

Margo had to smile, but she also felt a pang of commiseration.

"Be nice, Jodie. I will be there in a flash."

"Okay, love you Mom." Her daughter hung up.

Herb had really worked the custody laws to his favor. He was never one to be too concerned about what was actually best for Frank and Jodie. He had set things up precisely counter to what would have worked best for the kids.

His primary concern always seemed aimed at ensuring that an entire situation was as painful as possible for everyone – with his second wife as a co-conspirator. The woman did not even like children, let alone their kids. Margo avoided contact with her at all costs. Any attempt to communicate with her guaranteed confrontations that were sure to upset the children.

Margo sighed.

At this point, there was not a lot that could be done to rectify the situation. Both she and Herb were beyond hope for civility. Besides, Herb's spiteful intractability meant that he was utterly inflexible when it came to any changes in the custody schedule, unless of course he initiated a request to accommodate his own needs.

As she pulled into Herb's neighborhood, she decided a heads up call to Laura might be in order. She hit her private office number on the cell phone.

She was relieved when the line picked up, and she heard Laura's crisp voice answering on the other end.

"Margaret Maxwell's office, this is Laura speaking."

"Laura, thank goodness I caught you before you left."

"Margo, it's good to hear a friendly voice. Sounds like you are in your car. Where are you?"

"I am back in Sacramento. I am just my way to pick up the kids."

"Give them a hug from me."

"Listen, I know it's getting late, but could you do one last thing for me before leaving? I wouldn't ask, but it's pretty important."

"Sure. You know for you it's not a problem."

"Well, we are going to need to go through the project files with a fine tooth comb. I am not really sure what we are looking for yet, but there is some fishy things going on that I need to get to the bottom of right away."

"Fishy, as in it stinks."

"That's about the size of it!"

"Don't tell me, our friend Andrew Benton has left us a surprise?"

"Well, I am not sure yet, but want to get as much data as I can get to get started."

"I am on it."

"Pull all the related files and financials together on our top donations over the past five years. You can e-mail them to me."

"Okay, that sounds simple enough."

"I want to do some searches tonight for any clues on anything that might look out of place. Then we can go from there next week."

"You are not going to work on this tonight, are you? Laura was incredulous.

"Maybe."

"Why don't you just relax and have some fun with the kids. This can wait until Monday."

"Don't worry. I plan to do something with the kids this weekend."

"You need to spend more time with them."

"I am going to have to work on this, as much as I would like to spend more time with them."

"Okay, I will see what I can do. Some of those files are thick and go back a ways."

"I am counting on your magical skills to get me something in the next couple of hours."

"A couple of hours, you say."

"I know, and I love you for doing this," laughed Margo as she was wheeling through the great iron gates of Herb's exclusive gated community.

"Dig up as much as you can on advisory committees and contacts that Ross and Benton may have referenced in recommending the international grants," she continued.

Laura got serious.

"We don't have anything to worry about, do we? I mean our documentation and filings are always solid."

"I hope not, but I want to have data and make sure we can explain any discrepancies if questions come up for reviews or audits."

"Will do, Margo, anything else you need?"

"Yes, for you to then go home and enjoy the weekend."

"Plan to do just that."

"I will see you on Monday."

Margo honked the horn. The kids, who had been looking through the living room window for a sign of her car driving up, immediately spilled out of the front door.

They both ran barefoot to the car, shoes and miscellaneous items in hand.

They threw all their gear into the trunk and then climbed into the back seat. Frankie handed his mother a business size white envelope with her name printed on it in large bold font.

"Great." Margo thought another of Herb's mandates.

She hated getting these intermittent declarations. He always communicated in writing with a copy to his attorney. He refused to meet face to face to chat about anything that had to do with the kids, so the alternative was his impersonal correspondence that only perpetuated the hostilities between them.

She had at least recovered enough from the pain of the divorce that she no longer got a tight knot in her stomach when she saw one of the ominous envelopes. She tucked it in the side pocket of her door. It could wait.

"Hey guys, what about take out for dinner tonight?"

She wanted to have some time to spend with Jodie and Frank, and did not relish the thought of spending much time in the kitchen.

Frankie brushed his dark hair back.

"We already ate at Dad's," he said.

Margo looked at her watch. She had not realized how quickly the evening was wearing away.

"Good, how about just stopping for some desert, then? We can swing by *Vic's.*"

The kids liked that idea. She was relieved that she was excused from worrying about dinner at all.

She had been on the go so much lately that at times felt guilty that she was losing touch with the children.

Daily video calls could not replace being with them. She knew they missed her very much while she was on the road.

Margo saw her hectic schedule as a temporary means to an end. Being a successful professional certainly had its merits, but was a challenge for a single mom.

Frank would be starting high school in the fall, and Jodie was only two years behind. Before she knew it, they would soon be in college.

"So, how was your week?" she asked them as they sat down at the small square booths of the nineteen fifties style local ice cream parlor.

The establishment was a neighborhood landmark. The walls plastered with articles and pictures from more than fifty years of reviews in the Sacramento Bee newspaper.

In the hot Sacramento summer evenings, it was a normal to see a long line out the door of the small shop.

Young parents walked their babies in strollers or dogs on leashes to enjoy a cool treat to counter the still heat of the valley. Seniors reminisced over years of memories and first dates enjoyed in the parlor. Even now, in the early spring, business was brisk. All the booths were filled with teenagers stopping by on the way to the Friday evening movie.

"It was okay, Mom, except for being on restriction again."

Her son responded between bites of his fresh made chocolate ice cream covered with Oreo cookie bits.

His smart remarks, typical of the junior high aged adolescents got him nowhere at his Dad's house, but that seemed a hard lesson for him to learn.

"Oh, Mom, guess what?" he continued.

"What Frankie?"

"Some kid got busted at school today. That was pretty cool."

"Yeah, that is about as cool as that fat pimple on your chin!"

"Funny, but your looks aren't everything, Miss Wire Mouth."

"That is enough, both of you. Frankie, are you saying that the student was arrested?"

Margo was alarmed at the news, and heading off one of the routine bickering sessions.

Frank nodded.

"Uh, huh, they had cuffs on and everything. It scared the shit out of us all."

Margo definitely did not like the sound of either the situation or her son's recent addiction to swearing.

"First, young man, clean up your mouth, and second tell me what happened?"

Can you believe the cops came into the classroom and took him away?"

"Probably had a gun or drugs or something," offered the younger Jodie as she delved into her ice cream sundae.

"Jodie, don't exaggerate," said Margo more to reassure herself than to think it wasn't out of the realm of possibility.

"Well, I wouldn't be surprised," said Frank. "School's always making us do those stupid drills in case someone shoots us all up. Maybe they got him before he could do anything".

Margo thought back on a prophetic conversation she had with Mrs. Smith, Frankie's middle school teacher the year before.

The teacher had not tried to gloss things over and was quite vocal on the current problems facing the city schools during the school's parent evening. She had articulated a dismal forecast if things were not turned around. She had requested that parents please stay alert regarding their children's friends and activities.

Many of her prophecies were now a part of the everyday lives of the school children and their families all over the country. Sadly, most school gun occurrences had become so regular, even shootings with loss of life, that they barely made headlines or evening news.

Violence was the new normal.

As much as she wanted to change the subject with the children, Margo knew that ignoring the problems would not make them go away. She would need to talk to them once again about staying safe and looking out for each other.

"So, what did you learn from this?"

Frankie laughed, "Not to get caught!"

"…Being an idiot." retorted Jodie.

"Now listen, both of you, these episodes are not a joking or laughing matter. And I would think you would have learned at least to know enough to stay safe and as far away from situations like that as possible."

They had been through these discussions before, but could always use a refresher course.

Both kids straightened up and never said another word. They picked up on the serious look on her face. They knew mom was not to be messed with any more on this subject.

"That's it for ice cream. Put your trash in the wastebasket. We need to get home."

Once at home, they continued to chatter about various school and soccer details and how their week had gone at their Dad's house.

Frankie was every bit as bright as his sister, but he had reached the age where hormones were winning the battle over common sense. She thought that sometimes his brain cells were turning into mush.

Margo was worn from the long drive and was still running on nervous energy. She asked the children to get ready for bed. She needed peace and time to go over the files Laura had already sent, and went to the kitchen to fix a pot of strong coffee

Then a wave of fatigue kicked in from the past couple of days. It seemed more than she could handle. She decided to cancel the coffee, and call it an early night.

The file could wait until morning.

Instead, at least in this moment she could take pleasure in a well deserved night cap before setting the alarm for four in the morning. She would have quiet time to begin wading through the documents long before the kids would think about waking up.

London, England

Andrew Benton caught the early morning British Airways flight from Frankfurt, and arrived into London's Heathrow by nine in the morning.

The grey overcast sky matched his mood. Having been briefly lifted in spirits by the previous evening's meal at the Hackteufel, he was now once again preoccupied with the issues at hand. He was certainly not looking forward to the day's events in the damp and drizzly English weather.

Who was it who said rain is the one thing the British do better than anyone else? He thought as he stepped out of the tube station and pulled up his coat collar at the posh Sloane Square area of Knightsbridge.

With only his overnight bag and briefcase in hand, Schwartz's luggage having been safely deposited the in a private locker at the Club in the German airport, he set off for the short walk to the nearby hotel.

He arrived a few minutes later at the posh Cadogan Hotel in the Chelsea district. He liked this hotel for his regular stay over on trips to London.

The Head Concierge cheered up on recognizing him, and welcomed him back.

"Good morning, Mr. Benton, it's a pleasure to see you again. Staying a while with us, we hope."

"Hello, Joe. No, it is just a quick stop this time. I will only be here one night."

"Right then, Gov, then let's get you settled in shall we?" smiled Joe in his local cockney style.

"Thank you."

The Cadogan was built by William Willet in 1887 at the height of the Victorian age. Recently having undergone a major renovation, it boasts its famous past clientele.

The two most notable guests were Lilly Langtry, the actress and reported close friend of Edward VII, and the the other, Oscar Wilde, the playwright.

Miss Langtry's long stay at the hotel was reportedly a happy one. The fate of her friend Oscar Wilde was less fortunate.

He was arrested in room 118 in 1895, and then convicted in criminal court for offences against young men. After serving a two-year prison term with hard labor, he was released. He died five years later in Paris separated from his family and bankrupt.

His plays, however, continue to be popular in the London theatre to this day.

Benton retreated to his stately room, located just along the corridor from the fateful arrest of Mr. Wilde's.

He called the number of Geoff Collins at the Harcourt Building Society, needing to arrange a lunch engagement with him. He decided on the Harvey Nicholas' fifth floor restaurant nearby.

Benton wanted a casual and open space to deal with Collins. The hustle and noisy public atmosphere of Harvy Nics was perfect. The young lad would think it was just a friendly get together.

Benton took a quick glance at Rolf's phone to see if there were any voice mail or text messages. Happily it signaled that the box was empty.

The lanky framed and toothy grin of Geoff Collins was immediately recognizable to him through the waiting crowds of the popular eatery. He signaled with a nod to the cheerful youth to join him at the small corner table.

Collins was the handsome twenty-four year old son of a former Pacific Rim Telecom executive who had worked for Benton in San Francisco.

He had been living in a flat on Browning Street for the past couple of years, and working as an accountant at the Building Society. He was a math whiz, and had been well on his way to a business degree at Stanford when his father had unceremoniously shipped him off to England. He had bailed him out of the Palo Alto jail on minor marijuana violation.

His father, a play by the rules strictly disciplined Brit, wanted no further trouble from his son. He felt an immediate departure from the Silicon Valley would do him good. He wanted him to straighten up at a safe enough distance to sever unsavory associations from Stanford drop outs itching to make millions on the next cool app.

Stanford could wait his father had said. He was footing the bill for his son's education so he held control. He had no concerns about him returning to the university if he provided a hefty donation for the renovation of a computer engineering lab.

Geoff's dual citizenship came in handy, and his father made sure who it was in the family that still made the rules.

Geoff had not spoken with his father since, but kept in touch with his mother through intermittent texts. He had once called her on Mother's Day, but preferred not to risk a telephone call that his father might overhear.

He was still seething over what he felt was his father's dictatorial approach to problem solving. There was never any reasoning with him. His father did, thankfully, still send him a small monthly stipend deposited to his trust account. The allowance nicely supplemented the entry level accountant wages he made at the bank.

At first, he expected that things would cool off enough to return home for the fall semester at Stanford. But the air still ran hot between him and his dad. The marijuana excuse always thrown in the son's face as the cause.

The chance presented itself and the youth decided to develop an alternative plan by crunching numbers at the Building Society. However, he devised a much more lucrative income insurance policy after going into cahoots with Benton.

Benton wasn't particularly fond of Geoff, but persevered as it served his own interests.

Geoff, however, saw in Benton all the traits lacking in his father. In some way he had formed an emotional dependency, perceiving him as a substitute for his estranged parent. He was gullible to the suggestions and schemes of the older mentor.

Benton was fully aware of his influence, and used the ill placed trust to further manipulate and control the lopsided association.

The young Collins was aware that the international accounting he had set up for Benton at best skirted the law. In his naïveté had no idea of the enormity of the international crimes to which he was an accessory.

Benton had done a proficient job of manipulating Rolf at one end of his scheme and Geoff Collins at the other. He carefully concealed the identities of his co-conspirators from each other.

"Hello, Mr. Benton," chimed the upbeat Collins as he pushed back a thick mop of black hair from his forehead.

Benton smiled at the affable you.

"It's good to see you again, sir".

He always addressed his senior by his surname. He never advanced to a first name friendly basis. Perhaps it had something to do with his father's preference for the formal after all.

"Yes, nice to see you, as well, Geoff. How is the UK treating you?"

"I can't complain, but I must say I do miss a good hamburger and fries. The Brits have improved, but only sitting on the Santa Cruz boardwalk staring at the ocean does it taste just right!"

"I cannot argue with you there, Geoff."

"But I must say this is the best place in London to satisfy my French fries addiction. Good choice."

"Well then, let's order, and make sure you are taken care of right way," added Benton.

"That's a first class plan!"

Benton chit chatted with Geoff, filling him in on a few newsworthy matters from the States. He brought him up to date on family topics, mentioning a recent evening reception that his mother had hosted at their swanky Saint Francis Wood home in San Francisco.

It had been a fundraiser for the mayoral candidate of the city. Benton had been more than happy to give a small contribution to be able to attend and network with the up and coming.

"It sounds like not much has changed on the home front. I am sure Dad is happy to have me six thousand miles away so that I don't tarnish his veneer," he said spitefully.

"I am sure he misses you."

He definitely wouldn't want me to get in the way of any political plans by giving the wrong impression at one of their ritzy cocktail parties."

"Oh, I think they miss you, Geoff."

"I doubt it, maybe mom misses me a little."

"You shouldn't be so hard on your folks."

"Right, Mr. Benton! You have been more understanding than Dad has ever been.

"He can't possibly understand that he has put me in exile here. But believe me, I am ready to head home the day I have enough to live in style and not have to depend on him ever again.

I have had enough fish and chips and wimpy showers to last me a lifetime!"

Benton seeing the boy was getting a bit carried away, and seeing an opening changed tone.

"If that is what you are content on doing, Geoff, then we really need to talk about transitioning our business accounts to best accommodate your return plans."

"I'm glad you brought that up, Mr. Benton."

"Oh, and why is that?"

"There was a bit of weird activity the past couple of days on the accounts."

"What do you mean *weird?*"

Benton blared out in an unexpected reaction, totally taking Collins by surprise.

"Well I am not really sure yet, but nothing I can't handle."

"Why didn't you call me?"

" I was keeping an eye on it before raising any red flags."

"Tell me now what it is."

"It seems like there was some sort of attempt at unauthorized access to the accounts. It was probably only hackers trying to get in. It's pretty common anymore all over."

"Common or not, Geoff, this worries me."

"I have set up fail safe firewalls, so no need to worry; it's just that it surprised me a bit."

"So nothing is missing?"

"No funds were moved in or out, but it was obvious that someone was poking around."

"This does not sound good to me."

"I figured it may be internal, so I did a little checking. It was all clear."

"That means it is from the outside, shit."

"Don't you worry. I am on it, and we're safe."

"How do you know it was not internal?"

"Well, I am pretty familiar with the software and probed the data to make the authorization code and pathway available to me for any inquiries. You see, the software automatically captures all employees' access codes and movements."

"And so that makes you sure it is external?"

"It was definitely a remote access attempt. That's why I think it may have been hackers."

"Hackers from where?"

"Who knows, but China or Russia are all over these days."

"So you are telling me a Russian or Chinese hacker may be into our files and accounts?"

"Well that may be jumping the gun a bit."

"Jesus, Geoff, and you didn't think this was a red flag enough to let me know before now?'

"I figured it was a probe event, and gave it a security fix, so not to worry Mr. Benton. This shit goes on all the time. I would be calling you a dozen times a day if I worried about every one of them."

"Well figure it out, and secure us, and quick."

Benton was beginning to perspire and get more agitated at the cavalier attitude of the boy.

"My guess is that it is nothing, and we don't have to worry about government agencies and the mob!" he replied with a wink, clearly not worried about anything serious.

"But you know, tax investigators or laundering investigators at the FBI try that sort of thing. They have pretty sophisticated intelligence software, and can pick up irregularities."

Geoff added, more as an afterthought than worry.

"What are you trying to say?"

"Well, nothing really, but with the transfers from your product distribution lines being deposited internationally to your account, perhaps Uncle Sam is on a fishing expedition to check on assets and taxes. It is for sure an invasion of privacy, but never the less goes on."

Benton was becoming unnerved.

The account had more activity than usual over the past few months due to an upswing in the profits from lucrative exports. His intention for the meeting had been to speak to Geoff about devising a way to facilitate easy access to some of the cash, thinking that the situation in Germany may expedite his need.

Another concern that loomed in the back of his mind was that Ross could still be snooping around.

Ross was no fool, and he would not hesitate to destroy Benton given the slightest chance. But from what Geoff was saying, it sounded more complicated than that. If were the feds or IRS on his tail then that was a far different matter.

Unknown to Schwartz and Ross he had been adding an extra leg to the Miami transport operation. He had been diluting the strength of the pharmaceutical products by twenty-five percent.

The diluted products were then given a new generic label. Legitimate customers in the states were unaware that some of the brand products they were shipped had only seventy-five percent of the recommended formula or dosage.

The slipshod control and quality standards in the supply chain enabled him to manufacture his illegal merchandise into a generic product for a secondary oversees distribution.

His unashamed name-dropping of Senator Hollingsworth had been fortuitous in facilitating the right connections to winning lucrative federal procurement contracts. Through those contracts he exported the high demand products as generic drugs to developing countries.

Essentially, the government provided him the legal cover and necessary paperwork to export his unlawfully gained products at a fine profit.

His direct payments, according to the government procurement contract terms of payment, were deposited into the Building Society account.

Products were siphoned and manufactured from the original legally acquired raw materials, paid for by federal grants.

It was a brilliant system, no investment, no overhead, just like adding a little water to the liquor bottle in dad's bar.

Neither Ross nor Hollingsworth had a clue of the operation.

But it seemed from Geoff's information that someone was onto the scheme.

He was convinced this was more than an incidental hack.

Flamingo, Costa Rica

Javier shouted, "*Señora Helena, teléfono.*"

His voice was loud enough for Helen to hear him clearly above the loud sound of the salsa music playing on the radio.

"*Gracias, Javier, voy,*" responded Helen.

She turned down the volume on the portable radio, and headed inside to answer the telephone.

Helen liked to relax on the patio in the late afternoon sun, listening to what she referred to as *happy* music, unbothered by anyone.

It was another way of calming down, and following her doctor's orders to take life easy.

"Helen?"

"Yes, this is Helen. Who is calling?"

"This is Maureen Sloan, Helen."

"Maureen, what a nice surprise to hear from you."

"How are you?"

"I'm fine, thank you. I am just taking it easy in beautiful Flamingo."

"That is good to hear. It's the usual rat race here in Los Angeles, so you are lucky to be away from it all."

"I am sure it is."

" I envy you."

"Well, what's stopping you from coming down here? I have invited you enough times."

"Yes, I know, Helen."

"The welcome mat is always out for you."

"I appreciate that Helen, and believe me one day I am going to take you up on the offer!"

"Good, well then, I will plan on that. So, you are not calling to tell me you are paying the overdue visit."

"Not this time, no."

"What may I ask, then, prompts this unexpected pleasure?"

"I need to pick your brain a little about a couple of mutual friends, namely Jonathan Ross and Andrew Benton."

"And you use the word *friends* quite liberally, joked Helen.

"It seems that Holly is nervous the dynamic duo might have been up to something unsavory over the past few years."

"That, my dear does not surprise me one bit."

'We want to make sure that the rest of us are not hung out to dry."

"Well, well, well. This is certainly the week for bombshells from the Foundation."

"What do you mean?"

"Ross called me only yesterday saying he wanted to get together, and I have already agreed to meet him in San Jose tomorrow afternoon."

"Yesterday, that is quite interesting."

"Then I see a blurb in the local newspaper mentioning that Rosario Ortega's bank account has been frozen by the government."

"Are you serious?"

"Quite. It seems that wise old Holly's worries might indeed lead to some revelations."

"Why would Ross want to meet with you?"

"I am not sure."

"It seems odd to me.

"I haven't even been actively involved in the Board for a while, as you know. Really, Mo, getting myself sorted here has been enough. You can't imagine what it takes to make a big move at my age!

"And you know, going through all those boxes, well, I tell you, I found pictures and stuff that I couldn't part with. Everything has its memory, you know.

"I found a little broken cup in the back of my closet that my little granddaughter gave me once when I took her to the beach. I think she was only five, and ….."

Mo could see this trip down memory lane might last a while with Helen.

"Helen, I know this has been a crazy time for you, but back to Jonathan, if you can."

Sorry, Mo, I do get going, don't I?

"No problem."

"Anyway, I am certain that Ross travels quite regularly to the Arenal research facility. But to tell you the truth, I never had much interest in going there with him, even though it is only about three hours or so from here."

"Why not?"

"I just do not like the drive, and my doctor says the stress of driving is much too much for me. I am not even looking forward to the trip tomorrow.

I went one time to Arenal. That was only because Rolf asked me to go along."

"Why would Rolf want you do go?"

"I am not sure, but Jonathan was going to be there, with an old university buddy visiting from China. He was a nice guy working on some research thing with vaccines."

"Helen, did you mention to Jonathan the article you saw in the paper?"

"No, in fact it was after his call that I noticed it. But I was going to see if he had any more information."

"Helen, please keep that to yourself when you meet with him."

"Oh."

"Holly might be on to something here. We don't want to give Jonathan a clue that you are suspicious. This whole affair sounds like it could get complicated."

"Maureen, I hope that this is nothing serious. I am getting a bit worried."

"Have your meeting Helen, and we will see where this leads."

" What could they have been up to?"

"That's what I intend to find out, believe me. Helen, be careful tomorrow."

"I will be careful, not to worry."

"Will you call me when you get back from meeting?"

"Of course, my dear, maybe we will have time then to catch up on some other more positive things. You know, I miss our little chats."

"Right then, we'll talk early in the week. In the meantime, I have a couple of other phone calls to make to see what else I can find out."

"Okay, then. Bye for now."

"Goodbye."

Helen stood staring out across the still ocean. She noticed that the small fishing boats were headed back to the harbor, and that large black rain clouds were forming on the horizon.

They portended a late afternoon thunderstorm. She hoped that was not an omen of things to come.

*****

Maureen turned to her computer screen, and clicked the mouse. Her e-mail system immediately popped to life.

Opening the contacts list, she found Jack O'Riley's name. He was her long time friend at the *Los Angeles Times*.

Jack had been the reporter covering the piece on the research facility in Costa Rica.

He must have met Rosario Ortega, and perhaps he had a clue to what was up.

Dear Jack,

Nice piece on the rain forest cures. Did you have the chance to meet the director, Rosario Ortega? It appears from the latest news that he has gotten himself in some hot water with his banking account. Any data? Our Foundation has supported the operation, and I would be grateful for any light you can shed on this.

Warm regards,

Mo

Maureen clicked the send icon, and the message instantly disappeared into cyberspace.

If anyone, Jack may be able to help me dig up some info, she thought.

*****

Helen was up at the crack of dawn to the loud wail of a Howler Monkey in the tall palm tree adjacent to her patio. He was advertising his territory to competing troupes.

The Howlers are conspicuous in the dry jungle area. They live in troupes of up to twenty family members, and forage the lush vegetation for their daily diet. Although they are mainly arboreal, rarely descending to the ground, frequently a bold member may decide to bond with humans.

She had not slept well all night, and certainly was not looking forward to the journey to San Jose.

The first part of the journey was not what bothered her, as the coastal peninsula meandered through delightful villages and rolling hills. She could take her time, and pull off for an occasional bathroom stop and fruit drink.

It was the last part when the road merged into the main highway, and intimidating trucks and speeders dominated the route.

At best, it would take her five or six hours. She had already made up her mind that after the meeting she would spend the night in the capitol city.

No way could she complete a round trip in one day, so she thought she might as well make the best of the opportunity to visit Multi-Plaza a shopping mall in Escazu. It was situated next to the onramp of the toll highway, so a perfect destination on her return journey. She would pick up a few items that were hard to find in Flamingo.

Why am I doing this at all? Might as well enjoy it.

One of the brightest spots on the main highway to San Jose from Flamingo was a stop about an hour away at a German style bakery.

It is located across from the new international airport of Liberia and just outside of the town bearing the same name. Travelers either on the route north to Nicaragua or south to San Jose used it as a rest stop.

Johann, the rather hippy looking proprietor, was the son of a *Meister Bäcker* from Munich. He had mastered the art of baking fresh bread using the ancient wood burning oven method.

Skillfully using this log fire technique of baking, he had valiantly conquered a lethal combination of intense high temperatures of the oven and the extreme tropical heat in the diminutive kitchen. Like an artist he turned out wonderfully tasty gastronomic delights. The selection of pastries and cakes were works of art.

I will treat myself to a coffee and cake.

Johann, the proprietor, had fallen in love with the out of the way location about ten years before as he was touring his Harley through Central America.

Finding the location, and considering it a diamond in the rough, he never gave a second thought to returning to Germany.

He had built a life in Costa Rica, and was expanding his reach to supermarket deliveries along with daily deliveries to hotels and homes in the nearby beach communities. He married a local, and she marketed his product with the same determination and skill he put into the baking.

To this day, the motorcycle remained securely chained to the iron fence adjacent to the bakery's brick chimney.

Helen had observed the establishment grow. She remembered the rustic roadside stand, and the gradual progression to profitable restaurant and bakery delivery service. Johann was a smart guy, and had timed it just right to take advantage of growing tourist industry

He was now owned two large delivery trucks. She heard that folks were talking about him opening a large factory location closer to the tourist center emerging in the beach community of Tamarindo.

Helen parked the car on the gravel pathway in front of the establishment and walked in.

It was an open air style seating area with a roof constructed of thatched palm leaves. The high bar was built from bamboo.

It had been designed so that as you ordered coffee you were able to view all the delicious choices in the glass case below. A shiny new espresso cappuccino maker on the bar caught Helen's eye. She took great pleasure in ordering large café mocha along with opting for a delicious looking mango tart.

"Is Johann here," she questioned the slight girl serving the customers from behind the spotless counter.

"No, señora, he left early to check on his deliveries to the hotels."

"Well give him my regards, and tell him to add a strawberry torte to my order on Wednesday."

"Si, senora", replied the waitress, placing Helen's coffee and tart on the small black wrought iron table nestled under a sprawling Guanacaste tree.

*****

Jonathan Ross was already standing under the hotel canopy, and waved as Helen drove into the opulent circular driveway. A young valet, clad in a pristine white jacket, took her keys and drove her vehicle off to the parking lot.

"Helen, you look terrific as always, this tropical lifestyle does you well!"

"Thanks, Jonathan. You look well yourself."

"Let's go inside. I have already reserved a table for us on the terrace, and since you don't have to drive home tonight you can join me for an afternoon cocktail."

"That sounds delightful. My doctor says an occasional drink is good for my heart."

Jonathan politely took Helen's arm, and led her through the colonial style lobby to the outdoor veranda of the bar.

Along the way, Helen admired the beautiful floral arrangements adorning the tables and reception counter. It was amazing how beautifully the red, yellow, orange and vibrant green colors brought the outside tropical life indoors.

The duo settled into two comfortable armchairs that faced the golf course and infinity swimming pool of the resort. The magnificent view through the lush palm trees was serene and calming, but Helen had her antenna on full alert.

The incongruity of the situation, along with Mo's warnings kept her on guard. The urgency of the call had her spooked about the purpose of the rendezvous.

"Let me get right to the point of my trip down here, Helen," said Ross suddenly.

She was a bit surprised at his rush to business.

"Zenkon is contemplating pulling funding support for the Arenal research facility."

"Oh? Why is that Jonathan? I thought things were going well with the project?"

"To be honest, we think it has been a successful venture, and has grown to a point of being able to survive independently of our investments."

"I see."

"It is ready to be completely independent of ties to us. We think the work is very important. But quite frankly there are a number of other organizations that would fill the gap if we decided to reallocate our priorities to other needy projects."

Helen just listened, allowing Jonathan go on.

"I wanted you to be aware of this since you live here. You may need to respond to inquiries regarding the change in strategy."

"Do you think it will give us bad press here?"

"We don't think it will cause problems, but one needs to be prepared."

"How does Mr. Ortega feel about this change in plans?"

"That's just the thing, and part of the rationale."

"Go on."

"Rosario is ready to resign from the operation to tend to his own business interests. He thinks that he has given enough time to the philanthropic side of things, and is ready for other things."

"Other things, that is a surprise development."

"Frankly, I couldn't agree more with his decision. He seems to have become more interested in private international investments lately than the work of the project.

"So you see, Helen, the timing is probably right for our Foundation to move on as well."

Helen picked up on the subtle rift that had apparently developed in the relationship between Ortega and Ross. She wondered what the root cause was really about. It was obviously more than Ross was willing to reveal.

"I see, Jonathan. Well, as you know, I have confidence in the decisions of the Board"

"Thank you, Helen."

"I am sure you will operate in the best interests of the mission. But, of course, there are a number of other worthy projects in Central America that could easily benefit from support. I would certainly like to see funds continued to be invested in the region."

"Of course, as a matter of fact that gets to my main point."

"Your main point?"

"I have taken the liberty to set up a private *sociedad anonima* for future opportunities."

"A new company?"

"Right now it is merely a shell corporation but I was hoping that you might want to become an active shareholder."

"I am not sure about that at this stage, Jonathan."

"It could, you know, give you some additional cash flow along with leverage in decisions about future Foundation investments down here."

"And how would that be, Jon?"

"I would be more than happy to propose a consulting contract to the Foundation Board to the new company to have you oversee our ventures in the region."

"My goodness, this sounds ambitious."

"Your dedication to the Foundation Board is unquestioned, Helen. I am sure they would have total confidence in your involvement. Of course, Helen you would need to resign from the Board to avoid a conflict of interest. But you have been moving in that direction for a while now anyway."

Helen was obviously taken back with the quick moving proposals and said nothing.

"What do you think?"

"This is quite unexpected."

"I know, Helen. But in a sense it could be very beneficial to you."

"How is that, Jonathan?"

"As a consultant you would in essence just oversee the operation from time to time and essentially keep an eye on things. In fact, you would be able to live the life, without really much of your time being needed. And at the same time we continue similar social interests but through our own private corporation."

"So you are proposing more of a silent partner arrangement?"

"In a sense, yes I am."

"And what's in it then for you, Jonathan?"

"Like you, Helen, I have grown very fond of this country. Having an operating consulting business here certainly opens up possibilities for the future. If I decide, like you, to live out of the states."

"My goodness, I had no idea you were interested in leaving the Bay Area, let alone the United States!"

"Of course, I am not talking about today or tomorrow. But one must always keep ones options open in life," smiled Ross.

Helen was on her highest alert, and definitely knew he was up to something.

"Why don't you think on this over night? I have taken the liberty to write up a letter of resignation for you that can be presented to the Board."

"You are asking for my resignation?"

"It would be best to complete this step before formalizing the consulting arrangement. I am sure there would be no problem getting the support of the members. They are all very fond of you, Helen."

Suddenly, she had no appetite to stay for lunch with Jonathan. She needed to rethink the conversation that had just transpired.

Helen's heart was racing and she was sure that he could see it beating through her blouse. His direct pitch and unexpected move had caught her off guard.

"Jonathan, this is a lot to take in."

"I understand, Helen."

"I need to think about all this. If you don't mind please give me a chance to work all this through."

"Of course, it is a big step, but I think a good one."

"Maybe, but after all, becoming a consultant might be more than I want to take on at my age."

"Helen, you have always been much younger than your age. I am sure you can do this."

"Let me give it some thought, okay?"

"Sure, Helen, I understand completely. Take your time."

Helen politely excused herself and headed to her room.

*****

"Maureen, this is Helen."

"Hello, my dear. I thought you were going to meet with Jonathan Ross today. I wasn't expecting you to call until Monday."

"I know. I am with him right now at the hotel in San Jose. Well, I mean he is not here in my room with me, but we met earlier.

Helen sounded quite flustered, and Mo picked up on it right away.

"Helen, calm down."

"Yes, I am a bit nervous right now."

"Tell me what our Mr. Ross had to say to upset you."

"Well, he has given me quite a set back today. He is obviously up to something, Mo."

"I knew it!"

"He has my resignation from the Board with him. It's all typed and ready for me to sign!"

"I don't believe it."

"Oh yes, and there is more. He has generously offered to set me up in a joint consulting business with lucrative contracts to follow from the Zenkon Board."

"My goodness, the snake does have something up his sleeve!"

"Yes, and from what he said, it seems there has apparently been a break up between him and his pal Rosario Ortega. Ross is planning on shutting down the Arenal environmental facility."

"Shutting it down?"

"It seems that Andrew Benton may have been his first victim on the chopping block, and now appears that Mr. Ortega is slotted for next in line."

"Well, Helen. This is all very disturbing."

"I know. I just came back to my room for a while to absorb all this."

"Just play along with our friend Ross. Do not sign the resignation."

"I have no intention of signing anything."

"Give him the impression that you are seriously contemplating his offer."

"All right, but I don't like it."

"No, but he thinks you are out of the communication loop. You may be our best bet to keep tabs on what he is up to."

"I will give you a call when I get home tomorrow evening."

"Thanks. And be careful."

California

Margo spent the better part of the weekend combing through the documents that Laura had sent to her via e-mail. Her frustration level was nearing its high point.

So far she could not see anything that raised red flags for activities Holly might be concerned about. Whatever nefarious scheme Ross and Benton may have been playing would need much more investigation. Their activities were definitely more deeply concealed from the official Foundation records.

She was about to throw in the towel for the day when the phone rang. Maureen was calling to report her conversation with Helen.

"That is too much of a coincidence, Mo. And you know, the fact that he had already set up a private company for himself is an even more disturbing angle."

"I agree. It may be why you haven't been able to find anything so far in the Foundation files."

"I don't trust him at all; it all has to be connected to some scheme he's had going. Something has spooked him, so he thinks he needs to move quickly."

"Margo, forcing Helen off the Board and setting her up with some bogus consulting arrangement to keep her in line is just plain weird."

"I agree."

"Keep digging and see what you can come up with."

"I will."

"By the way, I sent a note to Jack O'Riley at the *Times*. He may come back with some insights, as well."

The call set Margo's juices going, and invigorated her efforts. She decided to approach her search from a different perspective. Perhaps it was not the projects or the grants that the Foundation funded that were a problem, but rather other contractual relationships that led to side deals for Ross.

Perhaps keeping the Foundation clean on the surface, and then running some other operation through secondary projects or third parties was the game.

They were not stupid, so of course they would want to keep the tax status with the IRS clean. Audits or annual filings would not necessarily pick up on all the different affiliations grant recipients may have with international companies or foreign government operations.

She sent an e-mail to Laura to tell her to begin pulling the files on subcontracts between Zenkon and any international vendors or consultants. She asked her to pay particular interest to any dealings in place with Central America.

It was likely to be a long list given the volume of federal grants they were now managing, but she was determined to get to the bottom of this.

*****

Bob Harris had spent a long boring weekend in his dreary motel, not venturing even once from the downtown budget lodge. On a skimpy per diem determined by federal regulation, the renovated Vagabond was about all the luxury his reimbursement covered. He had no intention of turning in an expense sheet, but he knew Ramsey was frugal.

He made it through the weekend by suffering the noise of the ceaseless traffic flow on the myriad of connecting freeway overpasses overhead. He ordered room service from a take out at the Veranda Restaurant in the Old Sacramento gold rush town just across the way. The only consolation was that the food was fairly decent.

He was definitely not in a tourist mood, so had no inclination to meander among the variety of old fashioned shops or restaurants the area had to offer. He preferred to hole himself up in the miserable surroundings of the hotel. He was beginning to feel generally sorry for himself.

He owed Henry Ramsey a favor, and this covert field assignment was payback.

As far as the Justice Department office staff knew, he was on a long overdue fishing vacation in Northern California for three weeks.

Ramsey wanted no one to know about the file he was building on Hollingsworth. It would be Ramsey's ace in the hole to use for the Administration's political strategy against the Democratic leadership in the upcoming primaries.

Ramsey believed it was also a guarantee that he would be a shoe in for appointment to the position of

Chief White House Counsel once the election was secured. He had a lot at stake, and intended to report directly to the Vice President on this one.

Bob Harris was the only one he trusted not to leak information by shooting off his mouth, or give some snooping reporter reason to think there might be a story. Competition for breaking news always had newbie journalists hanging around bars and restaurants on the chance of overhearing something.

Harris could keep his mouth shut, and was loyal.

Bob, a stereotypical conservative raised on an east Texas ranch, was happy to play a part in Ramsey's plot to bring down the icon of liberal politics. A side benefit, of course, would be the pleasure of seeing all the former young Silicon Valley upstarts squirm as word got out on *CNN* of their tax evasion scams.

They would have more to worry about that stock devaluation and irate shareholders once the IRS got wind of their dealings. As Harris saw it, at least it might take the fake media, and climate change crowd off the backs of Texas oil companies and their Midwestern fracking partners long enough to make it successfully through the bitter reelection campaign.

Margaret Maxwell must know what has been going on, thought Harris. She was after all the mastermind of the Foundation from the beginning. She is either totally involved or has been operating with visors over her eyes from the start.

Whatever it was, he intended to find out. Maxwell would either lead them to the information they needed, or go down with the rest of them.

He was fine with either outcome. Ramsey had said that he was sure Hollingsworth had alerted her after his late night warning call, and it was just a matter of picking up on what her next movements would be.

*****

Ramsey had stumbled onto the Foundation lead quite incidentally during a conversation with his oldest son Dennis. The two had been talking about the inflated costs of prescription drugs that distributors were charging to Medicare.

Dennis, a North Carolina highway patrol cop, had just returned from a visit to his grandmother in a local nursing home. She had a fall, and he had been talking with nurses at the facility about all the drugs she was taking and the high costs on the family budget.

He then went on to mention to his Dad about a traffic stop in which a well-dressed speeding violator had seemed quite nervous. Picking up on this, along with suspicions about the Florida license plate, he had requested that the speeder open the trunk.

The man had done so without incident, displaying commercially labeled cases with vials of a natural serum made from rain forest herbs. He had a distribution permit, so it all appeared legal.

Dennis then asked the guy if he could maybe have a vial for his grandmother, off the record of course, as might help her with some of her aches and the upcoming flu season. So the guy gave him a sample.

But Dennis told his Dad that he had felt uneasy about the episode. He actually thought about holding the guy and his products on suspicion of moving illegal substances across state lines.

As a precaution he did call into the station and got confirmation that the stuff was legal. Since the distribution license was in order, and the substance was not illegal, the North Carolina highway patrol had no grounds to follow up.

But Dennis told his father that something just seemed fishy, and that he had the sample run at the lab just for the heck of it.

Tests did confirm some form of natural energy remedy, but the lab report showed that the formula was only about twenty five percent of the strength indicated on the manufacturing label.

Dennis suggested to his father that perhaps Justice should at least investigate why the product was diluted.

Ramsey had followed up after speaking with his son.

The label identified a partnership between the manufacturer and a small nonprofit organization.

He easily discovered that the nonprofit organization was substantially supported by grants from the Zenkon Foundation, and operated under the direction of a Mr. Rosario Ortega out of Costa Rica.

Most interestingly, however, was that Senator Lawrence Hollingsworth was on the Zenkon Foundation Board as an advisor.

Further probing turned up the name of the herbal product on the procurement list for export products through HHC. It seems that the company also had a lucrative contract from the federal agency to export the natural serum to third world countries.

Ramsey was not one to believe in coincidences.

Perhaps the incorrect labeling was not a ground for arrest in North Carolina, but Ramsey knew that if the bad labels were then being shipped with products under an HHC federal grants program then he had something.

Lawrence Hollingsworth's name appearing twice on the data search was enough of a red flag to warrant his digging more deeply into Zenkon's activities.

If something on the squeaky-clean Senator were to turn up, it would indeed be a feather in his political cap.

*****

"Maureen, how are you, Jack O'Riley."

"Jack, it's great to hear from you."

"Listen, thanks for the lead on Rosario Ortega."

"You are welcome."

"I have been doing a little more mining for information on our Latin American friend. It seems his background is quite colorful, and his roots spread widely."

"Tell me more."

"Bud Watson, an old retired associate of mine freelances at the *Tico Times*. He lives in Costa Rica, and keeps his pencil sharpened to occupy his time. Once an investigative reporter, always an investigative reporter, they say."

"Go on."

"Bud says the banks that froze Ortega's assets were under, shall we say, very heavy pressure."

"Meaning what?"

"In Costa Rica that probably means from the highest level, perhaps with some major arm twisting from Washington."

" Something is up then, Jack."

"I can guarantee that either the Feds or Justice is involved. If there is enough clout to have the Ticos put a freeze a citizen's account then, yes, something is up."

"So we are correct."

"I am not sure yet where this will lead, but I'm hot on the trail. Besides the frozen bank accounts, my contact tells me that the government is examining all of Ortega's personal holdings that they can get their hands on down there."

"Seriously?"

"Apparently many may be registered through anonymous societies, a way for private citizens to hide corporate assets. Obviously, they seem to think they may have something on him. He has never had too many friends in high places, but never seemed to be short on cash, either."

"My question is how does this all fit with us?"

"If Washington is involved you can bet that it something to do with the partisan political games going on. I'll keep you posted."

Jack hung up, and Maureen gave an exasperated sigh, *great, now I know for sure that Holly has reason to be concerned.*

Washington, D.C.

Henry Ramsey smiled smugly as he straightened his crimson colored tie. It had been a while since he had a meeting at the White House, and never alone with the Chief of Staff for the Vice President. He was looking forward to the occasion, and would be meeting in one of the Vice President's private conference rooms in the Old Executive Office Building.

The Eisenhower building, as it was known, was a magnificent venue, but it did not have the status of working in the West Wing with insiders. The West Wing office space was gold, but the less prestigious meeting venue did not bother him one bit.

The driver would still be instructed to drive to the White House with instructions for the 17th Street entrance, and perception of being in with the big boys was all that mattered inside the Beltway.

Ramsey was confident the information he had on Senator Hollingsworth's ties to Zenkon and the nonprofit's possible misuse of federal funds for an illegal manufacturing operation would ingratiate him with the reelection strategists.

The President's media attack campaign needed a boost in the arm, and pinning major scandal on the Democratic Party leadership was just the ticket to get the hounds sniffing on a new trail.

He was certain this would cement his ambitions for White House Counsel in the post-election line up.

He was hedging his bets that the information was on target, and had instructed a couple of his underlings to gather additional information on Hollingsworth's time and activities with the Foundation.

He knew nothing was solid yet, but getting a few nuggets of suspicion circulated was all he needed. By the time the information was picked up by a few radio hosts and twisted into conspiracy theories on websites, it would be too late to worry about whether it was actually true or not.

No one really cared anyway; it was all a game to get red meat out there in order to control the next breaking news banner on either *Fox* or *CNN*. The truth in politics no longer mattered, lies became the truth, and there was no shame in lying, nor apologies or retractions offered when caught.

The country had become politically and culturally divided with a very short memory span, influenced by fomented tribal beliefs. It was politics and all politicians were the same, and the next news or poll number was all that mattered.

The intercom buzzer interrupted his reverie as his secretary announced that the driver was ready to transport him the short distance to Pennsylvania Avenue.

He self-assuredly stuffed the red manila folder that Harris had sent via overnight express mail into his black briefcase, and then headed for the meeting he believed would change his future.

At the other end of Pennsylvania Avenue Hollingsworth was pacing back and forth in his Senate office. His aides were starting to get nervous since their boss was preoccupied, and questioning him made him even shorter with them, something was up.

Holly was impatient with no news from either Scott or Margo, but was determined to keep this low key until he could find out something concrete. He planned to fly home at the end of the week, and would definitely talk to Scott then. In fact, maybe he would have him drive out to the ranch.

A light knock sounded at his door, and his secretary, Aretha walked in with a worried look on her face.

She was a middle aged African American woman who had been with the Senator for years. She was more than competent to play gatekeeper to the numerous lobbyists and staff constantly trying to get access to the precious time on his calendar.

She had grown up street smart in Baltimore, worked her way through college on student loans, while raising two teenagers alone. She hadn't seen their father for years. Last she heard he was locked up forever on a three strikes and you're out charge. Life had been tough for her, and as she would say *I take no shit from no one*, and she didn't.

"Rethie, you look a little edgy, anything wrong?"

"Senator, it's those men from Justice, again."

"Again, I thought you told them to go to hell."

"They have been pestering the staff all week with questions and requests for information. Now they are calling and want to schedule some time to talk directly with you."

"Not to worry, my dear." He said, trying to keep a low profile on the whole affair.

"I'm sure it's one of the usual fishing expeditions they dream up to keep them busy."

"Well then, sounds like they are not prime time for getting any time on your calendar."

"Certainly not! Say I am totally booked and headed out to the west coast this week."

"Don't you worry, sir, their attitude set me off from the start, so leave it to me. I will send them packing, don't you worry."

She had no fondness for anyone having to do with the Federal Justice System, as far as she was concerned the senator's concurrence gave her a little bit of an upper hand in telling them to piss off.

"I have no worries at all Rethie, am sure you will know just how to handle our friends."

Aretha gave a conspiratorial wink as she departed. She had the okay to give the bothersome investigators a rough time."

Germany

Helga had been quite pleased when two days before Rolf had called her saying he had arranged for a ride to the airport the next morning, and she no longer needed to drive him.

She was not fond of early rising nor the drive to Frankfurt. She far preferred to linger in the late morning with her Brötchen and steamed coffee while reading the daily Bild Zeitung.

The newspaper arrived faithfully on her step at around eight, and she looked forward to the juicy stories of the latest madness in modern European society. She had no inclination to get up more than fifteen minutes before its arrival at the front door.

Helga and Rolf were twins, but by all accounts it seemed that different blood ran in their veins.

Rolf, the scientist and intellectual, had made a name for himself as one of the world's top medical researchers. He was a seasoned traveler with a lust for life and a pioneering spirit.

Helga, never had any ambition to leave their Bavarian hamlet, and had been more than happy with her long time employment in the local florist shop where she knew everyone in town on a first name basis, and felt blessed with life, knowing that she could enjoy the beauty and fragrance the fresh flowers each day.

She had nothing in common with Rolf.

Both had drifted apart as soon as Rolf had left for university. His resolute dedication to research, and his chosen lifestyle was something she would never understand, but had come to accept.

Rolf's passion for scientific research began when he was only six years old. He never forgot the day the American soldiers approached the snow covered terrace of his grandmother's small farm. It was just days before the end of the War in 1945.

The soldiers were special agents on elite missions from the British and American military. They were looking for his uncle Rudolf who had been hiding there for several weeks. He had escaped from the allied forces after being holed up in Nordhausen, a small city in the center of the country.

Rudolf was one of the prized German rocket scientists who had worked on secret and significant aerospace technology throughout the war. The advanced research was coveted by the British, American, and Russian governments. The race to capture the intellectual work of the scientists became more vital as the fall of the Reich became more obvious.

Fearing captivity and death from the Russians, many top scientists fled to high mountain retreats in Bavaria, waiting to surrender to the British and Americans by using the scientific knowledge as a bargaining chip to save their lives.

During those brief days with his uncle, young Rolf learned about the underground rocket production factory hidden in the hills of Nordhausen. Rudolph told him about the assembly lines of intact weapons, a technological treasure trove labored on by captured prisoners. He learned about how the German scientists had invented rocket powered engines and completed sophisticated aviation engineering and design that would lead the world for decades to come.

Rolf was too young at that time to understand that the sudden disappearance of his uncle after the visit of the American soldiers. Years later he would find out that he was transported to a secret project far away that would be known as the Manhattan Project.

But those short hours spent at his uncle's knee had planted the seeds of inquiry and scientific research that would remain with him for the rest of his life.

It had only been in recent years that the twins had renewed their relationship. The reunion came after the death of Fritz.

Rolf had returned to their village from Heidelberg after his partner's death. Helga had never met Fritz. She had only tried to approach the subject of her brother's private life once, years earlier. It had been painful for both of them, and so the awkward subject was dropped. The contact with each other gradually distanced.

Rolf had been the one to reinitiate their relationship, asking her to attend the funeral. Helga had at once sensed the emotional suffering of her brother in his time of need, and reciprocated in renewing their long quiescent bonds.

She had since been a loyal sibling at his side. They were an unlikely duo in every respect other than having come from the same womb.

She was actually already missing him now that he had left on his latest project. This would be the longest separation since he had moved back home, and until this moment she had not realized their emotional dependency on each other.

Perhaps she should have insisted on driving him to the airport, rather than jumping at the chance to be liberated from the responsibility. Never mind, he no doubt would call her as soon as he was settled in San Jose.

Perhaps I will pop around to the cottage and make sure that he had locked everything up properly.

He had asked her to keep an eye on things, and she intended to take in the mail every week or so.

She knew the place would be spotless, but no harm in giving a quick once over just in case.

Yes, that is a good idea. I will stop by on my way home from the florist shop.

*****

Rolf's seventeenth century chalet was located not too far from Nuremberg.

The find had been Helga's doing. The effort she took for him helped cement their sibling bond, and the twin brother considered himself very lucky to have it.

It had stood nestled a mile or so from the main village for more than four hundred years. Even when it was built, nearby Nuremberg was already a developed city of craftsmen and patricians, and commerce.

Today, Nuremberg is a major producer of optical and electrical products, as well as a center for paper and textile industries. Its institutions of higher learning and technology are world renowned. Schwartz found solace in building intellectual relationships with learned researchers and scientists after relocating from Heidelberg.

In fact, he quietly held a once a month social at his cottage with distinguished guests during which they clandestinely debated the latest research trends and political implications and pressures regarding vaccine and drug development.

They were beginning to worry that science and data was being politicized by profit and global politics. Rolf had never mentioned these covert encounters to his sister other than casually mentioning gatherings with friends.

The tight group had been disappointed that their organizer was going to be gone for so long. Rolf had graciously offered the chalet in his absence to continue the meetings on the first Monday of each month. The small group had been delighted to accept the offer, and pledged to make sure his home was left in pristine order after each gathering. Rolf had no doubts about that; each and every scientist would be meticulous about detail and order.

Rolf did, however, feel obliged to inform his sister that an occasional associate or two from the university may drop by his home, and not for her to worry that it was perfectly all right.

He felt this was sufficient detail to inform her without divulging any information on the purpose of their meetings.

It was just an undisclosed private concern that he preferred to keep to himself.

*****

Helga decided to stop by her own house before walking on to Rolf's chalet. It was not too much of a detour, and her old Doberman, Maxi, would enjoy running up the trails during the brisk walk.

Helga also felt a little safer with Maxi at her side during evening strolls. In times past, she would not have given a second thought, everywhere was considered safe. But like the rest of the world, things had changed, and folks were less trusting and on their guard.

There was an eerie silence to the cottage as Helga approached the front door. She felt a momentary chill up her spine and contributed it to the creeping cool night air and emptiness of the surroundings created by Rolf's departure.

She was used to seeing his wide grin and outstretched arms in the door frame with a tasty treat in hand for Maxi.

Maxi was disappointed, too, racing agitatedly around the house, and finally coming to a stop in the living room. Sitting in the middle of the floor she let out a hysterical whine, nearly causing Helga to jump out of her shoes.

Her owner raced in to see what was going on with her.

"Maxi, will you settle down for heaven's sake, nothing's wrong. Rolf has just gone away for a while".

The dog was not to be settled, and continued her disconcerting rant.

Helga went to the doggie treat jar to find a morsel to calm her down. No luck. Maxi was not interested, at all, and continued to fret and whine.

Seeing that everything appeared in order, other than with Maxi, Helga decided to make a quick departure.

"Maxi, let's go."

The dog remained in the center of the room, and couched down on the command to leave.

Normally, one time is all it took to have her obey. This time she was obviously naughty and upset about Rolf's absence.

"No Maxi, do not be a bad girl. I know you miss Rolf, but we have to go."

She put the leash on the dog, and literally dragged her through the front door.

Well if that's how she reacts to coming up here while my brother is out of town, we won't be checking in very often. Rolf's friends can take care of that.

With that, the pair left for home.

London

Geoff Collins was intensely focused on the streams of data running across the laptop screen. He was equally oblivious to the dirty dishes that were piled on the counter of the cramped kitchenette.

The rented Browning Street council flat was a mess of discarded take away food boxes, untidily thrown on the floor and scattered on top of the coffee table.

His London lifestyle was exactly opposite to the pristine and ceremonial residence his parents maintained in their fashionable San Francisco home. He rather enjoyed the contradictory lifestyle. It seemed a rebellious act towards his father, and the girls he picked up at the local club never complained.

His good looks and American accent got their attention; along with his creativeness as an enthusiastic lover. The untidiness of his dwelling was never a problem; at least he had never heard any complaints.

Geoff's attention was directed completely on the numbers and codes his vigorous search demanded.

He was determined to uncover who had been accessing the account. The reaction Mr. Benton had to news of the trespass was cause for concern.

Geoff had total confidence that he would be able to fix it.

Mr. Benton had been his only friend when his father had abandoned him, and he felt it his responsibility to protect his assets. He was fully aware of the older man's shady dealings, but his money came from was his business. He paid him a good fee to make sure his financial affairs were kept hidden.

Hell, he had seen enough in San Francisco with tit for tat that at least on this one he was getting a little piece of the action.

"Bingo!" He cried out as the screen displayed the data he needed.

Well, well, well. Mr. Benton is not going to like this shit one bit.

*****

"Mr. Benton, you have a telephone call at the desk." the concierge announced with a nod and bow from the waist.

"Thank you, Joe. I'll take it here in the lobby, please."

"Of course, Sir, I will fetch you a telephone straight away. By the way, Sir, it is a pleasure to have you stay with us longer than expected, again."

"Your lovely city is always worth extra days, if I can swing it", smiled Benton.

He had not expected to stay a day longer than he needed to clear up the account situation with Collins. The kid's revelation of the hacking had been quite a shock. He was certain that someone was on to them, and needed to put a fix on it as soon as possible.

"Here you go, Sir."

Benton took the phone.

He immediately recognized Ortega's accent.

"*Hola, Andrew.*"

"Are you out of your damn mind? What are you doing calling me here?"

"I had to let you know about Rolf. He hasn't arrived yet, and Ross is here already."

"Well, then, you don't need to worry about Rolf saying anything, do you?"

"Of course that's a help for right now."

"So no need for the call."

"But Ross is very suspicious of the reasons we gave him to expand Miami. He is calculating costs, and he can see it adds up to a lot more than they thought."

"Let him worry, just do not give him a hint you know something."

"We know that Rolf is on the same line of thinking so maybe they put their heads together and added things up."

Benton was convinced that Schwartz had not informed anyone of his suspicions. And he certainly wasn't about to talk to anyone now.

"Look, Ortega, you just take care of Ross. Satisfy him that his personal side deals are safe. You do not worry if the Miami operation is, shall we say, even more successful than we anticipated.

"Look, I spoke with Rolf a few days ago, and he got cold feet about going back to Costa Rica for so long, maybe he is rethinking the trip."

"So he may not come now?"

"Just let Ross know you heard that the *Deutsche Pharmaceutical* delayed Rolf's trip due to some crisis only he seemed to be able to fix."

"That helps a bit. At least I only have one person to worry about for the *momento*."

"Who else is worrying you?"

"Our Colombian amigos made it clear that they definitely do not want anyone asking questions. That was the deal, Andrew. No questions asked. No *problemas* for anyone."

"I know that, and you know that."

"As long as we have a smooth operation we make a tidy profit, and no one is the wiser. If we get them upset, they can be very angry operators. *Entiendes?*"

"Of course I understand."

"I just need to make that clear, Andrew. This is not a child's game."

"Fine, you are clear. Now do not call me again at the hotel, or anywhere for that matter. If I need to talk to you then I will call. Do you *entiendes?*"

Ortega was more than pissed at the attitude of Benton, pledging to make sure he needed to learn who was boss.

Andrew furiously ended his end of the conversation, regretting even more about getting involved with Ortega's crowd in the first place.

*****

"You are late." He barked at Collins.

Benton was still seething from Ortega's call.

"I'm sorry, Mr. Benton, but I was on to something, and figured taking time to follow the trail of the data would be worth the wait."

"Yes, well I am sorry. It's this damn drizzly weather that is getting the best of me. I will be glad to hopefully be on the plane home by tomorrow."

"For sure, these dreary days get to everyone, even the Brits.

"I wish I could take time for a little escape to Pismo Beach myself, great surfing, you know," smiled the easygoing lad.

"Anyway, I think I found out who has been sniffing around, or let's say at least I may know where the hack came from."

"So, where did it come from?"

"You won't believe this Mr. Benton – I had to go through about forty different layers of origination codes, and let me tell you it was a pretty sophisticated operation."

"Geoff, just get to the main point. Who is hacking our data?"

"Who – I cannot tell you for sure. From where – I can tell you that it came from Bogota, Colombia."

Benton tried not to explode, not wanting to give any indication to Collins that he was more than alarmed than he seemed about this new information.

"Oh well, sure, that takes a lot of pressure of us then. Colombia, jeez it must be some hotshot kid with access to an Internet connection!"

Geoff was taken back with Benton's sarcastic tone, and let him continue.

"Thank God the IRS is not on to us. I feel a hell of a lot better," he ranted mockingly.

Geoff still wasn't too alarmed, it was all data traffic and numbers on a screen to him, but Bogota certainly wasn't a reputable city.

Someone prying into bank accounts seemed like trouble to Geoff as well, but nothing was missing. He figured his talents could keep a track on it. But maybe he had seen too many late night drug movies.

"To be safe, Mr. Benton, we should go ahead and move everything to another account."

"Yes, do it immediately. It may not be the IRS, but by the same token we don't want this guy thinking he is playing us like some damn video game."

"You are right on it there, sir."

"You need to get on this pronto. Close out all the Halifax links."

"That is exactly what I planned to do."

"I trust you will be able to finagle the right process, but better to use the Swiss account to park the funds for the moment."

"It's as good as done, Mr. Benton."

"You know how to reach me if any more red flags come up. Hopefully, it is the end of a hacker kid, and we can move on."

"Right, Mr. Benton, you got it!

"Say hello to Mom for me. You can give Dad the finger."

"Take care of things, and I will be in touch."

Benton had no intention of contacting his parents, he never did.

Geoff headed for the nearest tube entrance while Benton hurriedly returned to his room to collect his belongings.

*****

Fuck, Benton said to himself as he sat in the seat of the black taxi cab taking him Heathrow. He swore that no South American hacker was going to get the better of him.

Ortega was right, the Colombians were checking up on him. But it was bad news that they had been able to find his accounts. If they had wanted to empty the account, they would have already done so.

They were up to something else, and he had to stay ahead of them.

With any luck the kid would work some account transfer magic fast before the Colombians cleaned him out. He was so close to executing his plan, and for sure needed no one screwing it up now, not even the Cartel.

Jesus, what has Ortega gotten me into?

*****

He settled into the business class cabin of the flight to Miami. He would have preferred a direct route to San Francisco, but convinced himself that he needed to first stop in Miami and check on the distribution operation.

There were too many unexpected problems right now, and he wanted to make sure that nothing else went wrong. He had come too far now to blow it. In a few short weeks he would be able to take a permanent retirement in his Swiss estate.

He blamed that damn Ortega's greed for getting them in this bind. True, they had all been dipping in the cookie jar over the years, but never anything too illegal or too dangerous.

But messing around with Colombian drug lords was way out of his league. He began to sweat nervously, even thinking about it again.

Ortega had insisted that the Colombians had no interest in either Rolf's research operation or Benton's screwing of Uncle Sam with the exports of diluted flu vaccines.

He said it was a simple clean operation. All they cared about was a highly regarded middleman for transporting hard stuff from Central America to Miami.

The shipments of herbal remedies, right under the feds noses, were a perfect set up to hide other illegal drugs being shipped out of South America.

It had worked for a while, and they had all made a nice cut. Then the Colombians figured out a better plan.

It was Ortega's loud boasting, always needing to play the big shot that had let things get out of hand. He was the one that told the younger Maldonado brother about Zenkon's partnership with the federal grants. He ran his mouth about redistribution of the herbal medications to the third world countries.

Maldonado was no fool, and saw his opportunity to show his stuff with the Cartel.

He pitched using Miami as the origination hub of export to Eastern Europe by leveraging the current operation in Miami. He persuaded them that by structuring a triangular trade scheme with Africa as a midpoint between Miami and Eastern Europe that they could operate right under the noses of the DEA.

The plan was to repackage their drugs on arrival in Miami. They would forget the US domestic distribution, that market was getting saturated. They would instead focus on Eastern Europe.

The feds would in a sense be partners since Zenkon already had the contract to supply drugs to developing countries. The shipments would be stamped with US seal of approval.

It was genius that the gringo tax dollars would not only simplify the customs inspections, but would finance the transport from Miami to Cameroon.

Of course, it would mean diluting Ortega's products again on arrival in Africa, before shipment to Prague for a waiting market. The Czechs adore natural and organic remedies, and wouldn't know the difference. New labels would indicate that the natural ingredients came from the tropics of Cameroon.

Benton had been furious and nervous from the beginning. Ortega and he had almost come to blows when he learned of the deal with the Maldonado brother.

As soon as Maldonado had walked into his San Francisco office, Benton realized there was no way out.

The Colombian had the appearance of a thug and the arrogance that comes with corrupt power, albeit nonchalantly disguised in his Armani suit.

It was clear from the onset that Benton had been sucked into something that was way over his head. Unless he cooperated with the brute federal prison for the HHS scheme would be the least of his worries.

He was way over his head, but the Cartel already had their teeth fully into it.

Maldonado made it clear that they were on the way to launch the operation within the next few months.

Ross, of course, had sensed something fishy was going on. He had no idea how illegal or how bad it could be for the Foundation.

Benton' growing edginess had tipped him off. Ross, always with his own self interest at heart, assumed he was being cut out of some lucrative action. The stupid idiot did not know that in this case he was actually better off in the dark and being protected for his own good.

Benton's escalating unfriendliness and disjointed communications caused a major row between them. This was what eventually led to his resignation.

Basically, dismissal by the Board was just a loss of face for Benton.

Ortega was still in place to keep an eye on the Costa Rican operation, and the distribution firm that Benton had set up out of Miami was an independent operation from the start.

In retrospect, leaving the nonprofit had probably been more of a blessing since he had enough troubles to deal with now.

Nonetheless, the embarrassment from wound Ross inflicted had been difficult to heal.

The plane was just about to back away from the gate as 's cell phone came to life in Andrew's briefcase below the seat. The ping was signaling a text startled him, and he immediately reached for the phone.

Andrew glanced at the text message on the scientist's mini display screen.

"*Rolf, please call - heard about your delay. Need to talk.*
Jonathan."

He turned off the phone, and settled in for the six-hour flight to Miami.

Los Angeles

Jack O'Riley had been digging for more information on Ortega's business since Maureen had called him the week before. Always one to sniff a good story, he sensed that this one had a big stink associated with it.

Why would Washington be pressuring the Costa Rican government to freeze the bank accounts of one of its most wealthy citizens?

Jack had put out a couple of feelers to close Washington sources that he knew he could still trust.

His liberal allies had been more than pleased to lend their old pal a hand in getting to the bottom of the mystery. The Administration had become close lipped and even hostile with the press, offering few opportunities for news conferences – nothing like the openness of the daily White House briefings and endless juicy stories of the Clintons.

The Clinton's had been a correspondent's dream.

The canned releases and identical quotes uttered from the mouths of all the current loyalists was enough to make the press desperate for the possibility of a crack in the dam.

Reporters were now like bloodhounds on the faintest scent to build up anything that had remote chance of turning the American pie image of any politician into tribal warfare and twitter gossip.

Uncle Sam forcing closure on bank accounts of private citizens of foreign governments with connections to American organizations had an appeal for a possible plot.

"Jack, its Ken Miller. I may have something for you. Give me a call."

Jack switched off his old twenty-year-old answering machine on the messy office desk. There were just some old technologies the old reporter would never replace, and his old desk phone was one of them. It was his comfort zone.

Ken was a top notched investigative reporter for the Washington Daily whom Jack had mentored in his first assignment at the *Times*. He moved from the Los Angeles newspaper to Washington with Jack's full support while he was still a young journalist. He was now a seasoned Washington correspondent, with sources in every bureaucratic nook and cranny.

He answered his return call on the first ring.

"Hi Ken."

He had no need to identify himself; his voice was always recognizable to his younger protégé.

"Glad you got back to me right away, Jack. I think you're on to something with this Ortega business."

"What do you have?"

"I have a source over in Justice who said Ramsey made the call. Not only that, but he pulled the all the HHS files that deal with anything to do with herbal drugs imported from Central America. It's probably not a coincidence that the lean was put on Ortega's accounts."

"Ramsey himself requested this?"

"Yes, that surprised me, too. There must be something to it, but no one seems to know what. Apparently, this is very close to the vest. Even Ramsey's key aides have nothing to do with it. Or at least that's what they are claiming."

"What would Justice be doing meddling in foreign citizen issues?"

"My thoughts exactly!" responded Ken.

"We are definitely on to something here."

"Especially since Ramsey seems to be focused on finding ammunition for the upcoming campaign."

"You are right on that."

"But there's more."

"Shoot."

"Another source told me that Intelligence has been poking around in the region where the natural herb facility Ortega runs is located."

"Intelligence down in Costa Rica?"

"That was a big surprise since their resources have been pretty much slashed, and what they have managed to salvage has been tied up with the South American drug and guerilla war situation. Could our Mr. Ortega be dabbling with the big guys?"

"Well, well, well. We may have stumbled onto a live one here."

"I'll keep on the trail, and let you know where it leads."

"Thanks, Ken. Let me know as soon as you have anything."

"Sure, Jack, anytime."

Jack leaned back in the old desk chair, and reached for a cigarette from the pack in the top left drawer. Some of his best thinking took place when he had a long satisfying drag of his Marlborough.

Some old newspaper habits could never be broken.

*****

"Jesus, Jack. What are you saying – that the Foundation might be involved in an international drug ring or something?"

"No, Maureen. I am just laying out the facts, and trying to put one and one together to see if it adds up to two."

"It sounds bad."

"All I know at this point is that the rain forest operation, the frozen bank accounts, Intelligence, Justice, and your foundation all have one common denominator. That is Mr. Rosario Ortega."

"Damn!"

"How that fits with Ross and Benton beats me, but I do intend to find out."

"Jack, this is getting far riskier than I ever expected. I think we might be playing a dangerous game."

"I must admit that it does not sound like it is leading to a good place."

"Helen is meeting with Ross as we speak, and she was pretty shook up when I spoke with her. He was trying to force her off the Board, nicely of course with an offer of other stuff. But then he let it drop that Ortega's days were numbered."

"That is another interesting piece to the puzzle."

" I think he knows something, or is up to his neck in this."

"Listen, Mo, leave the Costa Rican and investigative work to me. I do not want to put you in any danger. You and Margo need to focus on Benton and Ross."

"I have no problem there, Jack."

"Keep looking through the Foundation books and see what you come up with. There must be something you are overlooking."

"Okay, Jack. But be careful, too. These days I don't really trust anyone out there, and attacks on you guys are also getting serious."

"Oh, don't worry about me. I do the desk work these days."

"Who ever thought we would see the day when the media would be accused of being the enemy".

"Yea, it's rough, but remember I am an old tough bird."

"Right, but this sounds like we might be rubbing up to some very seedy characters, to say nothing about the potential involvement of drug cartels."

"That's why I want you and Margo as far from this as possible."

"What about Holly?"

"He needs to be told, definitely. Listen, he is due back in California later this week. Let's hold off for a couple of days until we have something more concrete."

"Okay."

"Perhaps once we firm up some facts we can all meet with Holly and Scott Jenkins to discuss damage control."

"That sounds reasonable. I'll give Margo a heads up."

"Hang in there, my dear."

"You take care, too Jack, ciao."

Costa Rica

Johann had just completed his rounds in the coastal port of Punta Arenas. He was headed back to Liberia, when all the commotion ahead on the main highway drew his attention.

A major accident had blocked both sides of the road just outside of the small town of Santa Rosa on the Inter American highway. Folks were standing at the side of their cars gaping at the crash.

Like magic, vendors had appeared like an army of ants. They were selling bags of mangoes and bottled water to the delayed motorists. This would be a long delay for sure.

Two big rig trucks were intertwined in a snarled disaster that had blocked all lanes of the highway. An old car was off to one side completely turned over, and a yellow tarp on the potholed asphalt covered what appeared to be a fatality.

The *policia* had completely stopped all traffic, and were now directing the northbound traffic to the left side of the road to avoid the accident victim and the mangled trucks.

Locals were taking it in stride, and helping the police clear the road of mounds of squashed bananas and pineapples.

A small pick up on the way to the market had evidently swerved to miss the crash, and in the process had dumped an entire load of fresh fruit. The clean up process would be efficient, and villagers would reap a benefit by salvaging any edible fruit for future sale or family meals.

The German baker's truck edged past the tragic scene as the police slowly resumed the flow of traffic.

His heart stopped, and he felt sweaty and sick to his stomach. Immediately recognizing the markings and color of the smashed vehicle, he knew to whom it belonged.

Quickly turning the bakery van off to the side, he jumped out and ran to the police near the covered body.

"Que paso?" He shouted desperately at the frenzied traffic policeman.

"Una viejita se murió." responded the young highway patrol officer.

"An old lady, yes, I know her – this is her car. Her name is Helen Nelson. She is from Flamingo, oh my God, what happened?"

"La viejita must have fallen asleep at the wheel, senor. Her car crossed over the line, right into the oncoming truck."

"Fell asleep at the wheel, my god."

" The truck driver said she was slumped over the wheel. He swerved to avoid her, but clipped the front end of the car, tipping it over."

"Ay Dios."

" The other truck then ran into the back of him. So early in the morning, *tal vez* the senora had been driving all night?"

"Poor Helen. She had a very bad heart. I think maybe it could have been a heart attack."

"Please, if the senora is a friend of yours will you come this way and give us her particulars?"

Johann walked to the patrol car with the policeman. He glanced back just as the rescue team was lifting Helen's limp corpse into the back of the emergency vehicle.

*****

About an hour's drive from the horrific scene, Jonathan Ross and Rosario Ortega were sipping a morning coffee as they sat on the impressive mountain deck of the guesthouse of *the Clínica Salud del Nuevo Milenio*.

Zenkon's research facility was located near the *Reserva Biologica Monteverde* along the inland mountainous region of Laguna of Arenal.

The incredible views and unspoiled luscious green mountain valleys provide a spectacular backdrop for the rustic buildings. Purple orchids, orange and red bromeliads, and deep green moss displayed a beautiful natural canvas of color.

The pastoral setting was another world from the loud noise and congested traffic of San Jose.

The *Centro Cientifico Tropical* a well-respected non-profit organization had first acquired more than ten thousand hectares of the area in the early sixties, and other endowments had added to the protected area over the years.

Scientists, researchers, and students from around the world were not uncommon in the mountainous region, and no one gave a second thought to the comings and goings of the *Clínica's* facilities administered by Ortega. In fact, the villagers from nearby Cerro Plano and Santa Elena provided cheap and reliable labor for the operation, and their families relied on the small business generated from the constant flow of the transient visitors.

The two small *farmacias* even proudly sold the herbal products to tourists, more of the brilliant *mom and pop operations* that Ortega and Ross had conveniently arranged on the side.

"I thought that Rolf would have been here by now."

"He was scheduled to arrive two days ago. I thought perhaps he would come with you, Jonathan."

"Yes, well that was the plan. But when he hadn't arrived by late yesterday I decided to drive up here alone. Perhaps there is some last minute urgent business he needs to complete before he leaves Germany. I have left a message with the hotel to have him call as soon as he checks in."

"It is no problem. I am sure he must have lots of last minute details to arrange when he is leaving his home for six months."

"I can imagine that is true, Rosario."

" He will no doubt be here by evening. We can take advantage of the privacy to discuss the urgency of your trip. I gather it has to do with the bank situation on my private affairs, a small bureaucratic mistake, I assure you. We can clear that up right away. Believe me, there is no need to worry about the reputation of the *Clínica*."

"All in good time, *mi amigo*. I would rather leave the business discussion until Rolf arrives."

"As you wish."

"Let us instead spend the day going over the progress of the *Clínica*. You have certainly expanded the operation since I was last here just a few months ago. I would like to know what new benefactors you have that made this possible, and what your plans are for the future. I want to make sure I give an excellent report to the Foundation Board."

"Of course, *con mucho placer*."

*****

The telephone rang for the fifth time in the kitchen of Helen Nelson's small beach house in Flamingo.

Maureen Sloan did not bother to leave a message. There were already three messages from earlier calls.

Something was definitely wrong.

Helen had promised she would be in touch on her return from meeting with Ross. Maureen was extremely worried about the safety of her aged friend, and instinctively knew that the non-responsiveness at the other end of the phone line was a portent of very troubling news.

The conversation with Jack had unsettled her, and she was certain that Ross was somehow wrapped up in the whole affair.

*****

In the lobby reception area at the Marriott Hotel a desk clerk was checking the display screen of his computer, while an international caller was on hold.

After carefully searching the guest list, he returned to the caller.

"No, senora, el Dr. Schwartz is not checked in at the hotel."

"Are you sure? Or perhaps he has left already. He was supposed to arrive there a couple of days ago. I am his sister."

"One moment, senora, I will check the reservations from earlier in the week."

"Ah, we had a reservation for the doctor; however, he did not arrive at the hotel on the evening to check in for his booking. That is all I can tell you."

"Thank you. You have been most helpful."

Helga thought it strange that Rolf had not at least called her to say he had arrived safely, and even more strange that he had not checked into the hotel.

He most likely decided to go directly to the *Clínica*, rather than spending the night in the capitol city.

He was probably very busy if he has not had time to call me. Besides, there is really no urgency.

Washington, D.C.

It is only a short few blocks drive from the Department of Justice office building to the White House east gate. He could have easily walked the short distance faster than the maneuvering the driver had to deal with on the crowded streets.

A simple drop off in front of the White House had been impossible for years since the large concrete barriers had been erected in the post 9/11 days.

The black SUV with its black tinted windows momentarily caught the interest of ever-present press corps as Ramsey stepped out of the car and onto the curb in front of the guarded gate.

No one important, they thought, and went on with their conversations.

The brief ride gave him a few minutes to glance over the memo once again, and gather his thoughts. He relished sharing the information on Hollingsworth with the White House staffers, and was sure it would be the key to ingratiating him for his goal of a West Wing assignment after the election.

He knew he deserved it. His confidence grew that he would be short listed for several key posts.

After all, years earlier it had been in large part his doing that a recount in Florida made the difference in a tight election. There was no argument that his maneuvers regarding the absentee ballot count had narrowed the candidate percentage margin just enough to open the door for a recount.

He felt he was instrumental in securing the United States Senate seat for the Administration. He was owed, and this latest news was just the icing on the cake.

He had cooled his heels for three years as Associate Attorney General, the third ranking official at Department of Justice, and a member of the Senior Management team. As far as he was concerned, this was only a placeholder to prove his loyalty and trust.

He wanted White House Chief Legal Counsel, but a senior legal advisor to the President would be alright as a backup plan, and he intended to make sure it finally happened.

The merging of the Bureau of Narcotics and Dangerous Drugs in the Treasury Department and various other offices of Federal Drug Administration and United States Customs had formed the Department of Justice in its present configuration in 1973. Its reach was immense, and it now operated virtually unchecked both nationally and internationally.

Once his son had tipped him off about the Costa Rican herbal manufacturing operation it had been fairly simple for him to then make a few inquiries through the immense DOJ data file. In no time, he was able to connect the dots to Hollingsworth's committee appropriations and the HHS oversight of the federal grant supporting the developing countries.

Even at this stage, he knew he had enough solid information to support the feeding frenzy of the press corps, and the rest could take care of itself. Liberal press would go wild to learn that their icon

Senator had funded a project that was providing diluted products.

The added morsel of Hollingsworth serving on the Foundation Board could raise perceived conflict or ethical questions, whether valid or not, worth a fortune in re-election campaign opposition research.

Ramsey took a deep breath as he put the clearance lanyard around his neck and passed through the security check. The process was familiar to him, but each time he entered the hallway the symbol power of the setting afforded him an adrenalin rush.

Despite his lofty title, he was a minor player in the pecking order of the Washington establishment.

Assistant Directors are a dime a dozen. As a rule he attended White House meetings as a side kick to the Attorney General, expected to keep his mouth shut unless asked something specifically.

He could hardly wait for the day when he would be an insider in his own right, and the one pressuring DOJ, asking the questions, and then providing the advice to the most powerful politician in the world. He hungered for that moment, as he ascended the circular staircase that would take him to the second floor meeting.

*****

His blood pressure was probably off the charts. He had returned to his office furious, taking it out on anyone who happened to get in his range. Everything they needed to nail Hollingsworth was right in his hands, and the self centered bastard had the nerve to cancel his meeting.

On arrival, he had been unceremoniously told to wait in the outer office of the Deputy Chief of Staff, Jim Murray. He kept his impatience in toe for nearly an hour.

Then hearing from an intern, no less, that Mr. Murray had been called urgently to the West Wing, and that his meeting would need to be rescheduled he nearly lost his cool.

He had no option, and now could do nothing for two days, the soonest available fifteen-minute slot the young intern had given him.

It was nothing but a put down, and typical posturing and power play, as far as he was concerned.

*****

A half our prior to Ramsey's arrival at the White House, Murray had been given the directive to cancel the meeting.

The directive had come from the top.

He was also instructed to then head over to Justice to speak directly with the Attorney General, or AG.

There are no secrets in the DOJ. Someone looking for a boost in career will always leak information to leverage their position, and Ramsey had been the victim this time.

A whiff of his intensions had been passed on to the AG while he was waiting for the meeting. It instantly put the brakes on any ideas he might have to work with the Vice President's office without his boss's approval.

He did not know it yet but his plans were already dead in the water.

*****

Three thousand miles away Bob Harris was also getting impatient with what seemed like his never-ending surveillance assignment of Margaret Maxwell.

He had already decided that she was a boring bitch. For nearly a week now she had done nothing exciting, even his peeping Tom act was giving him nothing to get encouraged about.

H i, Scott, this is Margo."

"Margo, it's good to hear from you."

"Well, I am not so sure about that when you find out what Mo and I found out. We definitely need to talk."

"I am all ears."

"Listen, I am on my cell phone right now. Are you going to be around in about an hour so we can go over all of the details?"

"Sure, I'll be here. Give me a call back."

Scott sat facing the sun set through the immense westward facing window of his office. The desk was covered in printouts from searches he had been doing all day on the Internet.

He was trying to find anything linked to the Zenkon Foundation, Benton, or Ross that would give a clue as to what they had been up to, it had been slow and tedious going.

The clouds were picking up over the Channel Islands, and were casting dark shadows over the expanse of ocean. He decided to take a break and stretch his back, so he headed for the living room, where he decided to light a fire in the hearth to warm things up before Megan arrived from the Center.

Just as the logs caught fire, the phone rang again, and this time it was from Holly.

"Scott. My staffers tell me that Ramsey is up to no good. He had some justice attorney over here asking aides numerous questions about Zenkon activities. I do not trust him one bit. Have you got news from our friends out there?"

"It seems that they are on to something, as well. Margo and I will be talking in about an hour. I can report back to you then with an update."

"That sounds fine. Ramsey had a couple of legal types over here this afternoon upsetting my aides with questions about my Foundation activities. I do not like this one bit, Scott."

"I understand, Sir."

"The last thing I need right now is some fishing trip from Justice. You know how they can make mountains out of molehills. The Party has enough to worry about in this re-election campaign without some hot shot trying to gain favor at my expense. Get this under control, Scott."

"I will sir, and will get back to you as soon as I can."

"Thanks, Scott. I am depending on you."

Scott ran his fingers through his thick, slightly graying, blond hair, and wondered why he got himself involved in these things.

He had moved to Santa Barbara at Megan's insistence to escape the vicious back stabbing of Beltway politics. The consultancy with Holly had attracted him only because of his long friendship and the Senator's pending retirement and clean-cut record. He figured this would be a piece of cake. As usual, nothing was a sure thing in politics, and everything ended up dirty when it came to campaigns and money.

To top it off, Megan's constant conflicts with local politics and immigration issues at the Center made both of their lives more of a roller coaster than the pleasant merry go round they had both planned.

He should have known better.

*****

Margo made a brief stop at the house of Mike Bergmann a trusted friend whom she had met shortly after her divorce from Herb. They were more than friends, but had decided to keep the relationship at a distance for a while longer because of Frankie and Jodie. It worked well that way for both of them.

Mike worked out of his rustic lodge-style home on along the Garden Highway of the Sacramento River. He was a very private person, and preferred communicating with friends around the globe rather than building a social circle in Sacramento.

He had never married, preferring to travel the globe in his position as commercial architect. He now enjoyed the quiet river front life, living in style on the substantial real estate investments he had been able to make over the years.

Margo was his window to the outside world, and as far as he was concerned his hope for the future. He knew that he had to give her time and space to realize they were meant to be together. And he was a very patient man.

She smiled to herself reflecting on how they had first met, and how far they had come since then. When folks asked how they met, she would lightheartedly say that he came with a chair, making them prod her for more information.

In fact, they met in a consignment store, and were bickering over an old glider chair that they both wanted. Being the gentleman, he gave in to her, and actually carried it to the trunk of her car. She thanked him by joking he would have to come over to her place to sit in it.

His response caught her off guard when he replied, "sure, I will bring the cognac."

He was true to the promise, and it was the start of her first relationship following the divorce from Herb. The chair still sits in her bedroom, and is her favorite spot to delve into a good book.

Mike was seated in a large contemporary style recliner, his long legs stretched out in front of him. He had been listening unwearyingly to Margo's interpretation of the happenings with the Foundation. As she finished her account he handed her a glass of wine that had been sitting in front of her.

"Here, my dear. It sounds like you need to relax a bit. And you haven't touched a drop"

"Oh, thanks, Mike. You think we are all crazy, don't you?"

"Of course not, Margo," he responded, flashing his blue eyes at her.

"But you must keep your emotions aside and deal with the facts." He stated in his usual self-controlled way.

"If Holly and Scott Jenkins are as sensible as you say, and the Senator is uncharacteristically alarmed about the proceedings from Ramsey, then there is something you need to find out."

"We are trying, Mike, believe me."

"Keep looking, and something will materialize. In the meantime, do not let it spin out of control, or have you all upset. You will not do yourself or anyone else any good in that state."

Of course he was right. Margo enjoyed a little sip of the wine, placed the glass on the table, gave him a quick hug, and headed out the door."

"Hey, that's all I get is a little peck on the cheek, and you didn't even finish your drink. That therapy session would have cost you about a hundred dollars from a shrink."

"Ah well, hang in there my friend, and we'll see what we can work out for a longer session this weekend!"

She left, slinging her handbag over her shoulder and grinning at him on her way out.

*****

Harris' hopes for a little action were raised to some extent when Margo went into the posh house on the river, but optimism died shortly when she was in and out in less than half an hour. Certainly, not long enough for him to assume anything spicy was going on.

He decided that if she were the one to lead them to anything then the road would be endless and unexciting as far as he was concerned. Still, he had made a commitment to Ramsey to follow the broad, and intended to stick with it.

He kept a safe distance along the levy highway of the river as he followed her home. It looked like she was settling in for the night with the kids.

He was hoping the wireless tap he had decided to use would bring him better luck than following her around like an invisible shadow. No sense in ignoring the technology if it got results.

He knew it was illegal, but what the hell the entire mission was off the books.

*****

"Margo, I have called at least half a dozen times to Helen's house. There is no answer. Something is terribly wrong. Oh, just a minute there is another call coming in…. Hello?"

"This is Johann calling from Costa Rica. May I please speak with a lady called Mo."

"Please hold on a moment. Margo, I will call you back it is apparently someone calling me from Costa Rica.

"Yes, Mr. Johann, this is Maureen Sloan. May I help you?"

"Oh, I was looking for someone named Mo."

"Speaking! People call me Mo."

"I see. I got your message from Helena's answering machine here in her house. I thought with so many messages you must be a friend of hers, so I have found your number in her phone book."

"Yes, she is a good friend. But I do not understand. Who are you?"

"I am the baker."

"Is she all right? Where is she? What are you doing in her house?"

"I am afraid that I have some very bad news. There has been a terrible accident. I am very sorry to tell you that Helena has been killed in a car crash."

Maureen felt her blood rush south and her entire body collapsing. Her legs gave underneath her, and she fell backwards onto the couch.

Dead!

It could not be happening. The room was spinning, and she began to tremble.

"Hello, are you still there?"

"Yes, I am here." She replied faintly.

"I need a moment, please. I cannot believe this. When and how did this happen? I just spoke with her when she was at the hotel in San Jose. She promised to call me when she got back home."

"She never made it home. The accident was on the road from San Jose to Flamingo."

"But what happened?"

"The police say she fell asleep at the wheel. But I suspect that she might have had a heart attack. Her heart was very weak you know."

"Yes. I know."

"It is very sad news for us."

"It is news that I never could have expected. What can I do to help? Is there anything we need to do? Poor, poor Helen, what a loss this is."

"Please let her other friends know of the tragedy. I have already called her family in the United States. They are already making arrangements to travel here tomorrow. They will take care of all arrangements."

"Yes, her family, of course."

"I am very sorry for the loss. We all loved Helena here."

"She loved being there, too. I am sure her life was full there."

"Goodbye, senora."

"Goodbye, and thank you for calling and letting me know."

Maureen broke down uncontrollably.

How could this be happening? She was sure there was a nefarious cause for Helen's death and that Jonathan Ross was stage center with something to do with it.

This had gone far beyond his cooking the books. They could now be dealing with murder, as far as she was concerned, and that meant whatever was being covered up was even more serious than they had ever imagined.

Nothing in the past, even being detained in communist Russia had ever really frightened her. But she now shuddered with fear.

*****

Harris listened in again as Margo made another phone call to Scott Jenkins.

"Scott, this is Margo again. Is this a good time?"

"Perfect, Megan is tied up again at the Center, so I am here alone enjoying the fire and view."

"It sounds lovely. Mo has already been in touch with Helen Nelson, and it seems from what she is saying that Ross is up to something. She is about to call me back in a few minutes with more details about their conversation. Oh, hang on. I think that's her now, hold on will you…

"Hello …

"Oh, Margo, something really terrible has happened. Helen is dead."

"Dead, my god, Mo! Let me get off the phone with Scott."

"Scott. I have to get back to you. Helen is dead! Mo is on the other line. This is awful. I'll call you back as soon as I can."

She disconnected from Scott before she heard his reaction.

Mo was still shaking, and understandably unable to speak coherently.

"They say it was a traffic accident, Margo, but I just know that Ross is involved somehow."

"It is very sad, Mo, and I am sure this is all linked together some way."

"Jack has uncovered some other things on possible drug activity. This is getting all so dreadful, Margo."

"More than that, Mo, it is way over our heads with drugs and now the death of poor Helen."

"Jack wants to have all of us meet when Holly is in town. Arrange it with Scott. I have to go; this is too much for me." She abruptly hung up still in tears.

Margo was stunned at the news.

My god, Helen dead, some sort of drug involvement. Her hand trembled as she picked up the phone again to fill Scott in on the awful events, and confirm the group meeting with Holly.

*****

At last, now we are on to something solid to give this exercise a boost.

Harris pulled out the head phones, and connected with Henry Ramsey right away.

Costa Rica

Jonathan Ross found it hard to get out of the comfortable guest house bed. He had stayed up late with Ortega, and drinking into the night was not something he was used to anymore. On the other hand, Ortega seemed to show little effect from the alcohol.

He would have to watch that.

Ortega had droned on the whole day about the new operation at the *Clínica*. His fast-talking and justifications for the expanded facilities had not fooled Ross one bit. He was clearly up to something illegal, and Ross was no fool. He could guess that he was into some drug manufacturing operation.

This came as no surprise. He had figured as much when the Costa Rican had come to the states shortly after the New Year talking about his big plans for expanding the operation.

Ross had already decided to pull the plug at that point.

This trip was just to confirm the already troubling suspicions.

Jonathan was used to walking in the gray zone on side deals, but big time drugs were not even in the cards for anything to do with either him or the Foundation.

He had his own political aspirations for the future, and he was smart enough to know where to draw the line. That definitely meant keeping clean away from any Latin American drug mafia. As far as he was concerned, Ortega's operations were headed into new territory that definitely crossed the line.

He planned to cut Ortega loose as soon as possible, and the convenient freezing of his assets had given him a legitimate cause for that.

Reasons unknown, it was still a blessing. Ross envisioned going solo with business returning to a semblance of normalcy with Helen Nelson playing the silent partner. He figured life was getting less complex, first with Benton out of the way, and then with Ortega off on his own trip.

Too bad Rolf had not arrived yet. His call the week before had confirmed that his suspicions about Ortega were on target. Rolf suspected something was going on, and planned to get to the bottom of it.

Rolf had agreed that it was probably wise to have someone on site for a while to better monitor the situation. He had been more than happy to trade in the gray skies of Germany for the tropics for a few months.

Maybe he would call today when he received the message. It was unlike him not to at least return a call. He was always one of appropriate manners and formalities.

Ross pulled himself together just as the maid knocked on his door.

"Señor, buenos días. Tengo desayuno y café para usted."

Ross opened the door to find the petite maid smiling at him with a breakfast tray laden with fresh coffee, *gallo pinto* topped with a fried egg, and fresh bread, the morning newspaper was tucked under her arm.

What a civilized country, he thought.

She put the tray and newspaper on the desk, and shyly left the room without another word.

Ross looked at the picture staring at him on the front page of the paper with distaste.

Why do they always have to make the morning news by showing the gory details of car accidents.

He poured himself a cup of coffee, picked up the paper as he walked onto the veranda of the guesthouse.

Taking a further look at the picture, his face went a chalk white. He had enough grasp of the Spanish language to understand that the caption indicated that Helena Nelson from Flamingo had died instantly in the horrific crash.

Ross was numb.

He could not believe that Helena was dead. He had spoken with her not more than twenty-four hours before.

He hastily showered, dressed and ran to find Ortega so that he could translate the details of the accident for him.

*****

Ortega had already been up for several hours. He was also finishing a steaming coffee, and was deep in conversation with Maldonado. He had arrived at the facility in the early hours after landing in the cover of darkness via private jet from Bogotá.

Maldonado's arrival into Liberia Airport was virtually unobserved. It was a much more secure passage than through the country's main airport in San Jose.

The subtropical area surrounding Liberia had made a name for itself as a clandestine landing strip during the American Iran-Contra affair of the 1980s.

The American military had fervently denied that they were ever involved in military operations from Costa Rica during the Central American civil wars. But the airport legacy, now an up and coming international airport, was a testament to the contrary.

"It had to be done, mi amigo. I doubt that she knew anything."

"Perhaps, but our sources are reliable, and so we know she was meeting with your friend Ross in San Jose."

The two men were obviously discussing Helen's death. Maldonado looked at Ortega and continued.

"We could not take the chance that he had alerted her to any suspicions. He is looking for specific information, and his behavior had us – shall we say – in a preventive measure mode. He won't be discussing anything with *la viejita* now."

"But they say it looked like a heart attack."

"Of course, *compadre*, her heart was the perfect cover. No sense in raising suspicions about what happened. You know how these peace loving *Ticos* are about *violencia*. They are pansies my friend, complaining in their newspapers about too much penetration of Colombian traffic, yet, they gladly take our money into their banks, and sell us their fancy houses at inflated prices."

Ortega remained silent.

"No, we eliminate problems quickly and in ways so that we do not offend our Tico friends. *Entiendes?*"

Maldonado finished with a contemptuous grin that unmistakably sent a direct signal, and turned Ortega's blood cold."

"We must also address how to take care of our other snooping gringo. His visit here is not, shall we say, welcome. You must resolve that situation right away," Maldonado continued.

As he turned to face Ortega he saw Ross heading hastily toward the outside patio deck with his morning newspaper folded in hand.

"Rosario! Have you seen this article about Helen in the paper?" He shouted breathlessly and waving the publication in front of him.

"Yes, a very unfortunate accident for senora Nelson."

"What does it say here about how it happened? Please, translate what it says for me." Ross anxiously handed the paper to Ortega, catching the figure of Maldonado from the corner of his eye."

"Ah, senor Ross. Permit me to introduce myself. Jose Luis Maldonado."

"Mr. Maldonado is one of our Latin American donors, Jonathan. He has been very supportive of the facility, and like you he is also here for a visit."

"I am pleased to meet you, Mr. Maldonado. I apologize, but Helen Nelson was one of my Board members who lived here in Costa Rica. I have known her for years, and am shocked at this terrible news of her death."

"My condolences, Mr. Ross, I did not know she was a friend."

"Yes, she just recently retired."

"The paper this morning, I believe it says a heart attack caused her to crash into oncoming traffic on the main highway."

Jonathan was shaken, responding to the additional information that Maldonado provided.

"A heart attack, yes, well that makes sense she had a very bad coronary condition. Poor soul, but it is a terrible way to go nevertheless. We met on Board business just a couple of days ago. It seems hard to believe that she is dead."

"Yes," responded Maldonado, "these things are most unfortunate. Gracias a Dios it appears it was a blessing that it was such an instant death."

"Yes, a blessing" replied Ross.

Shit now what do I do.

Ortega handed Ross another coffee from the buffet. All three stood quietly on the veranda, looking out over the green valley. Each deep in separate thoughts of deception.

"Why don't all three of us take a walk through the facility?" suggested Maldonado, the first to break the silence.

"It will help take your mind off your friend's misfortune, Sr. Ross, and give us a chance to get to know each other a little better. We are both major contributors in this center so perhaps we can offer some advice to Rosario on future plans."

"I really should make some calls to the United States and let the Foundation staff know about Helen. Perhaps later in the day would be better."

"It is still early in California, surely it will keep a while longer," responded the Colombian in a rather detached and somewhat commanding tone.

"You are right, Mr. Maldonado. A walk for an hour or so may clear my head, but first I must at least call our Executive Director to let her know the situation."

"Of course, I understand. We will wait for you in the reception lobby. Please, take all the time you need."

"Thank you."

*****

"Margo, Jonathan here. I am in Costa Rica."

"Jonathan," she repeated, truly taken aback by the unexpected call.

"Yes. Margo, I have some terrible news. Helen Nelson died in a car accident here in Costa Rica."

"Oh my God," she exclaimed, not wanting to give any indication that Mo had informed her the night before of the tragedy.

"What happened?"

"It seems she had a heart attack while driving home to Flamingo from San Jose. I had met with her the day before to go over some Foundation reports. My God, Margo, I cannot believe she is dead. It was front page in the paper this morning!"

"Poor Helen, she was such a dear. Let's hope that she didn't suffer too much."

"Listen Margo, this trip has really opened my eyes to this Arenal operation. I do not want to go into it now on the telephone, but we have to talk when I get back."

"I see."

"I was hoping to meet yesterday with Rolf, but he has not arrived yet. Have you heard anything from him at all up there?"

"No. Why should I? I wasn't even aware he was going to meet with you in Costa Rica?"

"It was last minute really. He had some concerns regarding the facility, and we decided to have him meet me here for an inspection. He offered to stay on for a few months after that to keep an eye on things."

"This is news to me, Jonathan."

"It is not like him to not call when he is late. Can I ask a favor and see if you can track him down? There is a lot going on down here, and I am not feeling too good about it."

"What do you mean, Jon?"

Margo was trying her best to sound as though this was all new information to her, and a bit surprised that he would be the one to offer any information given all they were learning.

"Not sure, Margo, but I have a feeling that Benton may be somehow connected to whatever it is, but it's just a hunch. No data at the moment. Let's just say that Helen's death, Rolf's disappearance, and some heavy duty activity here at the site have me more than a little shook up."

"It's takes a lot to shake you up, Jonathan. I will see what I can do to find out about Rolf, and make calls to the other Board members to break the news about Helen, such a dreadful loss to all of us."

"Margo, thanks, listen, I know that we have had our differences all along the way. But I am hoping that we can put that aside right now. Remember how we worked together on this project at the beginning?"

"Yes….." said Margo, wondering where this was going.

"Well, if you can stick with me here, I think that there is major funny business we need to sort out. I really need your help to get to the bottom of it."

"Jonathan, you are sounding a bit paranoid, maybe the shock of Helen's accident has thrown you off tilt."

"That is true as well. But Margo, I think there is something nefarious going on that could give the Foundation a black eye."

"More than your usual shenanigans, Jon?" she said half seriously, but trying to lighten the tone.

"Okay, Margo, I concede that I deserve that once in awhile. Nevertheless, you and I both know that there is a limit to my personal games. I do have some sense of ethics."

"Jonathan, you can't be a little bit pregnant, either you are or your not. We both know you have used the Foundation to advance your self interests for a long time. Legal maybe, but you are pushing the envelope, and you know it. It sounds like your games might be catching up with you."

"I will confess that I have leveraged my position Margo, but believe me there are some dealings that I think are more dangerous than any of us know about. Certainly things that are out of my league. I think that Andrew knew what was up, and maybe he left us all holding a very dirty bag."

"What are you saying, Jonathan, that you are an innocent bystander that is now caught in some wicked web?" she was now getting angry at him.

I know you are angry over a lot of things, Margo."

"Do not play Mr. Clean with me. If the Foundation is in a mess because of some illegal scheme, then I am sure you are at the heart of it as much as Benton or anyone else."

"Margo, I can understand your resentment. But believe me, there is something else here that we have to sort out. Please, work with me on this, or we will all lose out."

Margo sensed a tone of desperation in Ross' voice, but did not trust him at all. Something had alarmed him, and he was now trying to cover his tracks, or pin all the blame on Benton.

She decided to play along and see where it would lead.

"Okay, Jonathan, let's assume something is up. If you and Rolf both think that, then there may be fire to go with the smoke."

"Thank you."

"I will see if I can track Rolf down. I am going to bring Mo in on this discussion. I will get back to you."

"Thanks, Margo. I have no problem with you discussing my concerns with Maureen. Honestly, Margo, there is more to this than even I could dream up. I can feel it, and it's giving me chills."

"Talk to you later, Jonathan." Margo hung up the telephone, and lay back in her bed.

She was perplexed that Ross would share any fears with her, and she had to admit that the snake did sound quite alarmed.

She decided to follow up on the suggestion to call Rolf, and see if he could shed any light on the situation.

*****

The kids were still asleep. She slipped on her well-worn blue bath slippers and her favorite robe, and quietly tip toed into the kitchen to get her first taste of fresh coffee before making the call.

The usual aroma of fresh brewed coffee that denoted her morning ritual was missing. The rich java fragrance always helped provide a pleasant start to the day. She was instantly disappointed by the sterile kitchen air that greeted her.

Remembering that she had adjusted the automaker for seven since she planned on an extra hour in bed, she groaned with disappointment.

Jonathan's call had spoiled her plan, and even the coffee maker seemed to have deserted her. Irritated, she pushed the red button to start the brewing process manually.

The telephone rang again.

Good Lord, this is like Grand Central Station.

"Margo, it's Mo. Are you up yet?"

"Oh, yes, I'm up. No doubt about that. I think I am pulling the plug on this phone. Yours is the last call before eight!"

"My, we do sound a bit off color this morning. Of course, I understand with the shock we had about Helen last night. I did not sleep a wink, either."

"Yes, well it is all really overwhelming."

"Did you get a chance to talk with Scott about everything?"

"Yes, Scott is almost up to speed. He said he would let Holly know about Helen. We also decided to meet at Holly's place tomorrow about lunchtime.

212

We can evaluate where we are. Can you make it on such short notice?"

"Yes, of course."

"Great."

"I have invited Jack O'Riley to meet with us, as well. Holly knows him, and I have a feeling that his investigative mind will be needed. I will give Holly a call in advance to clear it."

"Thanks, Mo, that helps."

"So if I am the last call this early, who was the first, your hunk, Mike?"

"Ha ha, no such luck.

"The slime bag Ross called from Costa Rica to let me know about Helen. Of course, I didn't let on that I had already heard from you."

"So what did he have to say?"

"Actually, he seemed quite shook up. He thinks there is some covert plot going on that will give us all grief. He is claiming that Benton may have set us all up, and he is the victim or innocent bystander!"

"Of course he would."

"Anyway, his call has given me proof that something is up. We are definitely on to uncovering something serious, perhaps serious enough to even get Helen killed."

"It is really terrible."

"Oh, I almost forgot. It seems Rolf has pulled a disappearing act. He never showed up in Costa Rica. I am going to see if I can find out what's up with that."

"Give me a call, and let me know what you find out. And I will see you tomorrow at Holly's."

"Okay, I'll let you know if I find out anything. Otherwise, I will plan on seeing you and Jack there tomorrow."

Margo was unaware of the soft click as Harris disconnected his listening device from the line. She was momentarily distracted by the soft dripping of the coffee maker.

*****

Ortega had been eavesdropping on the conversation outside the door. Maldonado was not going to be pleased if he found out that Ross was acting like a loose cannon about to blow the whole operation.

This was sure to stir up enough trouble to make the Colombians edgy, and they had a way of eliminating problems that even hinted of trouble.

Ortega certainly did not want to go down with Ross, he had to think. Guilt by association was not a sentence he wanted imposed on him. He knew the consequences of that.

Slipping unseen into the thick bushes near the door, he followed the dirt path back to the main building. The humidity in the air was rising along with the heat of the day. By the time he arrived at the expansive trees adorning each side of the entrance, his shirt was damp and sticky, more from his own sweat and nerves than the heavy tropical moisture.

He managed to hide his worries for the time being in order to avoid raising concerns to Maldonado who had been waiting for both him and Ross to return for the tour.

Rosario Ortega knew that he had everything to lose, including his life. All his life he had pushed for power and recognition. He had climbed the ladder of success – financially and socially within his *campesino* class. However, enough was never enough for him.

Ironically, the golden grail of unlimited riches that he had envisioned in the deal he cut with the cartel now had him trapped in an extremely dangerous game. He was late to realize that he would never be more than a lowly dispensable pawn in a club that you could never turn in your membership.

One false step and the ruthless Colombians would have no problem eliminating him or Ross.

It was now a matter of survival. Ross had to understand that just as Benton had come to understand it.

London

There was no doubt about it. The account showed twenty one million dollars in balance. He had checked the figures more than four times and the number still appeared as twenty one million dollars. It was no mistake.

A deposit of seventeen million had been wired through an intricate network of international banking transfers, landing squarely in their account. Geoff Collins wiped his brow, but the sweat still ran down his back making the blue and white striped shirt damp and sticky against his skin.

Hacking into their account by some Colombian hot shot was one thing. He figured he could take care of that with some firewalls, but using the account to move major funds was definitely something else.

This was very high-level stuff. The hacker was a serious player. It was no wet behind the ears kid at a computer playing pranks. This was serious money laundering, and out of Colombia that meant trouble.

He needed to get hold of Benton right away, or, perhaps he didn't need to get hold of him at all, he was not thinking straight.

Shaking himself out, he decided the best approach would be to take care of this alone and see how it played out. After all, what could Benton do anyway?

Perhaps his instincts had been right, and Benton was too offhand about the Colombian connection. No, he decided, his protector had been straight with him, he was sure, but maybe not. He didn't know what to think at the moment.

Follow the money.

Benton had promised him a ten percent management fee for the original transfers. Nearly half a million had then seemed fantastic for easy work.

But now he was looking at a balance of twenty one million, a figure hard for him to fathom. They were both mega rich at this precise moment. But unless he could figure out how the money got there, and who was laundering, it could as quickly disappear.

He leaned back on the couch, rubbing his fingers through his hair, and let out a whistle to himself. Never would he have thought he would be looking at this much money.

Doubts entered his mind again about Benton. What if he had been up to something, and playing him for a fool?

Why not cover all bases. I will leave half of it there, and set up my own account. Hell, Benton would still be sitting on over ten million, and besides, I've done most of the work why shouldn't I be an equal partner.

Yes, that was it.

He would create a separate account for himself, before letting Benton know of the windfall they had unexpectedly accumulated. If Benton were playing it straight with him then he would still be sitting on a cool ten million, and if he had taken him for a ride all along, then he owed him anyway.

Pleased with his own ingenuity, he stood up, stretched his back, and returned to the keyboard, and his fingers raced over the keys.

He quickly accessed the bank's internal system once again without difficulty. In less than half an hour, he had successfully transferred more than ten million to a new account he had set up for himself.

Via a complex web of international wire transfers, facilitated by mega computers all around the globe, he was now according to the numbers displayed on the screen a multi-millionaire.

The hacker in Colombia would be enraged that his laundered stash had evaporated. Collins was certain his process would make it virtually impossible to figure out to where the money had gone.

He was quite pleased with himself.

He looked at his watch, and saw that it was still in the early hours in Miami. It was too early to give Benton the good news about his new balance of ten million.

The call to Benton would have to wait.

Grabbing his jacket from the couch, he headed to buy a take away meal from the neighborhood fish and chip shop.

The line at the "*chippy*" was as usual out the door catering to the crowds on their way home from work. Like most of the fish and chip shops throughout England a Chinese family owned it. This particular establishment was well known for the perfect batter and crispy cod cooked to perfection.

The smell of the fish and vinegar greeted Geoff's nostrils at just about the same time as the broken cockney voice of the Chinese immigrant shouted, *"three fish and two bangers"* to a young girl, perhaps thirteen or fourteen, standing in front of the deep vat of hot oil.

She obediently dropped the orders, along with two extra battered fish, into the scalding deep fry. She then expertly flipped a batch of crispy cod and fish cakes into the greasy display window so that the hungry line of patrons could work up even bigger appetites.

There is no doubt that the Brits love their fish and chips, indulging in the custom from mid day to long after the pubs closed late at night. Geoff had gladly adopted the ritual. His favorite time was after a good night out. There was something about walking home from the pub, warm chips drenched in salt and vinegar then wrapped in paper, on a cold damp London eve that gave a whole new meaning to the expression comfort food.

One Fish, chips and mushy peas he announced to the owner as he drew near to the front of the line.

Orders were called in about three or four down the line, so that they would be deep fried, wrapped, and doused ready for pick up by the time he handed over his cash. It was a fast food operation that dated long before the McDonald's days.

"Hiya, Geoff," came an enthusiastic greeting from farther back in the line.

The voice of the female *scouser* was easily recognizable. Pat Price was a true born and bred *Liverpudlian*. The sexy red haired blue eyed lass came from Irish grandparents and a huge catholic family. Her father worked double shifts in the Ford motor car plant near Liverpool to provide for his own family and that of several other siblings. Her mother was a bar maid in one of the numerous clubs in an industrial town just outside the city, and made ends meet for the family by working Saturday and Sunday nights.

Pat and her little sister, Olivia, had survived by taking care of themselves since they were toddlers.

Her beautiful looks and shapely figure were quite stunning, and she knew exactly how to use her assets to get gentleman friends, young and old, around her little finger. Liverpool was known as a rough town, and Pat had total confidence in handling any situation quite well. She was definitely a live wire, and had taken quite a fancy to the young American.

Geoff had met her in the *Rose and Crown* pub a few weeks before when she had come straight to his table and quite forwardly puckered up and said that she had always wondered what it would be like to steal a kiss from a yank. Leaning over she landed him one, much to his surprise and pleasure.

Since then during their brief fling she had been the one to give him a few lessons in carnal pleasures. He had to admit that she was quite a kick and pleasant handful; he was getting to like her a lot.

"Pat, what a lovely surprise it is to run into you, what's up?"

"The sky is up, my love, and hopefully other things if I can get you alone again."

She unabashedly laughed out, joined by several onlookers in the queue. Geoff, not quite used to such public displays, immediately turned bright red.

"Make his order two of everything, and wrap it together," she ordered the young Chinese girl before Geoff had the chance to object.

"No sense in wasting extra paper," she joked as she winked at him.

"Let's celebrate at your flat, why don't we?"

"What are we celebrating?"

"The night, my love, we are celebrating the moment. I am back in dear old London Town after a bloody long week visiting my crazy family. We shall eat, drink, and be merry, and then in our dreams we will sail away to faraway lands."

Pat had grown up on an industrial estate just a few miles outside of Liverpool. It was working class, and rough. Rows of identical council houses and ugly flats interspersed with dozens of factories became home to thousands of poor families, many with four or more kids. Housing was scarce in English cities after the bombings. New housing was touted by the post-war government as the key to the future.

Her grandparents had been among the first to move out of the city in the 1950's thinking they would make a better life for a young family in this newly developing area that boasted jobs and housing.

The family was typical, several kids, her grandmother working in the Kraft factory at night packing cheese, and grandfather leaving early in the morning to catch the double decker bus headed to the docks for his day shift. The kids basically took care of themselves, older ones making sure the little ones got off to school. Pat's mother inherited the same future, and there she stayed.

Pat grew up as second generation there, and learned how to take care of herself. But she knew she had to get out.

Even for her grandmother, the town proved to be more a nightmare than a dream. She saw how the once promising council houses and blocks of ten and twenty story flats transformed into havens for petty criminals and ruffians, and encouraged her granddaughter to be smart and move away.

Pat learned to take care of herself, and as soon as she finished secondary school, without looking back, headed for London to make her own dreams. Her heart was still back home with the family, but she knew that her life was destined for other shores.

"Actually, Pat, I am a bit tied up on some work this evening."

"Do not fret, pet. We will have this nice meal, and then I will relax you with an unforgettable massage. You know what they say – healthy body healthy mind. So then you can get on with the work while I have a nice bubble soak in your bath."

"Go on, give the girl a chance," chimed in a little white haired old lady in line.

"All work and no play makes Jack a dull boy," she laughed toothlessly.

"Brilliant! Right, then we're on?" smiled Pat before any other objections could be made.

Geoff paid for the order then linked arm in arm with his unexpected date, smiled as they headed back to the flat, encouraged by a few whistles and thumbs up signs from the waiting crowd.

California

B ob Harris figured he was finally getting somewhere on this tiresome assignment of surveillance of Maxwell. The conversation with Jonathan Ross certainly seemed to imply that something was up, and she seemed to be playing him along. There were more twists and turns in this saga than the California coastal highway.

Nelson's death now certainly added a gruesome element to the picture, particularly if it had not been as innocent as a heart attack.

He was sure than Margaret Maxwell and Jonathan Ross were engaging in a cat and mouse game with each other. Both were probably involved in one or more schemes with Hollingsworth and Benton.

He was feeling a bit better that the thread was unwinding, and he would get a break on something shortly. This meeting at Hollingsworth's place was crucial. He had to figure how to get inside his place.

Ramsey would no doubt know something more about the Rolf character.

His boss had not been in a great mood when they had spoken the night before.

His meeting with Bob Murray at the White House had again been postponed, and his frustration was quite obvious. The power plays between the Justice

Department and White House senior staff, as usual, being played out to the full. He was glad he did not have to participate in the Beltway games too much longer – all about posturing and power plays. Once he was through with this last favor for Ramsey, he planned to be permanently out of it. The rest of them could get their jollies at back stabbing each other. He preferred his fishing and retirement.

At least Ramsey had perked up when he learned about the pending meeting with Hollingsworth and the whole team. Helen Nelson's death had also sparked more than a passing interest in the Assistant Attorney General. He did not believe in coincidences, and planned to make a few calls to the authorities in Costa Rica.

Harris tossed the small Styrofoam coffee cup into the wastebasket, and lit another cigarette. He hated drinking from these awful cups. He was no environmentalist, but if a motel wanted to give guests the pleasure of a morning java in the room by providing a coffee maker, the least they could do is provide a proper cup – something bigger than a thimble that did not leave a residue taste.

He decided to wait on contacting his boss with another update, putting it off until he had further information. Besides, it was way too early in the day to have to listen to more rants about Murray's games. He preferred to get himself ready and get out of this two-bit hotel room for some fresh air and a good breakfast.

*****

Holly and Eleanor arrived at noon into the small Monterey airport. The five-hour early morning flight from Washington's Dulles airport to San Francisco

224

International was uneventful, and they both always enjoyed the short connecting flight that regularly returned them home. The twenty-minute trip took them right over their own hillside property, and on a clear day, the view from the coastal range to the Pacific Ocean was spectacular.

This was such a day, and even after hundreds of these trips over the years, they both still marveled at the picturesque beauty and serenity of the Peninsula.

Springtime in the Central Valley gave birth to a velvet carpet of green hills highlighted with colorful yellow daffodils, orange poppies, and peach blossoms. Grape leaves were busily covering the twine getting ready to bear their succulent fruits.

In the distance the little town of Seaside sported white sand beaches dotted with the flowering purple and blue ice plants. Low buildings of the state university campus that Holly had fought so relentlessly to fund faced the ocean next to the large military base.

The entire area seemed to fit together in harmony and beauty, and the couple knew they were lucky to call it home.

The sprawling university campus had been carved out of federal property belonging to the Fort Ord military base. It was hidden from public view by the gentle sand dunes and windswept cypress trees along the Pacific Coast Highway. Many of the original old army buildings had been renovated and now housed classrooms and labs for students.

Former barracks still stood on the former base, bearing testament to their age and outdated function with the boarded up windows and peeling paint.

The land had been deeded to the State of California. As soon as the state budget permitted they would be demolished to make way for more modern facilities and additional student housing.

During the early years of the Clinton Administration, several California military bases were closed and offered for private development due to federal budget cutting measures.

The thousands of acres of beachfront property of Fort Ord had every developer in the country salivating. The real estate lobby envisioned multi-million dollar estates, golf courses and private beach clubs. Holly leveraged his seniority and championed the cause of preserving the natural environment of the community.

He worked with local and state community activists and environmentalists to create a long-term plan dedicating the entire area to the new university campus and environmental reserve. The new campus in the state university system would focus on the needs of the surrounding farming community as well as research into environmental issues and marine biology.

He smiled to himself as he remembered the tough battles and public debates. Then how proud he was finally sitting next to the President to watch him sign the legislation at the White House. He had won, and the President deeded the area to the interests of higher education.

He felt that this legacy was his proudest moment.

It was Holly's favorite time of year in his district. As a senator, he represented the whole state of California, but this was home. It was also his former congressional district where decades before he had been given the trust of the people to represent them in Congress. He had never lost sight or appreciation of that trust, and his constituents and neighbors held him in high regard.

He was troubled at what they would think if his image were tarnished by a scandal with the Foundation. How ironic, he thought, that such a relatively unimportant association might be a goliath that brought down his life of public service, tarnishing him on the eve of his retirement.

Eleanor sensed his sudden tension.

After years of marriage they could feel one another's' every emotion. She gently took his hand in hers, and gave it a loving squeeze as the jet pulled to a stop. Peeking out of the small window, she saw that their driver had already parked the limousine near the steps of the plane.

They would be quickly on their way to their home in the nearby hillside.

*****

Margo planned to leave mid morning for the meeting with Holly and the others. The kids had gotten off to school without any problem. On the way there, Frankie reminded her that she had not opened the letter from his dad from the week before. It was still in the car door pocket, and she knew that she had probably put it out of her mind intentionally to avoid the stress of reading its contents.

Now, as she stood alone in the brightly sunlit kitchen, she tore open the envelope.

As usual, there was no salutation on the letter, just a statement from her former husband along with the date and his signature. This time it detailed travel expenses he had incurred to take the children to the dentist's office and for their physicals while she had been in Washington the week before. All the medical expenses were covered on their insurance policies, but Herb was enclosing a bill for nine dollars and fifty-eight cents as her portion of his mileage costs for driving them back and forth to the appointments.

His mileage was calculated to the allowable federal tax rate per mile. He was unbelievable and shameless, but totally predictable. His idea of joint custody and splitting costs was always defined to a fine art of splitting microscopic hairs. She had long passed the point of arguing with him, and had even learned to laugh at his ludicrous behavior.

Get a life!

To save the peace she would give Frankie a check when they returned to their father's house the next time.

Years before she had gotten upset with his nickel and dime calculations of the day to day expenses, particularly since he earned more than a comfortable salary himself. She found it offensive to reduce the raising of their kids to a mathematical formula of microscopic costs. However, the arguments with him were never worth the trouble, so she just paid him his blood money, and went on.

It had not been an easy concession on her part – particularly since she never reciprocated with like bills to Herb. She had tried that method at first by trying to put a halt to it by showing him how silly it was. He did not get the point, and had merely sent her demand back with a list of deductibles, including a new toothbrush and toothpaste for Jodie and new shoelaces for Frankie.

At that point of lunacy, Mo convinced her that enough was enough, and Herb was insane.

From that moment on, she merely avoided conflict by merely sending him checks for the petty demands. These little payments, which she referred to as her *sanity dues*, were far easier to take care of than other demands that involved the bigger issues on which they were likewise never to agree.

She went into her office and noticed that the screen was indicating new e-mails and attachments.

Margo opened the e-mail from Laura. The content raised more questions in her mind than it provided in answers.

Margo, have gone with a fine toothcomb through the records, and nothing jumps out with Benton. One thing though, in his expense reimbursements to London he has charges for lunches with the son of Edward Collins. Maybe just checking up on a friend's kid, but I found it interesting. Wouldn't have noticed except I remembered a young man called here a couple of times from the UK asking for Benton. It seems an odd relationship.

I'll keep on looking, Laura

She stared at the message again. Edward Collins was a mover in the San Francisco social circles, and she recalled his rambunctious son had been a student at Stanford. He had quite abruptly been yanked from the university by his parents and shipped off to England, as she recalled.

But why would Benton be in close communication with him. As Laura said, perhaps it was no more than keeping an eye on a friend's kid, but Benton never seemed like the paternal type. She picked up the phone and dialed Mo.

"Hi, Mo, it's me, again."

"Hi me!" joked Maureen with more levity than their prior calls. "What can I do for you?"

"Do you know Edward Collins?"

"Sure, he is a big contributor in San Francisco, always throwing parties in his fancy home for the latest cause celeb. Why?"

"What about his son that went to Stanford?"

"Ah, yes, the young Geoff, a real rebel in his father's eye. His dad sent him off to learn a few lessons in civility from the Brits after some minor school pranks with marijuana parties and low key computer hacking shenanigans threatened the stately family image. From what I hear, the kid was a math and computer whiz at the university. I hear that Geoff broke off all contact with his dad."

"Hmmm then, why would someone like Andrew Benton decide to befriend him in London?"

"Don't have a clue on that one, Meg. Why, what do you know?"

"It's just that Laura uncovered several receipts for meals between him and Andrew Benton in London on the expense vouchers. I mean it could be his just checking on his whereabouts for the parents, but now that you mention his mastery of numbers, it makes me think that Benton may have been using him for other dealings."

"This is an easy one to check out. I know Mrs. Collins fairly well. Gina and I both sit on a state library board together. I could give her a call to check it out."

"It's probably nothing, but worth a call, anyway."

"You've got it. I can give her a call and let you know."

*****

Ken Miller called Jack O'Riley as soon as he had the report from his research intern.

"Jack, it seems our adventure with the Ortega case and the Colombian connection is taking a very interesting turn."

"Tell me more."

"Our bureau contact in San Jose informs us that Ortega was seen this week in the company of Jose Luis Maldonado, rumored to be one of the operatives for the Colombian cartel. I don't think it is any coincidence that our friend Ross is in the same area at the same time."

"But the questions is what are they exactly up to?"

"And what is the connection they are trying to pin on Holly in all of this."

"We found out that the so called herbal export business from this Arenal facility goes to a distributor in Miami. The distributor may have federal grants to export the manufactured process to third world countries under some of the HHS programs. Holly has supported those bills over the years."

"So they are trying to pin guilt by association on him."

"You got it."

"That helps a bit, Ken. But there must be a whole lot more to this. If Justice must think they have more to bring down a United States senator with as clean a scoring card as Holly."

"I agree, Jack. We will keep digging and let you know."

"Thanks pal. Oh, by the way, one of the Foundation Board members, Helen Nelson, died this week in a car wreck after meeting with Ross."

"This is getting hot."

"The reports are that it was a heart attack. Could you check with your bureau contact to see if we can get any more details?"

"Sure, my friend, the timing sounds a bit too convenient."

"Those were my thoughts exactly."

*****

Scott and Megan were lunching at a small ocean view restaurant in Pismo Beach. He had talked her into going with him to the meeting with Holly. He wanted her to leave the Center's problems behind them for a while. She had resisted at first, but then conceded to his pleas.

Now, sipping on a fruit punch and munching on the best cheeseburger she had tasted in years, she gave him a warm glance.

"You were right, Scott. We both needed to get away for a while. This is exactly what we came to California for and it's easy to lose sight of it."

"I know, my dear. Although this meeting with Holly and the troops is intense, there is no reason we cannot take the opportunity to relax a little on the way. All the others will arrive tomorrow, so we can take our time today, and arrive in time to visit with Eleanor and Holly this evening. We will take the coastal road. It's longer, but the views are stunning today."

"If you like, I can plan on doing something with Eleanor. It will give you a chance to be alone with Holly. I am sure he has concerns to share with you before the others arrive."

"You read my mind, sweetheart. I told them we would be there around five."

Scott walked over to the small window in the beachside shack and left a twenty to cover their tab and a tip.

The smiling teenager wished them a good day, and they continued their trip north.

*****

That morning, Bob Harris had waited for Margo to leave the house to pick up the kids at school. He knew that she would be gone only a short time, and so he only had about fifteen minutes to plant the listening devise in her briefcase.

It was a highly sensitive chip, and would transmit the conversation of the meeting the next day to his recording devise without any problem at all.

As she pulled out of the driveway, he walked up the side of the house wearing the uniform of the gas company, pretending to be checking the meter. As soon as he was out of site, he pushed open the sliding door on the patio. It was an easy entrance.

He had planned to force the lock, but was pleased that she had made it even easier by not even locking the door.

He quickly found the office where he had placed the earlier telephone bug, and now placed the tiny listening devise on the bottom of her briefcase. As a backup measure, he decided to place a second tiny chip on the inside of her overnight bag since she had already half packed it ready to go.

A back up measure never hurt anything he thought.

By the time she arrived home a few minutes later, Harris was already on his way back to the hotel.

He checked out and headed down south.

No need to follow her, and risk identification, the devises had a long range and would transmit all the information he needed.

Colombia

Coiled lines of barbed wire protected the entire wall surrounding the house in the Bogota slum. As an extra security measure slices of cut glass had been inserted on top of the wall in the cement between the wire barriers.

A pathetically skinny dog picked through the trash in the front courtyard, while two young boys kicked a soccer ball back and forth between the filth. There was no sign of modern life except for the telephone and electrical wires strung from the nearby utility pole to the window of the decrepit building. A guard with a rifle stood across the street, seeming to be unconnected with the broken down shack.

The inside was not much better. The only furnishings were a tattered old mattress that lay in one corner, and incongruously, the latest version of a Dell computer resting on a wooden plank supported by stacked gray colored cinder blocks.

Mario Garcia's fingers were flying expertly across the keyboard, as he fixated on the information screening across the monitor.

Mierda! What the fuck?

Displayed in front of him was the account bearing Andrew Benton' secret numbers with a balance showing over ten million less than he had transferred via electronic deposit only two days before.

He began to sweat profusely; missing money was no joke with his bosses. He had to figure out where the glitch in the system was, and fix it pronto.

Mario was twenty-nine years old but looked much younger. He had been educated in the finest universities in the United States. His family was from poor coffee plantation workers who had toiled for generations in the hills of Colombia, and he was destined for the same life.

At twelve or thirteen years of age, he and his friends would pool their few pesos, and go to a local Internet café. Surfing the net, and developing skills for hacking into systems just for fun was sport for them.

Mario had a gift for it, and he became a champion hacker. Jose Luis Maldonado noticed the kid's talent as he scouted for soldiers in his drug trafficking business. There was no doubt that Mario was a diamond in the rough, and could be useful.

The cartel put him through prep school in Colombia, and then sent him into an undergraduate technology program at Miami University. He had excelled, and successfully capped off his education earning a computer science Masters degree.

Any corporation or research institution would have hired him, nevertheless, he had to return to Colombia. There was no option. He was owned by his sponsors. He was now investment property, and their star performer. His talents of course were highly rewarded with a new home and salary, so he was able to release his parents from the life of coffee picking.

He had a luxurious residence in Bogota for himself and his young family.

The shack where he was currently sitting was merely one of the decoy locations that he used for conducting the global business operation of his *jefes*.

His personal bank account afforded much better lodgings for his wife and three-year-old son.

His phone sprang to life.

"*Hola*, Mario."

"*Hola, Jefe*. How are you?"

"Listen, is that transaction completed?"

Mario began to perspire again as he glanced at the alarmingly deficient account balance displayed before him on the screen.

"*Claro, todo esta bien.*"

No sense in raising alarms to Maldonado at this time, the problem would be fixed before anyone knew.

"*Esta bien*. We have business in Miami later today, and want to make sure there are no hold ups."

"*No, jefe*. Everything is fine."

He knew he only had a few hours to get a handle on it, and correct the account. He knew his life and the lives of his wife and son depended on it.

Washington, DC

L ook, our sources tell us that Ramsey is hot to take Hollingsworth down with this deal. He knows the Miami operation financed through the HHS grants. He thinks it will land him a gold star and the jewel in the crown of the next executive staff line up. Not that it would bother me one bit if we kicked the ass of the ever-pure Senator off its Holier than Thou pedestal, mind you.

"However, the pressure we are getting from the Florida party insiders to lay off this one is beginning to have an effect."

A small group remained silent in a conference room at the Hays Adams Hotel near the White House.

"This is a tough campaign, and we need to keep the funds from lots of happy Latinos flowing. I am not sure what the connection is right now, but believe me, when Florida talks in presidential politics our people listen. The word came in loud and clear this week that they want no Justice Department or DEA folks poking around.

"If the good Senator is on the Board of a Foundation that donated a few thousand dollars to an operation that is now reaping the benefits of Uncle Sam's "pork barrel" for an export operation then so be it. We have more to lose in campaign contributions than the retiring Senator has to lose over this one. Do I make myself clear?"

Several heads nodded in compliance as the head strategist of the reelection campaign coldly stared back at them.

They were seated around an oval conference table in the opulent setting known for political operations. Located within walking distance to most of their White House offices it was a convenient meeting space. There was no way he was about to discuss campaign fundraising on their home premises. There was too much risk in that, as others had discovered.

The cherry blossom trees around Lafayette Square were still short of a full bloom, and seemed to know that there was still a lingering nip of winter in the air.

But the campaign strategist's stern tongue-lashing was responsible for the noticeable chill in the room, not the cool spring weather outside.

His job was to make sure the mega dollars kept rolling in to the coffers, and no inconsequential ambitions of a Justice bureaucrat would stand in the way of major campaign contributors. If someone was making a little on the side from government grants, and a Senator was getting a kick back, it was all part of the politics as usual, as far as he was concerned.

"Hollingsworth is a big fish to catch. There is no doubt about that. But we have bigger fish to fry right now, so make sure you keep Ramsey and his investigation under wraps and in check."

"Are you saying to keep stalling Ramsey from meeting with us, then?" asked one of the staff, as he cleared his throat.

"No, we can't keep canceling meetings on him indefinitely. He will go over our heads, and then we will have a real mess on our hands. Appease him by listening to what he has to say. Humor him a little. Make him think we value his information. Do what you have to in order to plug this before we have the whole god damn situation get out of hand. You never know, Ramsey may in fact be on to something we can use later. At that point it is your worry, not mine. In the meantime, I need to get the all-clear signal to the folks in Florida that the heat is off. And I want no screw-ups over that. Got it?"

With that last word, the short meeting was over, and the group disbanded to follow orders.

The Maldonado brothers were well connected with their American cousins. They had built an extensive network of legitimate business interests in Florida and the Silicon Valley.

The problem with trying to weed out illegal drug laundering investments was more than complicated. Literally billions of dollars had been invested in stock of legal companies and real estate.

Federal investigations could open a far more serious can of worms for election campaigns.

As soon as the Colombians started using Zenkon affiliate to move product and launder more funds word was out among Florida officials that it was off limits.

The Maldonado brothers rubbed palms where necessary. Benton through their protection, operated freely.

News of Ramsey's nosing around spread like brushfire. Politicians in Florida's state and federal political circles took no time in telling them to back off.

Money is the engine of campaign fundraising operations, and it had only taken Maldonado one well-placed call to make sure the right message was delivered to the appropriate person.

*****

Ramsey was finally getting his hearing.

He had all the documentation he felt he needed. He was ready to nail Hollingsworth on Benton's distribution operation.

The additional information that Harris had provided regarding involvement of the Foundation and potential ties with Costa Rican operatives was his icing on the cake.

"So you see, Jim, it is a solid case of self dealing here, to say nothing of a potential drug laundering operation."

"Jesus, Henry, how believable is the White Knight of the United States Senate as a drug cartel operative?"

"I'm not saying that Hollingsworth is directly involved or into the drugs, Jim. However, the implications are there, and the media will have a field day with it. We checked into the Costa Ricans bank account, and there is no doubt that deposits made over the last year far exceed even his lucrative business deals."

"It is still a risk, Henry."

"He's in tight with the President of the Board of the Zenkon Foundation, and keeps company with the Maldonado family. What more circumstantial evidence do you want? It's exactly what we need, a collective public fear factor that senate leadership are in cahoots with violent South American drug Mafia."

"That may be a stretch for even the fake news guys!"

"Okay, then what about using tax dollars from hard working Americans to finance laundering operations. That is CNN news alert come true for us, and you know that it is what we need to get the damn media pressure off the President on this economy fiasco."

Jim Murray tapped the pen against his cheek.

"Okay, I'll get on it right away. We need a solid case to substantiate Hollingsworth's personal involvement in order to go public. But listen, in the meantime you are right that we need to keep digging into this. It has to be managed completely under the radar for a number of reasons. We are already getting signals from Florida that your DEA guys have already been asking some embarrassing questions. So can you just back off for a bit until we can get the spin-doctors involved? Understand?"

"Quite frankly, no I do not. What else do you need for God's sake? Hollingsworth is meeting in California this week with his band of thieves, and we need to catch them with their pants down."

"Hold on, you know that Hollingsworth has his backers as well, and they are formidable."

"Not as formidable as the whole damn DOJ."

"Just remember when we marched in on Clinton with the White Water deal, everyone thought it was a piece of cake. All we got was a fat bill for Ken Starr's time, reality show time with Lewinsky and the red dress, and the Clinton's walking away with a public relations slap on the wrist. Christ, his polling even went up!"

"I understand that, but times have changed."

"There is a lot riding on this election, Henry. Let us handle it from here. I will get a special team on it right away. You will get your due once it unfolds, have no doubt about it."

Ramsey was no fool.

He could see that he was being aced out of the lead role on the investigation for some reason. He would have to look like the loyal soldier, but have his own backup plan. Someone was on Murray's case, and so if that is how he wants to play it, so be it. But he was not going to let them run with this and then throw him under the bus.

"Fine, Jim. I understand. Just make sure that if anything new comes up that Justice is in the loop. We have given you the ammunition to check it out. Nevertheless, I want to be the DOJ guy that makes the hit on Hollingsworth once the right timing and approach is decided."

"That is not a problem Henry."

"I am not sitting on the sidelines. You know that for damn sure. He's one bastard that I would like to send into retirement with an appropriate farewell party."

"It goes without saying."

Both men halfhearted shook each other's hand and the meeting was over.

Costa Rica

Ross instantly took a dislike to Jose Luis Maldonado, and the feeling seemed to be mutual. Maldonado was smooth talking, but his hold over Rosario Ortega made Ross feel increasingly uneasy as to how much of the operation was already under the control of the Colombians.

Rolf's absence without a word worried him even more about the way in which the whole trip was shaping up.

He had already decided that he had seen enough at the research facility to confirm his previous analysis that it was time to pull out of committing any further Foundation funds. From the looks of the expansion facility, and the big plans that Maldonado had spoken about, the loss of Foundation financial support would have a minor impact on the new direction of any research needs.

Rosario had shrugged off the fact that his bank accounts were still frozen, but there was obviously more going on there as well. A chill went down Ross' back, and he was starting to wonder if Helen's death was an accident, and to feel afraid for his own safety.

He made up his mind that he would head back to San Jose early in the morning.

Just too be safe, he would make a stop at his bank in San Jose to arrange transfer of minor assets to an offshore account he had set up years earlier. He still had the problem of his main worth in the joint account with Ortega and his brother lawyer. Damn his mistake of allowing them to take the majority shareholder interest in the *sociedad*. Any withdrawals from that required two signatures.

He was furious with himself, but his fear and common sense told him to leave that as is for the time being. For safety sake alone he needed to catch the first flight to Miami.

He was thinking that he would get in touch with Rolf from Florida. Perhaps if he hadn't left Germany yet there was even a chance they could hook up in Miami.

There was no sense in putting him in jeopardy either, particularly if his gut feelings were on target.

Jonathan Ross was no saint, but he knew the difference between skirting the law and getting involved in an evil empire. He strongly sensed that everything Ortega touched was looking more and more corrupt. He needed to go into damage control.

Across the grounds, Maldonado and Ortega were in conference. The sun was already beginning its early set, and their shadows cast a dark shade over the terrace where the conversation was taking place.

"Ross is trouble, Rosario. He suspects more than he lets on to know."

"I can handle him. He has so many personal interests tied up here in Costa Rica. He is not going to just walk away from that. If nothing else, his own greed will keep him in check."

"Don't be too sure about that, mi amigo. I have learned that our Gringo friends tend to have a soft spot for morality that can even supersede their personal greed. You know their puritanical heritage is why they pride themselves on a so called democratic justice system."

"That is true."

"They elude themselves that democracy is incorruptible. They feel compelled to tell the truth just because they put a hand on the Bible and swear to it. Idiots! They never understood loyalty and brotherhood like we do."

They both stood in silence contemplating the next step.

Neither man noticed that Ross had been hidden in the shadows of the rain forest covering listening to their conversation.

"No, Rosario. It is decided.

"Our friend Mr. Ross must not be another problem like the *viejita*. And our problem, is your problem, *me entiendes?*"

Dear God! They did kill Helen, and I'm next! I have to get away from here, and fast. What the hell have I gotten myself involved in?

California

Margo tried several times to reach Rolf at his home number after she had spoken with Ross the previous day. There was never an answer.

She decided to give another number that Laura had found in his reference folder a try before heading off to the meeting with Holly.

The e-mail from Laura indicated that it was the number for his emergency contact, his sister, Helga Schwartz.

"*Guten Abend*," answered the voice on the second ring.

"Ms. Schwartz? This is Margaret Maxwell in the United States. I am a business associate of your brother Rolf."

"Rolf, you hear from him, ja?"

The woman responded in understandable English peppered with a heavy German accent.

"Actually, no we were hoping that you could help us locate him. You see he never arrived at our project in Costa Rica. Could it be that he changed his mind and cancelled the trip, or went somewhere else?"

"Nein. He went to his trip. His things are gone. I do not hear from him at all. It is very trouble not to hear. I worry about my brother greatly."

"I can completely understand. Please let me know if you hear from him. We are also worried about where he might be."

Margo gave the sister her number to reach her if she heard anything.

This was not good news and Margo was afraid for Rolf.

Helga was now even more disturbed that there was no word of Rolf.

She decided to go back to his house to see if there was any note she may have missed from her brother. Perhaps he left something indicating a change in destination and forgot to tell her. She was very concerned, and had a deep feeling that something awful had happened to her twin.

*****

Margo saved Helga's number to her contacts.

She rushed to put her overnight case into the trunk of her car. The morning was getting away from her, and she still had a quick stop along the river highway to pick up Mike. He had decided that he would enjoy the short trip to Monterey with her after Holly's wife had graciously called the night before suggesting that he come along.

Eleanor had convinced the Senator that they might enjoy getting their mind off the Foundation problems by having a small dinner party after the daylong business meeting.

It was rare that Margo and Mike got any time together without the kids, so he surprised Margo by agreeing to the idea of spending time with the political wonks, and even offered to drive.

She figured his lead foot would get them there all the faster.

Mike had never quite adjusted his speed from the German autobahns to the California freeways. Luckily, with budget cuts for personnel, speed traps and highway patrol were rare on the vast expanses of California highways, so he had been fortunate to have never been pulled over for speeding.

*****

It was late morning, and the group was already assembled in the library of the Senator's hillside ranch.

The sprawling home nestled in the foothills on about fifteen acres of prime property. Holly had invested in the property about twenty-five years earlier, after opting for more privacy than was possible in their Victorian style Monterey house.

Neither he nor Eleanor had ever regretted the move. The land formed a gentle sloping vale, dotted with oak and cypress trees. Over the years, he had added a barn for their horses, along with an assortment of fruit trees, and a large vegetable garden. He had gated and fenced in the entire property to ensure his privacy, and now thoroughly enjoyed the solitude of strolling around the land tending to his property and animals with no company other than that of Eleanor.

A small natural pond sported bass from a year round stream. This provided a home to an assortment of frogs and tadpoles. The property provided a serene backdrop through the large bay window in the library.

A tennis court, pool, and in ground spa had been added to the estate in the last few years, mostly all standing quietly, only waiting to be used for the enjoyment of the couple's children and grandchildren when visiting from Southern California. Although today, Mike had already decided to take complete advantage of the heated pool and spa while the others talked business.

The library was the only room on the lower level of the tri-level home, most folks would refer to it as a finished basement, but it seemed too elegant for that description.

It was the section of the house that had originally sealed the deal for Holly, personal pride and joy, and man cave way before the term became popular.

It was a refuge from Washington, the press, even the telephone, and all other public distractions. Science fiction novels stood side by side with legal tomes, and biographies. The walls were graced with photos bearing personal messages from Presidents. Holly fully intended to pass more time in the hideaway as he wrote his own memoires.

A large nineteenth century oak dining table served as a conference table. It had been covered with a thick beveled glass protective cover to preserve the wood below from dents and scratches. It was the one sentimental piece that had been with them since the first year of their marriage.

A fireplace mantel displayed a cluttered collection of family pictures, adding a warm touch to a corner seating area made up of a fifties style well-worn brown leather recliner chair. An end table was piled with books, half opened mail, and what looked like a small vase with an American flag perhaps made by one of the grandchildren. Everything combined gave the impression that this eclectic setting was where he passed a lot of time and pleasure.

Margo, Mo, Scott, Jack and the Senator were seated around the conference table ready to get down to business.

Holly rose and walked toward his new arrivals.

His tall frame and gray hair were silhouetted against the morning sky, and his deep, reassuring voice opened the session. He smiled and assertively took his seat at the head of the antique table where Scott and Mo were already informally chatting.

"Let me first welcome each of you to my home.

"It is a pleasure to have you here, even given the unfortunate circumstances that have brought us together today. My goal is to discuss in detail what we collectively know about this situation, and devise a strategy and sensible plan that will end any misguided speculation and also protect all our interests.

The Foundation has implemented some commendable projects around the world during its short existence. Thanks go to members of the Board that are dedicated to its philanthropic cause. And thanks to the tireless efforts of its Executive Director," he said acknowledging Margo.

"My involvement from the beginning was due to interest in global health and research. Believe me when I say that even in the midst of this current situation that my own commitment to the long term needs of developing countries still remains strong."

Margo and Mo glanced at one another with a shared sigh of relief. Until this moment their concern that the Senator may feel a need to distance himself from the organization had weighed heavily.

His public rededication and continued participation would be essential in protecting the Foundation's image; both gave him sincere look of appreciation.

"Unfortunately, we do not live in a Utopia, and there are always bad apples in a barrel that have the effect of contaminating the whole lot. Unless they are quickly removed, that is.

"My assessment of this situation is that we have a few bad apples, and even some worms. Both need to be removed. Let us dedicate our time today to assessing the overall situation and then from that we can agree on a plan to make sure we are on solid ground moving forward."

The meeting already had the tone of a congressional hearing, with the Senator in his familiar spot of Chair of the Committee. Knowing how he operated in this setting, each of the participants was comfortable knowing how the flow of the process would ensue from here.

So, it surprised no one when the Senator retained the floor.

"Scott, please lay out the overall situation for us and then detail the issue areas and information gaps before we open it to a group discussion."

"Of course, Senator," responded Scott, addressing Holly with is formal title since it sounded most appropriate given the setting.

"Here are the facts as we know them to date", he began.

"Andrew Benton and Jonathan Ross most likely had a falling out over Foundation issues that at this point we are not clear on. At the recommendation of Ross, Andrew Benton was removed from the Board earlier this year. At the time, the Board was led to believe that it may have been a conflict in management style and Foundation priorities that led to this, but Benton was not overly upset, it seemed, by moving on. We now believe that there may have been more serious underlying causes involved between the two that led to the conflict. But again, we do not know what they were.

"Next, we are fully aware that Henry Ramsey, assistant AG at the Department of Justice has been conducting a covert investigation into the Foundation operation and especially the Senator's interest in the health angle. He implies that he has evidence that the Senator has used his influence with HHS appropriations to serve his own interests by channeling grants for developing countries through the Foundation. Specifics of this remain unknown at this point.

"We are also aware that Jonathan Ross is currently in Costa Rica meeting with a Rosario Ortega who has directed the Zenkon foundation grant recipient in the country for several years. This is with financial support of the Board.

"During this trip, he met with Helen Nelson, asking her to resign from the Board so that she could supposedly work with him on other projects in Costa Rica as an independent consultant. According to Helen's own words to Maureen, he planned to have Zenkon fund her consulting contract. Two days later, Helen was dead, killed in a car accident, allegedly due to a heart attack while driving.

"Jonathan Ross then called Margo, appearing somewhat agitated, and implying that there may be more involved than accidental death in Helen's fatality. He further informed Margo that Rolf, one of the researchers from the German Pharmaceutical faculty under contract to Zenkon was expected in Costa Rica for a six month assignment. He is nowhere to be found at this point. Further calls to his family confirm that he left as planned for the trip."

As Scott outlined the series of events each of the members at the table kept their eyes locked on him. The picture he was painting somehow seemed even more sobering as he factually laid out the details without any judgmental comment or analysis.

Discussion would come during the Senator's questioning period - that was his style, so each of them allowed Scott to continue uninterrupted by comments.

"We know the bank assets of Rosario Ortega were frozen by the government."

He concluded by glancing at Jack and then continuing.

"Finally, we have information from sources indicating that Rosario Ortega and Ross have both been seen recently in the company of unsavory characters associated with Colombian drug trafficking. I think that about sums it up."

There was silence in the room.

Eyes shifted from Scott to the Senator waiting for the Senator's next request.

"Not a pretty picture," he said.

"Connecting the dots is important, but let's not jump to any conclusions at this point. The trial Scott has detailed may or may not lead us to the bottom of this. I don't want to act prematurely, but rather let's first go around the table, and ask each of you in turn to add any additional facts you have uncovered, comments for the cause, and questions we must consider that may add clarity to the litany Scott has outlined."

Everyone shifted a bit in their chairs, prepared to add their piece to the unfolding saga.

*****

Bob Harris could not have been more pleased as he sat in his car down the country road hidden from the security cameras on the Senator's estate.

His bug on the bottom of the briefcase was working like a charm, and through his headphones, he was more than astonished that he was about to get a complete readout of the whole affair. This was a surveillance dream assignment.

*****

"Margo, please begin with what you have to offer as an assessment of the current situation."

"Gladly, Senator," she responded, taking a deep breath, and then beginning with her account.

"Well we started combing through the records of the Foundation, and to this point have not discovered any misappropriations of funds by either Ross or Benton. Further this is no indication of potential illegal activity, or problems with our IRS standing for tax issues. Our accountants also inform us that past audits and filings are in good shape, so everything seems clean. This leads us to believe that if Benton or Ross were up to anything then there may have been independent operations set up entirely separate from us."

The Senator interjected.

"That is somewhat encouraging that we may be dealing with individual illegal activity, not Board involvement. Please continue, Margo."

"Jonathan Ross informed me directly that there was something going on at the Arenal facility that was over his head. He actually sounded quite afraid for his safety. When I spoke with him, he appeared concerned about the circumstances of Helen's death, and that Rolf had not made their meeting days earlier.

"He indicated that Benton was involved in whatever scheme was going on at Arenal. But of course, he could be covering his own you know what. We know him well enough for that."

There were a couple of nervous smiles around the table.

"But he sounded more like he was afraid and that his side activities had spun out of control. He seemed a bit desperate that he was now in way over his head. He asked me to try and track down Rolf."

Again the Senator stopped her.

"So we can assume he does not know where Rolf is?"

"Perhaps, so at his request followed up by making a call to Germany. I spoke with his sister. She has no idea where he is. She said that he had not called her since he left, which was unusual for them, and she is also worried.

"That's about all I have from my end."

"Thank you, Margo."

"Oh, one last detail that seems unconnected, but we might want to throw it into the discussion pot. It seems that Benton has befriended the son of Edward Collins, and regularly had lunch with him in London over the last year or so.

"It seems odd that he would spend so much time with the young man. But, on the other hand, Geoff Collins had a reputation for hacking online before his father shipped him off to England. I'm not sure what Benton would be socializing with him for, but my gut level sense is that it was not purely paternal, and perhaps even had something to do with his tech talents."

"Quite an interesting side bar, my dear.

"Let's move on to Maureen."

"Thanks, Holly," opened Maureen, always casual with the Senator.

"Jack and I have been tracking down some leads through very discrete and trustworthy off the record bureau sources. If we ultimately have a story on this then they want an exclusive." She winked.

"We know that Rosario Ortega has been in the company of some seedy characters, one namely Jose Luis Maldonado. He is widely reputed to be the front man for the Cartel in Central America, and a very nasty character. According to sources, he wants to ingratiate himself to the boss by seizing distribution via Miami into the Eastern European market. Not sure how that will line up with the Russians, but I suppose that is another story."

The participants bristled to hear about this detail.

"Anyway, for a while now he has been moving goods north to Costa Rica and then through a web of affiliations transporting from there to the US. Apparently, the heat was getting to them on more direct shipments; obviously the American drug eradication effort was getting a bit of traction in Colombia. Last year they even seized a homemade submarine vehicle, if you can believe it. No, it's fricking unbelievable, and now they're experimenting with drones for moving smaller amounts."

Maureen had a habit of giving the details, but adding a bit more of a dramatic tone to the story. She continued with her input to the discussion.

"Anyway, our sources say that he has taken a major interest in a company in Miami that ships herbal drugs to Europe. The main link, Senator, is that the company was awarded a sizable export grant from Commerce through HHS legislation to service African health projects. This may only be a coincidence, but we need to check it out. It could even be connected with the federal project Benton was overseeing for Zenkon Foundation at one time. The tie has me worried.

"Helen told me before she died that Ross was putting pressure on her to resign. She also knew before she met with him about the frozen bank accounts of Ortega.

Is that about it, Jack?"

"You did call Mrs. Collins to check out if there was some sort of friendly relationship on their part with Benton to keep an eye on the boy." Offered Margo.

"Oh, right almost forgot. It seems she knows nothing about this. Unlike her husband, she keeps in touch with her son occasionally. He has never once mentioned meeting with Benton. She knows her husband would never have approved any relationship between them. Andrew Benton and Mr. Collins were not on the best of terms when they were both worked at Pacific Rim Telecom.

"She did mention, though, that Geoff has been able to get on his feet quite well in the U.K. by working his way up the ranks at the Halifax Building Society. That is sort of the equivalent of a credit union here in the States. She was very proud that he always excelled so well in math and computers at Stanford."

"It seems that perhaps Mr. Benton has formed a convenient banking liaison in Europe," commented Holly.

Bob Harris also gave a little whistle of satisfaction on hearing this piece of interesting information.

"Jack, do you have anything else for the cause?"

"Senator, my sources, and they are pretty reliable, tell me that family connections of Maldonado are established legitimate Florida businessmen. They provide generous support for several congressional campaigns. Apparently, Ramsey's poking into the HHS business in Miami prompted some well placed calls to Washington to have them back off. Ramsey was then warned that it was out of his hands."

"So, obviously whatever Ramsey is after is not as important as some key donors," remarked the Senator, "or, poking around in whatever the Maldonado connection is to the operation could give them bigger problems than this gives me."

That seemed to be the last comment for the cause.

"I think we all need a short break. Let's process the information we have on the table, and discuss next steps.

"I do believe Eleanor has prepared a nice buffet lunch on the deck for us to enjoy. We will convene again in exactly one hour."

With that polite dismissal the group took a break.

Harris decided he could take off for a good hamburger and fries, and started up the engine of his rented blue Buick, heading for a nearby eatery.

Margo had just started on a delicious Asian noodle salad when her cell phone rang. Finding it buried at the bottom of her purse, she quickly retrieved it and saw that the caller identification indicated it was coming from the number she had programmed before she left home that morning.

She walked to the edge of the long deck, and anxiously answered on the fifth ring.

It was a very distressed accented voice on the line with news that turned Margo quite pale and sick to her stomach as she listening without a word.

Apparently, it was the missing rug that Helga had not noticed on her first trip to the chalet that now made her suspect that something untoward had happened at the house.

She could not find the oriental rug that her brother loved so much. He would not have moved it without letting her know. He consulted her on everything about the house.

On further examination of Rolf's bedroom she knew that he had never left home.

His picture of Fritz was still sitting on the end table besides the bed. Rolf would never leave on an extended trip without it. It was always the last thing that he lovingly placed in his briefcase before he went out the door.

Alarmed, she had immediately called the local German police.

Police had arrived almost immediately with a squad of detectives and police dogs. They had been at the house all day.

Now in the dark of night, lit only by portable strobe lights, a forensics team was removing the body of her brother that had been discovered by the police dogs.

Helga was hysterical with grief as she witnessed the coroner zipping the green tarp body bag enclosing the remains of Rolf. He was signaling to move it to the waiting van of the town coroner.

She had no idea who could have committed this terrible crime against her brother. He was gone again from her life, but this time he would not be back.

The police had questioned her extensively on Rolf's activities the days before departure. But she could only say that she did not notice anything unusual, except that he had left a text letting her know that he no longer needed a ride to the airport. He must have had another way of getting there.

Obviously, someone at the last minute must have made the offer. Did they think this person had killed him? She explained that his suitcases and briefcase were gone when she checked the house, and so she had no reason to believe anything was wrong.

She blamed herself for not paying more attention to the alarming behavior of Maxi when they had first come to the chalet. Perhaps they would have had a better chance of catching Rolf's murderer if she had paid more attention to Maxi and been quicker to report him missing.

How could she have known, she asked herself.

Even Rolf's friends from the university had not suspected anything when they came by the house earlier in the week. In fact, Marten, a research associate had even called her as a courtesy to let her know that they had been there.

The police were now on their way to Marten's home to question him further.

"Margo, what's wrong? You look like you have seen a ghost." Remarked Maureen, as her friend returned the cell phone to her purse.

"I have," she blurted out.

She burst into tears.

"Rolf's body was discovered earlier today by the German police under the floor boards of his house."

Complete silence fell over the entire group congregated on the outside deck.

Mike rushed over to hold Margo, who looked as though she were about to faint.

"This is now a completely different matter," remarked the Senator.

"A colleague of the Foundation has been murdered. This whole matter is far more serious than political mudslinging and side deals.

Scott, call Jeff Peterson right away."

Without question Scott immediately returned to the library to place a call to the home of the director of western regional office of the FBI.

Within minutes of the call, Peterson was in route to the estate from the Bay Area. Estimated arrival time was about ninety minutes or so from his home in San Mateo.

*****

Bob Harris, who had just returned from his lunch to overhear this latest development, hastily dialed Henry Ramsey's home telephone number.

Costa Rica

Jonathan's body was completely covered in welts from relentless insect bites. His face bore deep scratches from the branches he had collided with as he made his perilous escape down the side of the steep slopes of the thick forest during the dark of night.

He had been running for more than six hours, and the heat from the early morning sun coupled with dehydration was already adding to his aching body's overall distress.

About midnight he had silently crept to his rented four-wheel drive parked in front of the reception area. He had intended to put the car into neutral and cruise slowly down the mountainous slope and far away from the Arenal facility. His plans were thwarted when he saw two of Maldonado's soldiers with automatic rifles positioned on either side of his vehicle.

The thugs were not intending for him to go anywhere, not alive anyway.

He had no other alternative. The only way out was to traverse the rough terrain of the surrounding mountainside. The going was slow and arduous. He was covered in scrapes and bites, and still had a ways to go before reaching the nearest road where he figured on hitching a ride into San Jose from one of the many early morning truck drivers who would be heading southwards from Liberia to the capital city.

He was still coming to grips with the realization that he was dealing with ruthless murderers, and that Helen's death was no accident. They would stop at nothing to protect their interests, and his life could be wiped out as effortlessly as Helen's had been.

His heart began to pound again with fear as he thought of how close he had already come to being killed.

He was no hero, and making a nice profit for himself on the side over the years in no way translated for him any aspirations to be tied up with any cartel. And he was smart enough to know that involvement was not a voluntary choice on his part. He had already seen too much. He knew that, and knew he was a problem that these ruthless thugs would take care of with no more of a thought than stamping a cockroach on the forest soil.

As he pushed aside the lush vegetation on his slow advance toward the highway, his mind raced.

Had Rolf also discovered what was going on? Where was he now, and how did Andrew Benton fit into this whole repulsive scheme? Rolf had been adamant about wanting to keep a closer eye on Ortega. He must have known something was suspect with the shipments from Costa Rica to Miami. What was it? And more importantly, does it now have anything to do with his disappearance?

Mercifully, Jonathan sighted an old blue pickup truck making its way down the mountainside. There were a couple of coffee plantation workers riding in the front alongside the driver. The windows were down, and a loud radio was blasting Latino music from the local radio into the morning air. The pickup was half loaded with bags of coffee and bananas.

He nervously made his way to the side of the road and flagged down the driver.

"Senor, senor!"

"Buenos días, señor, que pasa?"

He heard from the guy behind the wheel.

In his broken Spanish, Jonathan was able to deceitfully convey that his car had broken down further back, and that he needed to get to San Jose *muy pronto*.

The driver smiled, understanding his dilemma, and offered him the passenger seat. He said something in Spanish to the passenger beside him, who then promptly gave up his seat and climbed in the back with the bags of coffee and fruit.

Jonathan thanked them, and breathed a small sigh of relief as they headed to the main highway.

The thugs at Arenal would soon discover him missing when he failed to show up for breakfast. He wanted to be well on his way before they caught up with him.

London

Geoff Collins smiled as he looked at Pat Wilson's stunning naked body asleep in his bed, her red hair spread like flames of fire across the pillows. The afternoon and evening had turned into quite a marathon. She was really something else. He had heard about the passion and lovemaking of some of the Liverpool girls, but he could now attest that his personal experience far exceeded expectations.

Hell, no wonder the Beatles had so much to sing about.

He thought as he made his way to the computer.

Pat's pleasant distraction had diverted him from his call to Benton. *No problem,* he thought, *he can wait.*

But he did want to give another check to his stash in the offshore account. He still didn't quite believe that he was sitting on a cool ten million. Perhaps he would even take Pat up on her fantasy and buy a sailboat to take off into the wild blue yonder.

Why not? He mused.

As he signed into his computer an instant message showed up that drained the blood from his face.

What have you done with it?

Move it back cabron, me entiendes?

Geoff immediately shut down the laptop and hastily deposited it inside the portable black leather computer case. He grabbed his passport and wallet. He shook Pat awake on the bed.

"Let's go my lovely. We are leaving, like right now."

"Mmmm," she whimpered, sluggishly waking up from a deep sleep.

"What's the matter, love? You should be out for another few hours after what we went through last night!"

"Ah, to the contrary, you have given me an energy boost, and inspired me to take you to wonderful places. Get dressed we are going to France."

"France, bloody hell. I have nothing appropriate to wear, as they say!"

"No need to worry about that. Haven't you heard that Paris is the best place for shopping, and you can have anything you want.

After last night, I will spoil you in style, okay? We can stop by your place, and pick up your passport and overnight stuff. And then as we say, *American Express don't leave home without it.* I'm good for you whatever else you need."

"Well, what happened to you? Did your lottery ticket come in while I was asleep?"

"Something like that, let's go."

She could see that he was really serious.

"If we are quick we can get a flight out of Heathrow, and be there in time for champagne lunch. I'm ready and able to get out of here."

Geoff figured if he were to be on the run then hiding as a couple would be far safer for him than a lone American.

"No arguments from me, love. You are a fast one, aren't you?" She remarked with a broad smile, as she pulled the green sweater over her unruly head of Irish hair.

Geoff was convinced that the e-mailer must know where he was. He knew that he had to get out of the flat fast before someone got to him.

His Spanish-speaking online buddy would no doubt be able to trace his IP address without any trouble at all, and in no time have his home address.

The good news was that although he had figured out who had moved the money that the Colombian still had no idea where it had been deposited. If he had, then there would have been no need for the message.

With the size of the cash at stake, it had to be an international cartel gang. He didn't want to take chances on running into other Colombians sure to be in London. From the message it sounded like the hacker was first hoping to scare him into returning the funds.

His neck was most likely also on the chopping block for screwing up so badly.

It was time to move on, pronto. Benton would just have to go into a holding pattern for right now. His own father be damned, it was time to pull a real disappearing act, for sure.

What better way than with his lovely companion. They made a real handsome couple.

Geoff had imagined a life with a fortune. He already was a step ahead of his computer challenger ready to activate one with his lovely redhead.

Miami

A ndrew Benton was hurting badly, his arms and legs tightly bound with duct tape to an old wooden chair. His left eye was swollen shut and dry blood covered his chin from the split lip. His bones and muscles ached from the severe kicking he had endured from the titanic hooligan and his creepy sidekick.

He had no idea what they were talking about regarding the missing money, but for the past two hours he had endured a severe beating. He again pleaded that he had no information on the missing millions, as once again the large brute began to rough him over.

Mario Garcia was taking no chances. He had traced Geoff Collins' e-mail address to his account through British Telecom. He was then was able to hack into his personal mailbox. He had found a couple of messages from Andrew Benton letting him know he would soon be in London. He put two and two together that the duo was in cahoots on stealing his *jefe's* money.

Benton had been easy to find at the Miami distribution plant, and Garcia quickly sent his own heavies to check him out before Maldonado got any wind on the missing funds.

He knew that regular payoffs to his old Miami street buddies were good long-term investments. He was now getting his just returns as the despicable emissaries continued to pound Benton for information on the missing money.

"Look," moaned Benton, "I have cooperated as much as I can on this deal. I haven't taken any funds from anyone. Jesus, you think I am stupid trying to steal from the Colombians?"

"Estupido, yes, mi amigo, if you think you can hide my *jefe's dinero.*"

"I don't know what the hell you are talking about. I have been more than straight through this whole damned operation." *To the point of killing someone I thought might squeal.* He licked more blood from his split lip, and envisioned the decaying body of the scientist below the floorboards of his house.

"Let's kill him now," interjected the sidekick.

"No, we wait for *el jefe* to call. If this prick knows what is good for him he will tell us before we have to take him apart piece by piece."

Andrew was more than completely terrified. He was petrified. He knew that these goons meant serious business, and he had no idea what they were talking about.

The two fortunately left him alone in the dilapidated room, giving him time to try to think through what the hell was going on. But he knew it was not for long before they returned wanting answers.

"What the hell were they talking about? What millions of dollars?

And then it slowly came to him, as he thought back on the conversation in London. Collins had moved the money. He had instructed him at their meeting to set up new accounts, and the fool had perhaps moved other laundered money, along with his own balance.

That had to be it. But how could he get hold of Geoff, and tell him to fix it? He needed to buy some time. His life, and probably Geoff's depended on it.

The thugs returned, more than ready to torture Benton again.

"Okay, listen," he said, pleading for mercy. I think I may know what you are talking about."

"Ah, your memory is improving, senor, we thought it might."

"Tell your boss that I need a couple of days to sort this out. It is a huge mistake. But we can fix it right away."

The big one laughed.

"Two days! No senor, you have hours to get my *jefe's dinero* right back where it belongs, no more.

"Today, esta bien?"

Andrew did not think he was in any position to negotiate terms. He nodded his aching head in compliance.

He needed to get hold of Geoff right away, and make sure that the money was right back where it belonged within hours.

Christ, how did I get mixed up in this in the first place?

He thought, lamenting his pathetic situation.

California

Special Agent in Charge, or SAC, of the San Francisco field office of the FBI, arrived precisely on time. He had known Holly for years, and never gave second thought to immediately heading to the ranch once summoned.

He had survived the last decade or so of the political backstabbing of the Agency during the course of both Republican and Democratic administrations, and so preferred to stay in the field operations in western regional offices in San Francisco.

He had his chance to move up the ladder but Beltway politics were not for him.

Peterson graduated second in class of twenty-three students from the then newly formed FBI National Academy in 1973. His tenure at the Agency began at one of the most turbulent junctures of its history.

The forty-eight year dynasty of the J. Edgar Hoover administration had just ended. It was followed by a succession of acting directors, each trying to implement policy change in the shadow of the Watergate scandal.

Three top White House aides resigned only three days after his new boss, Kelly, was appointed.

This preceded the political chaos of the resignation of the Vice President of the United States, Spiro Agnew, on tax evasion charges and evidence of widespread corruption.

He was replaced by Gerald Ford.

Then a year later, Richard M. Nixon became the first President of the United States to resign office.

Gerald Ford was elevated to President of the United States, and became the first person to serve as Vice President and President without being elected to either office.

Peterson, as a new recruit, was assigned to the Washington, DC headquarters of the agency, and served at that time as a low level liaison to Congressional staff. They were conducting hearings on the methods of the Agency for gathering intelligence.

The FBI was under fire in the post Watergate scandal, and a young Senator Lawrence Hollingsworth was at the core of the investigations on the Hill.

It was there that he first met the friendly young Peterson. They had hit it off, and after the years, and beyond, had remained in touch now and again, both now ready to ease into retirement.

The Senator trusted him, and was ready to include him in the current situation to seek his advice.

Maureen was still on the patio being comforted by Eleanor from the shock. Holly decided to leave them there, along with the others. He suggested a walk to Peterson around the grounds so that he could convey the unfolding events in private, and see what they needed to do next.

Bob Harris uttered a huge moan at the suggestion. He was going to lose his eavesdropping capability as soon as they moved away from the house.

For the next hour or so, they walked the perimeter, as the SAC agent was brought up to speed on all the sordid dealings. He even had to admit to that the situation seemed somewhat astounding.

They had gathered together for what they thought primarily amounted to making sure that the Senator's reputation was not going to be tarnished by mudslinging in the upcoming campaigns. The meeting had evolved to trying to make sense of how the pieces fit into an international drug operation and at least one confirmed murder.

"Understand, Jeff, that the Administration, whether it is directly involved or not in this mess, has far more to lose than I do, if all this gets out as being tied to any connections at the White House."

"I understand."

"Henry Ramsey needs to be called into this, right away. I want it to be clear to him where I stand. He needs to understand the political implications for both sides. He's your superior, I know, Jeff, so let me handle that call."

"No problem on that front, Senator."

"Good."

"In the meantime, Senator, I will get hold of our guys that deal with the Criminal Polizei in Berlin to see what they have on the Schwartz investigation."

"Definitely, we must be helpful to find this murderer."

"I also think I need to make a call to the agency contacts in Costa Rica. Hopefully, it is not too late to autopsy Helen Nelson's remains."

"See what you can do, Jeff. I will take personal responsibility for handling the political spin control with Scott. All three of us need to be a task squad on this and keep in close touch. I will direct Scott to brief me once a day minimal.

"Let's go back and reconvene. It's getting late, and I think we should call it a day. I think we have had all we can take for one day."

Shit what the hell is really going on?

Jeff thought as he kept his cool and nodded in agreement with the Senator.

With that, the two returned to the main house.

The Senator had no need to even mention to Eleanor that her dinner party would need to be postponed. She had anticipated as much, and had already instructed the chef prepare a small road snack for each of the guests.

Mike led Margo by the arm to the car, with Jack and Maureen in tow. Mike kindly offered to drop them off at the Monterey airport for their return flights home, the favor would not take them too far out of their way as they headed back to Sacramento.

As the group departed, Holly was already on his way to make the call to the Assistant Attorney General, Henry Ramsey, in Washington.

California

After dropping Maureen and Jack at the small Monterey municipal airport, Margo and Mike were headed north on Highway One flying past lush green fields filled with the spring crop of artichokes and strawberries.

Mexican laborers stooped over hoes while attending the back breaking work of harvesting. Most of the workers were seasonal migrant farmers who regularly made the treacherous border crossing north from Mexico to attend the fields.

In the past, primarily the men would migrate, sending their hard earned dollars back to families in Mexico and Central America. But for the last decades it was entire family migration, not only for work, but escaping the violence and drug wars in many Latin American countries.

It was thankless work that no Americans would take.

Undocumented immigration is a never ending political battle in California and other southern border states – thousands of workers necessary for the economy have migrated across the border for decades, farmers relying on the cheap labor and hard work.

Respect for the migrant workers' toil is overpowered by resentment and bitterness encouraged by tribal politics. Migrants, their families and children are trapped in a life of poverty and fear, as the melodramas play out.

The entire area now occupied by California was Mexican land until 1845. It was claimed as American territory from a weak and ineffectual government by only sixty-two armed American volunteers. This historical coup had taken place near this very spot in the Salinas Valley.

A year later in 1846, President James Polk sailed into the Monterey Bay with a force of two-hundred and fifty sailors and declared that *"henceforward California will be a portion of the United States"*.

Politically it became so, but geographically, linguistically, and culturally the state has always maintained strong ties to its Mexican heritage.

The cell phone rang, and thinking it might be Maureen again, Margo reached for her purse on the back seat.

She was disappointed to see that the message read that the call was from an unidentified caller, and nearly declined to answer. But she pressed the talk button giving Mike a startled look on hearing the voice of Jonathan Ross.

"Margo, thank God you are there, Jonathan here, you have to help me."

Ross clearly sounded panicked. This immediately sent more fear and alarm signals to Margo.

There had already been too many shocks for one day, she wasn't sure she could handle any more.

"Jonathan, calm down. You sound desperate."

"Desperate is putting it mildly, you have to help me!"

"What are you talking about?"

They are after me, and they have already killed Helen."

He was sounding even more out of control and frightened.

"Jonathan, get a grip, please. What are you talking about? Who is after you, and who killed Helen?"

Mike looked over at Margo with a watchful stare.

"Look, Margo, you have to help me. I had to escape from the Arenal facility before Ortega and his Colombian thugs killed me as well. I overheard them. They set Helena up. The car accident was no accident."

"Oh, my God, Jonathan, we thought as much here as well."

"You heard about it already? It was only in the papers this morning."

"Yes, well it seems that one of Helena's neighbors called Maureen with the bad news".

"Well, bad news does travel fast. And these guys are definitely bad news."

"So you are trying to tell me that it was a set up by some drug dealers, and the same guys are now after you?"

"That is right, Margo, no shit."

"Come on Jonathan. And you were just an innocent bystander who now needs our help."

She raised her voice, anger clearly beginning to take hold, as the thought of poor innocent Helena being murdered for no reason made her even more enraged.

"I know how it must sound, Margo."

"You bet you do. You go to Costa Rica to meet with Helena and Ortega. Helena gets murdered after meeting with you, and now you call us to help you!"

She was furious, and nearly yelling. Mike leaned over and gently placed his right hand on her arm to both show support and calm her.

"You have to believe me. I had nothing to do with Helena's accident."

"Helena's murder you mean."

"Yes, murder then. I came here only to set her up in a new business deal."

"You are such the choir boy, Jonathan."

"Margo that is it. I admit I have my weaknesses, and have not been a saint. But murder. Come on. Even you must admit that is way out of my league. Please, you have to help or you will have a second body to cope with."

"A third body to cope with, Jonathan."

"What are you talking about?"

"Rolf's body was found earlier today buried below the floorboards of his house."

"Jesus, Margo. These guys are after us all. You cannot believe that I had anything to do with Rolf's murder. I was expecting him here in Costa Rica. You are saying they got to him in Germany!

"That is right, Jonathan, now we have Interpol involved in this mess."

"Oh, God, they will get me if you don't help, Margo. Please, I don't know who else to call."

Margo had to admit that Jonathan was a snake, but it really was hard to see him as a murderer, more the self-centered opportunist and wimp. She decided to give him the benefit of the doubt for the time being.

"Okay, Jonathan, let's suppose you are the victim here. Where are you now? How can we help?"

"I literally had to run for my life from the facility through a bug infested rain forest. I hitched a ride on an old coffee truck with two guys from the fields, believe it or not."

"It sounds too damn fantastic to make up, go on."

"Anyway, the *campesinos* thankfully dropped me off at a small hotel near the San Jose airport. That is where I am right now. I have got to get out of here, Margo. As soon as they find that I am gone, which they probably already have, then they are going to be after me. I have only the clothes on my back."

"You do indeed sound very desperate, Jonathan."

"The airlines are telling me all the flights are full out of here for the next two days. I am not going to last that long, really Margo, you have to do something to help out."

He was raising his voice again on the verge of another panic attack.

"Jonathan, hold on and just calm down. I get the picture. I agree that we have to get you out of there. It will take some doing – we will probably need to call in a favor, and have someone place a call to the airlines."

"Margo, I will really owe you my life if you get me out of this one. I promise that I had nothing to do with Helena's death."

"Leave that for now, Jon. Let's get you back here, and then I am sure you will have questions to answer from authorities higher than me."

"I am sure of that. But my life is on the line right now, honestly."

Margo did not put much weight on honesty from Jonathan Ross, but had to admit he was clearly worried and extremely edgy.

"What about your passport?"

"That I have. Always keep that on me, luckily."

"Okay, let me make some calls and see if we can get you a ticket. How do I get hold of you?"

"I'll have to call you again later. I had to leave my cell phone and computer at Arenal."

"When is the next flight out?"

"There is one to Los Angeles leaving in about three hours."

"Get to the airport, and lay low. Plan on being on the flight, and call me in about an hour from the terminal to confirm."

"Thanks, you are a real lifesaver."

"Yea, well don't count your chickens yet. I will see what I can do."

She glanced at Mike who had got the drift from one end of the conversation.

"Well, it's a long story. But right now I need to take care of getting him a ticket out of Hades. The Casa de Fruta is just ahead. You got us here in record time. Pull off there, and you can buy us each a strong coffee while I make a few calls."

"Your wish is my command, sweetheart."

He said in his usual calm and collect way, pulling into the small tourist area of fruit stands and novelty shops at the side of the road.

Miami

The miserable situation was going from bad to worse for Andrew Benton. After inflicting further brutal damage to his body, the goons had locked him in a small dingy office at the back of the warehouse, and had given him twenty four hours to find the missing money.

His swollen leg was chained tightly to the bottom handle of a large black filing cabinet, and he was certain the fingers on his left hand were all broken.

The desk was empty except for his laptop and cell phone, which they left him to use to get the money, or else.

There was no water or place to relieve himself. The latter not being an immediate problem since his soaked pants were testament to what he had endured.

He had attempted to reach Geoff Collins at his London flat with no luck. Calls to his cell phone had gone unanswered, and his e-mails had bounced back three times as address undeliverable.

Obviously, he knew what was going on, and was already covering his tracks. For Benton, the future looked more and more miserable.

The Colombians had said ten million was missing. Geoff must have discovered additional laundered money parked in the account when he went back to transfer their own funds. Perhaps he thought he was getting screwed with the original deal, and decided to take what he thought was his fair share of the money. He must have transferred it to a new account and then disappeared.

No, not possible, he was solid on all their dealings.

More likely, he was cracking his balls with what he thought was a game with another hacker trying to outwit him. He was online gaming to take the prize of outsmarting him.

Whatever he was thinking, he was screwing up big time, and had no idea of the ruthlessness of the characters he was playing with.

In fact, he was fairly certain that Geoff would have only taken what he thought was a just split. He believed he would in some way communicate where the remaining funds had been transferred. Collins' basic sense of fair play would have left at least half for him. The light bulb went on for Benton.

Jesus Christ, there must have been at least twenty or more million being laundered through the account.

The kid would have no idea the fire he was playing with. He is messing with the Cartel at the highest level.

Worse, Ortega had really played him for a fool, he was obviously much deeper into the game than he could have imagined.

He knew his own life, and the kid's depended on finding him. To do that in a few hours would be impossible.

The phone in his briefcase beeped. He realized immediately that it was Rolf's phone. The shudder of another wave of panic passed ominously through his entire body, instantly inflaming excruciating pain in his hands and leg.

The small display indicated a short text message flashing on the screen. His limited German was able to interpret the message.

Hope you arrived safely, please confirm, Helga.

The German Polizei on discovering that the luggage, computer, and cell phone of the victim were missing from the house had figured that the killer must have taken the belongings with him to avert suspicion.

On a long shot, they speculated that perhaps the perpetrator had also been responding to Rolf's electronic messages to give the impression to colleagues that he was still alive. So they decided to test their theory and see if they could get a response to a text message sent by his sister.

Four thousand miles east of the Miami warehouse, Helga sadly looked at the police captain as she wiped her eyes.

"I hope that your trick may work, Captain. I will do anything to help you find the person that took Rolf away from me."

"We understand your pain, Helga. We will do our best. If you do not mind, we will take your phone with us so that we can track any response that might come."

"Of course I do not mind, whatever you need.

"Danke."

"Auf Wiedersehen," he said softly as he took the phone from her trembling hand. He headed for his patrol car.

She only could only give a weak stare in response.

*****

Oh, great. His sister is starting to get worried. Well, at least that means they know nothing of his whereabouts. She will just have to wait for a returned call.

The door was kicked open, breaking into his thoughts. Garcia's main thug came barging into the room looking ready to enjoy thrashing him once again.

"You not answer your message, senor? You afraid we might learn something new, *verdad?*"

"No, that is not true."

"We will decide what is true."

"It just is not an important message. I can wait to call back."

"Well, perhaps not, we shall see how important."

The thug sneered, as he once again punched him on the side of the head for good measure.

The phone dropped from his hands to the floor. It was immediately retrieved by the assailant, who hit the return call button, instantly connecting in the overcoat pocket of the German police officer.

"You talk," he said, roughly shoving the phone in the swollen face of his victim."

Benton seemed defeated.

"We will see who this is that wants to reach you, and who is not so important, *verdad?*"

Benton was visibly pale. He nervously took the phone and placed it near his ear hearing an accented voice from the other end.

"Hallo, Herr Reiner here," announced the officer.

"Yes, you were trying to reach me?" responded Benton.

He tried desperately to maintain a sense of calm and normalcy. He was caught off guard to hear the male voice rather than that of Rolf's sister.

The signal locator from the cell phone was simultaneously being tracked by satellite from Germany through a complex infrastructure of global wireless networks.

Within seconds a radius from the cell tower in the city where the call was being made would be identifiable to the authorities.

"Herr Reiner, do I know you? And what were you doing calling my phone?"

"No, not your phone, you know that you have Herr Schwartz's equipment. We have found him. You must identify yourself, and turn yourself in to our authorities immediately."

Benton trembled at the tone and command of the voice, responding fearfully.

"You must have the wrong number."

Benton then cut off the line."

It was enough time for the Colombian to see reaction on Benton' face that he was lying.

Grabbing the phone once again, he pushed the redial.

"Who is this?" he barked at the German officer.

"This is Herr Reiner of the German police. Who are you?"

"That, my friend, is not business of yours. But it seems that we both have business with Mr. Benton here."

Benton' legs gave way, as he realized his identity was now established. There was no way out. If the Colombians did not kill him first then the German's would surely lock him up for life.

"Mr. Benton you say. Who is this Mr. Benton? We have reason to believe that he is involved in the death of one of our German citizens. Please identify yourself to me."

"That, my friend, again, is none of your business. However, if and when we finish with our mutual friend here, be certain that we will notify your authorities with our pleasure."

He threw the phone to the floor, and for good measure stamped it to pieces with his foot.

"Well, well, senor, it seems you have for yourself many *problemas*."

Benton knew that for the first time in his life he had no one to turn to in this mess, and that he could not buy or manipulate saving his life. He was on his own with perhaps only his negotiating skills.

He figured that no matter how badly they beat him their bosses would not give the order to kill him until the location of the missing money was extracted from him.

If nothing else he may have just a bit of time.

Meanwhile in Germany the high powered tracking equipment had already identified the call in a cell tower in Miami.

German national police were without delay contacting the Florida FBI agents.

California

Bob Harris was convinced that he had plenty of information for his boss. He raced past the freeway exit ramp Maxwell's car used to pull off the highway into the *Casa de Fruta* shopping area, and continued driving on the mountainous pass towards Sacramento.

He was anxious to wrap up the assignment and get on with his real fishing trip in the northern California lake country, just a couple of hours more and he figured he would report his findings, and be through with his obligation to Ramsey.

Maxwell had placed the briefcase with the listening chip in the trunk of the car with other overnight bags, so unfortunately since leaving Monterey he was not party to the discussion that had been taking place in the car.

Nevertheless, it was clear from the information he had previously gathered that they were all involved in something disreputable with the Zenkon Foundation. Some sort of a cover up was taking place that put the Senator right in the middle of it.

Bob Harris was sure the news he had to report to Ramsey would be well received and would no doubt provide him with sufficient ammunition to wage a full scale smear campaign on the Senator.

Meanwhile, back at the ranch, Holly was pacing back and forth on the patio. In his usual methodical manner he was mentally revisiting all the different pieces of information before making the call to Ramsey.

*****

Margo had called Scott from the roadside coffee shop. He had reassured her that he would have Jeff Peterson handle the ticket to Miami for Jonathan. He said it would be the first test of the effectiveness of their small Task Force that the Senator had insisted upon.

Peterson, no doubt, would have an agent on the plane, and another to greet Mr. Ross on arrival in Miami.

Mike insisted that Margo put her feet up as soon as they arrived at his riverfront home. The strain was wearing on her, and he could see the stress lines in her face.

He handed her a hot cup of tea and a chocolate wafer, and insisted that she at least try to relax a little.

Mike was in his element when he had the rare opportunity to pamper her, and he gently massaged her feet as she sipped the tea.

She always seemed in control in her professional life, and rarely did colleagues understand the constant worry she was under being a single mom and dealing with two children and a hostile ex-husband.

Clearly though, all the usual stresses were overshadowed by the current affairs, and he was determined that she would listen to his advice and try to take it easy before she was pushed over the edge.

"Margo, this is a complex and dangerous situation. You have to make sure that it doesn't get the better of you."

"What do you mean, am I in way over my head?" She snapped back.

"Clearly it has gotten to the point where the police and authorities need to take over from here on out."

"Mike, this is our Foundation's reputation, and the credibility of Board members, the Senator, and me, too. I have to stay involved, along with the others.

"That may be, but it is a police situation."

"Yes, I agree that the authorities have to handle it. That is why Peterson is involved. But there are things that only Mo and I know about. We have to be involved."

"I understand that completely. But you have to admit that murder, cartels, and congressional investigations are even more than you, my dear, or Mo can handle."

She was listening to him.

"You especially need to consider that Jodie and Frankie need you to, too. And you can only stretch yourself so far."

"I hear what you are saying, but what do you want me to do? I can't just walk away from all this, and leave the others hanging."

"No, I am not saying that. I am just saying that you have a lot on your plate, and perhaps you should let me help out a little bit more on the home front."

He responded, sensing that a change of tactics might be in order.

"What do you mean?"

"Well, I could pick the kids up for you at times; drive them to their various activities. They love it here along the river, and so we could plan on a dinner once or twice a week. They would be safe, and it might take the pressure off you at the moment."

Mike had an expectant look on his face, and his soft blue eyes suddenly melted her heart, and calmed her down.

He and Margo had kept their relationship distanced from the kids, and she had been reluctant to move in the direction of establishing a new family bond with the scars of divorce still blistering.

"Oh, well, I suppose that might be possible," she softly. "Do you think it is too soon for the kids?"

"Margo, they are tougher than you think, and our relationship is no secret to them. Let's just take it a step at a time. I just want you to know that I am here for you, and more than willing to help out."

"That means a lot to me Mike."

"Well, particularly now that you are spread so thin, my first assignment will be to go and get the children, stop on the way for some Chinese, and then we eat here. You my dear will then have the next hour or so all to yourself."

She leaned over and kissed him gently, truly happy for his support.

She realized contentedly that their relationship had taken a serious step toward commitment.

*****

The short flight in the small plane between Monterey and Los Angeles had been turbulent. The clouds and the marine layer from the coast rolled in early, and the cross winds kept the pilot busy for the entire fifty-five minute trip.

Jack and Maureen used the flight time to go through all the data again, and see if they could come up with any answers. The reporter in Jack loved solving a good mystery, and this whole scenario more than fitted the bill.

"You know, Jack, there is much more to Andrew Benton' role in this than we know. Somehow I have the gut feeling that he is in deeper than Ross. The fall out between them over control of the Foundation was just the tip of a huge iceberg."

"I think you are right on that score. Benton has been laying low for the past several months, but my instincts are also that he is the connection somehow between Helena's death and Rolf's murder. But what is it that we are missing? What is the common denominator that ties it together? And why does Ramsey think that he has got Holly's head in a vice over it?"

"We know from what Ramsey said to Holly the night he called him that it had something to do with the Health and Human Services Committee, but what?"

"That is what we have to get more data on."

"From the balls it took to make the call to a ranking Senator, he must be thinking he has a scandal big enough to leverage something he wants really badly

"Listen Mo, I will talk again with Ken Miller back in Washington, and see if he has come up with any new information. He will be even more interested when he learns that Helena's death was no accident.

"He was already hot on the trail of the connection between Ortega and Maldonado and some herbal export business in Miami that received funds from HHSC. That has to be the link pin in this saga. We need to connect more of these dots on how Ross and Benton fit into it all? Was the break up all just a front to cover up something else the two had going on?"

"Perhaps, Jack."

I'll also check into that connection with the Collins kid in London. It sounds like a long shot, but my reporter antennas went up when Margo mentioned his banking job and hacking."

"Sounds like a good idea. You have to help us read all the tea leaves, not only for Holly's sake, but the credibility of all the Board members is on the line, and especially for Margo. She must be going out of her mind with worry on what she got us all into with this whole mess."

"If nothing, we have the network and resources to get to the bottom of this, and I am convinced we will."

The flight attendant asked them to make sure the seat belts were fastened, as they prepared to land at Los Angeles International Airport.

*****

Megan and Scott had arrived home after about a three hour drive south. Silence had dominated the atmosphere in the car, with Megan catatonically staring blankly out of the side window practically the entire trip.

She was prone to mood swings, and from the moment the car drove out of the long driveway of the

Senator's ranch she had brooded. Nothing Scott said got any kind of a conversational response, so after an hour or so he just gave up.

It did not help at all when the call from Margo came through asking him to help out with Jonathan Ross. He assured her that a quick call to Jeff Peterson at the Bureau would handle securing a ticket to Miami and most likely a police escort to make sure he did not evade custody. But the abrupt intrusion and follow up call added to Megan's festering mood.

He was used to dealing with her, and experience had taught him that better to back off and let it pass. Sometimes this might even take a day or so before she simmered down. He loved her, and figured this was all part of the territory when both of the partners had demanding careers and dominating personalities.

He knew exactly that Holly's stipulation that he play team leader on the investigation was the main reason she was upset. In her mind he was sliding back into the political morass they had been able to escape so effectively.

She was also under a lot of stress with her job as well, so she most likely thought this would be a pressure on both of them. Her moodiness did not help any potential job stresses either of them had to deal with, but that was Megan, and Scott knew he had to work through it.

In silence she sipped a glass of wine as she sat alone on the patio, hugging her knees as she sat with feet up on the lounge chair.

She perked a little to see that Scott was just about to join her to enjoy the late afternoon sky when the phone rang pulling his attention back into the kitchen.

Typical, here we go again.

She thought to herself remembering seven days a week and eighteen hour days during Scott's Washington days.

Washington, D.C.

They are a bunch of idiots, all of them, acting as if this is some damn reality show, and they are the heroes solving all the puzzles and saving the day. Jesus, they have no idea what a dangerous game they are playing. And as for Benton and Ross, two complete fools, they deserve what they get for being such stupid dupes as to think in the first place that it would be safe to nibble around the edges with cartels without ultimately getting a bullet in their heads.

Ramsey was thinking to himself after listening to Harris' narrative.

Their only saving grace, thank god, is that Hollingsworth had the sense to contact Peterson. He is a play by the book guy, so at least we move this from kindergarten into the hands of trained professionals before their remains are all found dissolved in vats of acid somewhere. Maldonado and his crowd won't give a second thought to ordering hits, his guys will have no qualms about taking care of anything the boss orders.

He decided to bite his time and wait for the call he knew would come soon from the Senator. That would be handled by playing unaware of course about what he had already learned from Harris' detailed briefing. He would definitely maneuver toward the need for DOJ and FBI involvement, perhaps even suggesting Peterson's involvement on special assignment to his ranch to protect the Senator. Peterson was already in the middle of the whole damn mess, and better to keep an eye on him.

Christ, what a fiasco.

It was the end of a long day, and evident that besides the chaos Hollingsworth's crowd his own scheme to leverage dirt with the Vice President's office was falling apart.

Not disturbing the sunshine state's prominent Latino business deals was a clear priority over whatever he might have for the campaign. It was the same old bullshit; he would need to rethink his own career strategy.

But one thing was certain; he still had some ethics, and he couldn't just look the other way if these fools had set themselves up to be eliminated by brutal criminals. Underhanded politics was pushing the envelope, but by not taking appropriate action to avert potential murders was a totally different category, and he had enough decency to not cross that line.

A soft knock on the door, and then the appearance of a senior agent from the Interpol Washington Division of DOJ stood before him.

"Sir, sorry to interrupt you, but we just got a call from Interpol in Germany. Apparently, they have picked up on a situation in Miami that seems quite serious. I thought you would like to know right away."

"Yes, of course. What do you have?"

It appears they picked up a cell location on a suspect wanted for the murder of a scientist in Germany. His body was found at his home.

Apparently, the killer still had the phone of the victim. He returned a set up text they sent from the victim's sister, obviously playing that the brother was still alive. But the stranger thing is that from the response the guy seemed to be in double trouble. After the text, a call came in from what sounded like a third party thug."

"Go on."

"Interpol said the guy had a Spanish accent. He wanted to know who sent the text, and then drops the name of the guy to the Germans. An Andrew Benton, who we found out, was the former head of a major nonprofit foundation out of Silicon Valley."

"Go on."

"Sounds like he is up to his ass in alligators from what Interpol surmised. They told us that from the tone of the call that our man Benton might already be getting pretty roughed up."

Ramsey nearly jumped out of his seat.

"Get the Florida FBI and DEA guys on it right away, and find him pronto. We need to know what this is all about."

"Already in motion, sir, you will be the first to know once we lock in the location".

"Thanks, keep on it".

This has to all be a part of this clown parade, but shit, how deep are these characters involved. Putting out fires here is one thing, but now with Interpol involved we have a damn international mess on our hands.

Colombia

Three muscle men with guns had burst into his house and snatched Mario in front of his terrified wife and kids. He was roughed up and then dumped into the back of a waiting black SUV with dark tinted windows. The two security guards at the front entrance lay dead in the driveway.

Few witnesses saw what happened, and those that did looked the other way and walked on quickly. They knew that this was something no one had seen, and if smart would repeat to no one. Too many of their friends and family had learned the hard way about keeping your mouth shut.

In a sad twist of fate, Benton had blurted out through his torture that the kid knew where the money was, just as moments later Maldonado, trailing him from Costa Rica, barged into the warehouse and overheard.

Instantly, he was on the phone to el jefe in Bogota, and Mario was nabbed from the street.

The ill-fated computer whiz was now blindfolded and tied to a chair, and had no illusions of his fate.

He figured they had taken him to a warehouse near the central market because the familiar diesel polluted air of the loud trucks combined with the pungent smell of thousands of kilos of fish was making him even sicker to his stomach.

He had tried for hours without success to find the money Geoff had stolen, but had been outdone by the Stanford dropout's skills at nefarious banking schemes and maneuvers. He knew as soon as they pushed him into the van that he was already a dead man, worrying only for the fate of his family.

His wife had been frantically clutching their son when he was dragged from their home, giving him some hope that they would have been killed already if the cartel wanted it done. He consoled in thinking she would perhaps be spared, and his son marked for years later. They never forgot.

His parents on the other hand must already be dead to remind the locals of the cost of getting out of line or ratting out. Mario silently recited a short prayer. Being a devout Catholic, made the sign of the cross in respect and sadness, as he resigned himself to what would come next.

He was too familiar with the process. He was well aware that they intended to painfully extract details from him. He prayed for mercy and a quick painless death.

It had been just bad luck on his part selecting the London account for what he thought would be a quick parking spot to launder the funds. He had no idea he was playing a dangerous game with such a formidable opponent. The unknown challenger had outsmarted him, and from the time he saw the empty account, he knew that he might be a dead man.

Time ran out. The error had been caught too late, and errors are fatal in the business.

He would pay a mortal price for that.

In a way, he admired his virtual opponent. He had been outsmarted, and knowing he would die anyway, decided that honor among thieves was in order.

He would meet his maker suffering the consequences and determined on maintaining silence.

The winner deserved his prize, and so would be left alone to prolong the game.

California

The curious passengers glared through the cabin windows as the United Airlines flight from San Jose taxied to a spot on the tarmac far from the usual gate at Los Angeles International Airport. A portable ramp was being towed to the door, and below blue lights of two flashing patrol cars, along with a small group of what were clearly law enforcement officers.

The scene gave the impression of some criminal intrigue.

The captain announced over the intercom that passengers must remain in their seats, and a short delay to the gate would postpone the arrival.

The door to the cabin opened, and two plain clothed law enforcement officers entered, indicating their mission without a word at the waiting captain.

Moving directly to the ninth row aisle seat occupied by a nattily looking Jonathan Ross, they promptly escorted him to the waiting vehicle below.

Ross was terrified, but actually relieved to be on US soil, and relatively speaking felt much safer than he had with the cartel on his tail.

He was certain that this could all be sorted out with authorities. He had involved himself in shameful goings on, but never pushed his private profiteering beyond limits of legality, and certainly had nothing to do with Helen's death.

The FBI operates more than fifty field offices throughout the United States and he was taken to the Los Angeles office located on Wilshire Boulevard. It is only a stone's throw from the airport.

Ross was now seated in a small interrogation room.

He had been provided with a telephone. He called Margo to let her know he was in protective custody.

The grapevine moved quickly. She in turn had called Mo, who was already home in her small craftsman style bungalow near the university campus. She lived handily minutes from where they had Ross.

Scott, the Senator, and Jack all were informed within minutes.

*****

The Costa Rican authorities had informed the FBI that Helen's body had been cremated by her family the previous day. They were ruling it an accident.

The interrogation of Ross lasted about three hours, and by the time the FBI finished Mo was waiting to pick him up.

They threatened him with a continuing investigation into his connections to Benton and Schwartz. At this point they had nothing to charge him with.

They had released him, but assigned surveillance, most likely for his own good as well.

He knew though that while he had been unethical he had not committed a crime. FBI could search all they wanted.

He worried more about Ortega and Maldonado, but he would have to live with that for right now.

At least he was back in the States.

He looked like he needed a hot bath, cortisone cream for the bug bites which had now swollen to bright red, and some clean clothes. Maureen had already prepared her guest room with a few amenities. He would be staying with her for the night, she insisted, not because she was fond at all of the guest, but wanted firsthand knowledge on what had happened in Costa Rica.

She intended to be relentless in extracting detailed information on how Jonathan for years had been more focused on his own self interest than that of the Foundation. She planned to get it out of him, and short of actually killing him, would be as ruthless as his pursuers may have been in finding out about all the ways he had screwed them all

*****

About thirty miles away in the San Fernando Valley, Jack was pouring himself a double bourbon on the rocks. He was processing the events from the arduous trip, when he remembered he needed to do one last thing before calling it a day.

"Ken, how are you", he said as he reached his source in DC.

"Jack, how did it go, any big scoop yet?"

"Maybe soon, Ken, but at the moment we are still putting the pieces together. Could you check on more hanging chad for me?"

"Sure, shoot!"

A kid named Geoff Collins may somehow factor into this. He lives in England, and is the son of some big donor Collins in San Francisco. We need to check him out, and see what he is up to. Apparently, has some connection to Andrew Benton – maybe just family link, but could be more."

"I'm on it Jack, and hopefully will be able to report something tomorrow. And take it easy, you sound tired."

"Yea must admit that the age thing must be catching up with me, not as sprite on the investigative beat as I once was you know, leaving that to the likes of you these days."

"And you can count on me, for sure."

With that, Jack, knowing it was in good hands, drained his glass and headed to bed.

*****

One hundred and twenty five miles north of San Fernando Valley, Scott and Megan were getting ready to call it a night. The past hour or so had been the silent treatment on Megan's part, so he was relieved to hear the phone ring as she came out of the bathroom.

"I will need to see who that is, could be Holly," he said.

She gave him the look he hated which without words told him she had no interest in the matter. She climbed into bed, and would be sound asleep, thankfully, when he got there.

The number indicated it was Holly, so he sat at his desk and answered. Before he was able to say a word, the senator began to speak.

"Scott, good, you made it home safely".

"Listen, I tried to call Ramsey after you left. Haven't been able to reach him yet, but will give it a go early in the morning. I heard from Mo that she has Ross sequestered at her place, so we should be able to shed more light on what the hell is going on with him and Benton soon."

Scott was about to say something, but the senator ended the quick call with, "so get a good night's rest, and we will pick this up tomorrow."

"Right, thanks Holly".

He wanted to wait a few more minutes so that he was sure Megan would be asleep when he got to their room, no sense in chancing more passive aggressive moments between them, the drive home had been enough.

On a whim, he reached out to Peterson to see if he had anything else, but the call went directly to his voice mail, most likely also sleeping thought Scott.

But he couldn't have been further from the truth.

Peterson was already clearing TSA at San Francisco International headed for a direct flight to Miami. He had been summoned by Ramsey, and had no time to touch bases with anyone before rushing for the redeye so that he could be there by sunrise.

Miami

The team of federal agents raided the warehouse just before dawn, and found a pristine scene with nothing but hundreds of shipping boxes marked for export. Those would be seized for inspection, but otherwise a sense of order in the large facility.

Tired of dealing with a worm such as Benton, and enraged with the local assassin's loose tongue tipping off the German cop, Maldonado swiftly drew a knife and cut out the tongue of the young thug, promptly stuffing it down his throat.

Then just as swiftly turned to Benton and sliced his nose completely off his face by slicing it from bottom to top. Leaving both men screaming and traumatized.

Maldonado then gave the sign to the second of Mario's pals, not a word, just the sign.

Two bullets at lightning speed hit accurately and fatally through the center temples of both men.

Benton and the goon were permanently silenced.

Neither victim had a warning what hit them. Then, it was a matter for the garbage patrol nothing more.

Maldonado was going to make sure that neither fool would make the same mistake twice. The millions were a loss for now, but nothing compared to protecting the entire operation.

He knew the feds would come down on the place, moved quickly to the clean up phase.

Stealthily, operating like a military special operations swat team, which in essence these armies of narco traffickers are, his specialist crew left the warehouse spotless. They then disappeared taking all evidence along with them.

The bodies were dissolving in drums containing an acid solution and travelling at seventy miles an hour in an unmarked big rig headed north on Highway 95.

The feds found nothing when they arrived.

Ramsey had been informed, and was furious that it had taken hours to get a warrant signed off.

Apparently, federal judges in Florida did not welcome being woken up in the middle of the night by a DOJ bureaucrat. This was especially true when the warrant involved searching properties of prominent citizens who made sure campaign contributions were well spent.

The delay had been more than enough time for the criminals to be tipped off. This was followed with an all clear call to Murray in Washington that Ramsey and his team had the go ahead to raid the warehouse.

Ramsey knew it was a tip off.

Benton was most likely dead. Being able to link all this to Hollingsworth was going to be a hell of a lot more difficult.

Peterson, sitting behind him in the black SUV, said nothing, but was thinking the same.

Interpol would still probe, but that could take months, far past the election.

Sacramento

Margo was in the bedroom reflecting on the beginnings of the collaboration with Ross. She had enjoyed working with him at the start, and now felt even a bit sorry, if not pity for him.

His zeal and belief in the greater good was what mutually drew them together. She believed the Zenkon Foundation was a perfect Petri dish for them not only to support worthy causes, but to build a satisfying career.

Obviously Jonathan had other ideas. He had taken it too far. Teamwork had evolved into mistrust and adversarial relationships.

A nonprofit had been used to conceal nefarious deeds.

She now worried if the consensus building model emulated by Foundation could be saved and allow the philanthropic work to continue.

Perhaps Ross and Benton, along with so many other competing self interests, had jeopardized the very survival of the nonprofit organization.

*****

Mike returned to the bedroom, barefooted clad in blue pajamas, and she cast him a caring smile, as she saw the two cups of coffee in his hands.

"Now I could get used to this," she greeted, as she took the coffee.

"Me too, and what I said last night still holds, so there you go," handing her the cup and smiling.

California

The senator initiated an early morning call to Ramsey, and received the news of Benton. He was somewhat relieved to know that his illegal schemes had mostly likely died with him, but got no joy from the thought of a decomposing body that would be found by no one.

He wasn't even sure if the man had a family. He had never really taken the time to get personal with him. He had always seemed to be standoffish and reserved.

None of the types Benton associated with would be volunteering any information. It seemed the criminal web in the southeastern state would want to let matters rest in order to avoid probes into their own dealings.

Reporters would have to chase a lower hanging fruit.

Scott and Peterson could sort out the ramifications for the Foundation with Margo and Mo. Eleanor had already convinced him to resign.

He agreed with her that he did not need more adventures or heart burn.

*****

Ken informed Jack that the parents had cut off contact with their son, and knew nothing on his current whereabouts. His source in London had traced him to a council flat he had been renting, but from there it was a dead end. Seemed he pretty much kept to himself and made ends meet with the job at a bank. Neighbors said he had pulled up and left without notice, but had an attractive young woman at the flat a few times before he left, probably took off for better prospects with the girl.

He could have gotten spooked about whatever he thought Benton might be up to, bailing before finding himself in trouble. He could have learned his lesson in San Francisco, and did not want another run in with the law. Hard to say, but the kids these days seem to have shallow roots, picking up and leaving all the time.

The bank said he gave no notice, just failed to show up for work one day, sounded like that was pretty common.

He would do more digging if Jack needed, but appeared to be a young kid bailing out and off to the next job. They left it there for now.

*****

Holly and Maureen, both feigning a desire for retirement, turned in their resignations to the Board. They agreed to be available on an advisory basis.

A subsequent recommendation came from Margo to sunset the Foundation as an alternative, claiming that the Foundation had put in its time. Zenkon Foundation had supported many worthwhile projects, and perhaps it was time to pass the baton.

315

Others on the Board were already dedicating efforts to new ventures, and agreed that without Holly, Mo and Helen the Board would never be the same.

Holly suggested that the recommendation be taken under consideration, and requested a review of where remaining funds and assets could be allocated.

A unanimous vote was taken to direct Margo to work a plan and a list of appropriate grantees.

Ross, with his tail between his legs, kept silent during the discussion. He knew that his future political aspirations required it; he had gotten off easy this time.

He planned no future trips anywhere in Latin America, no, for him his San Francisco home was just fine, with its gateway to the Pacific.

Margo was contemplating a proposal Scott had offered.

He suggested they team up to form a consulting firm in California. She would direct operations from Sacramento in the north, and he would manage clients in the south from Santa Barbara.

It sounded tempting, and she was ready for a change and less travel. As Scott had found, the long flights and unrelenting tribal politics of Washington would continue to become even more partisan and corrupt.

She intended to take a well earned break and then make a decision.

Nonprofits come and go, and this one had served its mission well.

Besides, the incorporation rules of nonprofit organizations allowed use of the same federal identification number for reorganization.

The name, goals, mission, bylaws, and the members of the board could be reconstituted for other activities.

It was all legal.

She had a lot to think about.

Epilogue - Three Years Later

Monterey, California

The funeral for Holly was held at the Unity of Monterey Church in the Central California town he proudly called home, and the countryside he had loved all his life.

The casket was draped with the Stars and Stripes to honor Senator Lawrence Hollingsworth's decades of public service, first as an officer in the United States Air Force, followed by years of service as the Congressman from the Monterey Bay Area, and ultimately as U.S. Senator for California.

Eleanor Hollingsworth had insisted that following the church service the hearse would follow a route through the downtown neighborhoods of Monterey, stopping briefly at the beautiful old Victorian style house facing the Pacific Ocean on Lighthouse Drive. The modest residence had been their first home nearly half a century before, and she was sure that the Senator would want one last stop on the way to his eternal resting place.

The beloved Senator passed away unexpectedly from pneumonia, after returning from a speaking tour to Hong Kong and Shanghai.

The solemn procession drew to a halt as the funeral vehicle paused directly in front of the old black iron gate, installed a year or so after the young couple had bought the house as a fixer upper, shortly after Holly had returned from Vietnam.

It was a retreat he needed, and working on the many projects the house needed helped him heal from the wounds and injustices he had witnessed in the war. His experience in Southeast Asia, and the lies the government inflicted upon the country, and deaths of so many of his friends contributed to his determination to make his first successful run for a seat in Congress.

His constituents rewarded him with a lifelong career.

The old house stood tall, as if it were waiting at attention to say goodbye. It was still pristine, and was now adorned by abundant white and red rose bushes. Some had wound themselves around the posts of the fence, and were now overhanging onto the sides of the gate in full bloom. Eleanor remembered planting the bushes from small cuttings given to them as a house warming gift by the next door neighbor.

She was assisted by a military guard in full dress as she descended the limousine bearing the body of her deceased husband.

She walked forward as the rear door to the hearse was opened, and then to gain her composure, took in a deep breath and exhaled. Like the pillar she had been to him in life, she stood next to him in a moment of silence, hand on his casket, knowing that he still felt her presence. She was as graceful in this heartfelt moment as she had been supportive holding his hand for decades. Eleanor sent Holly a silent message and wiped her eyes, returning to the sedan.

The solemn motorcade then proceeded through the picturesque streets of the beautiful seaside town which on this particular morning was lined with his former constituents and friends waving small flags. Many were also wiping a tear or two.

Eleanor was proud of his legacy, and knew he would be remembered.

Following the internment a private reception had been planned by the Senator's family at the ranch. Guests included family, political dignitaries, neighbors. Each in turn expressed condolences to Eleanor and family, as they shared personal stories and memories of his public life.

Two of the guests were from the Foundation for the Global Trust. Margaret Maxwell, President and Scott Jenkins, Chair of the Board.

Scott and Margo stood on the lower deck of the ranch just outside the panoramic windows of the office where the Senator had spent many hours. They could see through the glass walls plastered with reminders and tributes to his political days, and a mantel filled with photographs and keepsakes from his children and grandchildren. It was his special part of the house. It now loomed silent and empty of his commanding presence.

"Scott, do you remember the last time we stood here?"

"How could I forget? What a nightmare day that was when we learned of the mess the Zenkon Foundation was in. To to say nothing of the terrible murders of poor Helen and Rolf."

"Yes, we are so fortunate that the Senator was able to navigate that awful affair for us, even though it meant we had to sunset the original Foundation.

We really owe it to him that the Foundation for the Global Trust exists today. All could have as easily been lost if it were not for him deciding to reorganize and transfer all the assets."

"Yes, Margo, the advice that Holly and Mo gave us to distance ourselves from the vaccine work for a while was a good move.

"Of course, they could see that a new foundation that actually returned us to our roots of telecommunications access would be an important social cause in the twenty-first century in so many ways."

"More importantly, Margo, Holly had faith in us to take on that mission. We have to make sure for his sake that his work continues as a legacy to the lifelong dedication he made to social causes."

"Agreed, to Holly then, he was a special person and a good friend", remarked Scott, as they both glanced sadly into the large window of the silent office, and then returned to the upper deck to mingle with other guests.

Liverpool, England

Geoff was glowing at Pat, radiant in her clingy champagne colored dress, and obviously not one bit shy that she was showing off her very pregnant contours.

She was happy to be the center of attention at the full swing wedding reception. In true Liverpool style, the festivities were complete with great music and DJ. There was plenty of food and drink, and everyone was dressed to the hilt.

Paris and Switzerland were more than Pat had ever dreamed about. Geoff had made sure no expense was spared during the months they travelled Europe. She assumed she had lucked out finding a rich yank, and never really worried about where his affluence came from.

She believed his story about estranging from his wealthy San Francisco family and living on a trust left to him by his grandfather.

The pair enjoyed every minute with each other; initial chemistry had not waned a bit, but had rather bonded them as two free spirits with the world at their feet.

With a baby on the way, both were elated, and a life of commitment was a natural next step. They could not have been happier. His family and life in the states seemed far in his past.

Overlooking the River Mersey from the elegant setting in the majestic Liver Building, they were wrapped one around the other closely. Pat had insisted the wedding be held in Liverpool with her family and friends. She had joked with him that he could take the girl out of Liverpool, but would never take the city out of the girl.

Geoff loved her quick sense of humor, and had no argument with her choice of venue and guests.

Life turned out better than he ever imagined. He had been lucky, far luckier than hitting jackpot on the lottery, and for sure better than any of his former college buddies still searching desperately for that killer application to launch the next Google.

The account from the proceeds Colombian gaff was more than he would ever need; hell a cool ten million had been nothing to sneeze about.

Months would pass before he felt with confidence that the Bogota hacker was done with him and he could safely move on. Now that three years were behind them, he felt confident that their lives were secure.

During the three years he had carefully invested proceeds into a diversified stock portfolio. He was now enjoying building substantial assets in many reputable companies around the globe. His diversified assets included stock ownership in biomedical and pharmaceutical companies, Amazon, Facebook, Microsoft, AT&T, to name a few, and with the trend of legalization of marijuana he was now looking at investing in companies that were experimenting with production and manufacturing of natural products, treatments, foods and cosmetics from cannabis.

His stars had lined up, fortune, a wife, and a baby on the way. After the reception they would be headed to the property purchased in Suffolk to start married life and a family, as upstanding community members.

He turned to Pat, and gave her a kiss before returning to their guests.

As they walked back to the reception he had not noticed two figures among the crowds along the pier.

Geoff had never met the two customers dining at the Pump House Restaurant at the Albert Docks. But they knew who he was, and had been following his life for the past eighteen months.

He would have recognized the clear unmistakable features of Rosario Ortega and Juan Maldonado just finishing their meal.

It had taken the Cartel months to track him down. They were impressed with his online accounting skills, and the way he could effortlessly move and track assets. In fact, he was considered by the Colombians to have more talent than Mario. They had all eyes on him, and were impressed with how he was managing their money.

As long as it was growing, they considered it safely parked and working for them.

The Cartel owned him, and when they needed to let him know how things in their world worked then they would let him know.

Silicon Valley, California

Jonathan Ross, Chief Executive Officer of PanApp21 was seated in his spacious office. Ross had worked tirelessly to incorporate the company after the Zenkon Foundation was dissolved.

PanApp21 was funded with venture capital investment secured by Dr. Tom Yang, who had contacted his former roommate immediately with the idea.

Both men were identified as equal partners. Ross was not going to make the same mistake on ownership that he had with Rosario Ortega, and this company dwarfed the investments he had abandoned in Costa Rica.

After incorporation, Ross immediately applied for a federal contract identification status, and then used his extensive network of political contacts to secure federal funding grants for research and development in the health and public safety area.

The duo now operated virtual offices in California and China. Scientists and developers, under the direction of PanApp21, were awarded federal subcontracts to collaborate with World Health Organization, National Institute of Health, and other prominent research institutions on research to address pandemic control and mitigation.

The contracts allowed them to build upon the work meticulously chronicled by Dr. Rolf Schwartz, and form a coalition of global expertise in viruses and vaccine, allowing PanApp21 to acquire patents and trademarks for applications that could be used to trace outbreaks.

Jonathan Ross smiled and mused:

Well, Margo, we were right, in thinking that the greater good would be served as long as self interests are satisfied.

*****

Jonathan's partner, Tom Yang, thousands of miles away in a well funded government laboratory in the Chinese port city of Xiaman, was remotely supervising dozens of developers located throughout China.

Many of the young professionals had spent time at universities in the United States, and were now busy gathering global research and data used by PanApp21 to create applications capable of tracing virus epidemics if there were a global pandemic.

Their subcontracts were managed by PanApp21's corporation in the Silicon Valley, all legal.

Cyber space would be where a coming war would be won, and technology would be the key in the tracking and controlling an enemy global virus before it could affect billions of humans.

Yang knew that he was racing the clock, a fact that his superiors on the Standing Committee never let him forget. He had a good Citizen Social Credit Score, allowing him and his family to have passports and travel.

He was determined to be successful so that his standing was not jeopardized, and was well aware that the surveillance cameras constantly monitored his actions.

It was just a matter of time before the pandemic hit an unprepared world. Scientists had been warning of it for decades. PanApp21 was only one piece of a complex strategy and operational plan designed to win both the battle against a global micro enemy and a public relations war.

Highly populated cities had been selected to test effectiveness of mass human quarantine. State of the art manufacturing facilities were under construction for production of testing supplies. Hundreds of laboratories were standing ready for conversion to expeditious production of billions of doses of a vaccine or therapeutic. All details had been planned meticulously, and were monitored constantly.

When the time came, all citizens would comply with orders to vaccinate, or risk their score.

PanApp21 would be ready to report results on effective tracing and mitigation of the pandemic within their own borders; demonstrating foresight and leadership, and public global good to a thankful world.

Made in the USA
San Bernardino, CA
14 June 2020

73225655R00207